Best Wishes

Tony Ansell

2010

BLAIR ADAMS

THE PACKAGE

An FBI Thriller

A Novel by
TONY AUED

Bloomington, IN Milton Keynes, UK
authorHOUSE®

AuthorHouse™
1663 Liberty Drive, Suite 200
Bloomington, IN 47403
www.authorhouse.com
Phone: 1-800-839-8640

AuthorHouse™ UK Ltd.
500 Avebury Boulevard
Central Milton Keynes, MK9 2BE
www.authorhouse.co.uk
Phone: 08001974150

First published by AuthorHouse 12/02/2006

ISBN: 1-4259-5373-5 (sc)

Printed in the United States of America
Bloomington, Indiana

This book is printed on acid-free paper.

This is dedicated to my wife Kathy; you have always been there to support all my efforts. I can't ever repay you for all that you have done for us and our family. I thank you for everything. You are my best friend.

Special thanks to my daughter for her involvement, and I hope that she can read this and know how much I love her. I am very proud of you and how you have handled adversity. In memory of my Son-in-Law, know to his comrades as "Bama", you will be missed.

I want to acknowledge my son who helped give me advice and direction. Because writing is your life's work I have appreciated your guidance. I love all three of you.

In remembrance of the brave men and women of our armed forces.

ONE

The pilot's voice came on the overhead speaker announcing that he was making the initial approach to LAX and that they would be on the ground in a few minutes. Blair opened her eyes and could hardly believe that they had already made the trip from Philadelphia to Los Angeles. The past few weeks seemed to be a blur. She looked out of her window and the sky was a deep steely blue as it reflected off the ocean. The palm trees were just coming into view as the plane banked to the left in its final approach. The landscape was so different than that of the east coast that it almost seemed like a different world.

The stewardess voice was the next thing she heard requesting that everyone bring their seats and tray tables to the upright position. Hunter's funeral was all that she could think about as the plane glided to a stop on the runway. Could all of this really have happened? Is he really gone?

Blair started to gather her package from the overhead bin when the passenger next to her asked about the triangle folded American flag. Blair looked down and sadly said, "My husband was killed in Iraq."

Passengers overheard what she had told the lady and started to repeat it to others on the plane.

The lady expressed her sorrow and asked "when did it happen?"

"He was shot by a sniper a few weeks ago."

"I'm so sorry. You're so young to have lost someone."

Blair had tears in her eyes and swore that she would not cry again after so many tears the past few weeks. She made her way up the aisle as other passengers offered their condolences. Blair nodded a simple

thanks and departed the plane to head for the luggage area. She hoped
that the long walk would do her some good.

It was a typical day in Los Angeles, sunny and warm. The weather
was always great in the spring. Warm winds came across the San Gabriel
Mountains often trapping the low laying fog over the city. People from
the east coast would not understand her love for Southern California.
Blair and Hunter could be on the beach from their apartment in less
than ten minutes or in the mountains climbing in a few hours. They
both loved the mountains and often would take overnight trips to the
San Bernardino National Forest. Now that was only fond memories.
As she walked toward the baggage area the memory of their trip to
Catalina and the good times mountain climbing made her smile. It was
an anniversary surprise trip that Hunter had planned. He was good at
that sort of thing.

She held the triangle folded American flag tightly as she approached
the baggage carousel. The long walk through the terminal helped her
gather her composure. She had talked to her two best friends Ashley
and Blake and they said they would meet her near the baggage area.
Blair saw them waiting for her and they ran to greet each other.

Ashley had moved to Santa Monica from Dallas about the same
time that Blair had moved there. They met at The California Kitchen
an American Grille where both girls found their first Santa Monica
jobs. They became fast friends and because Hunter was gone so often
they looked out for each other. Ashley and Blair lived together for a
short time when Ashley was moving to another apartment. Hunter
was in South America at the time and Blair loved having someone with
her and Ashley was the perfect fit. They both loved jazz and big band
music and had similar backgrounds. Ashley was a beautiful girl and had
long curly black hair. Blair often would tell her that she would do well
in an acting career. Ashley had two cats named Lois and Clark from
the superman comics. Blair was a dog lover but enjoyed Ashley's two
cats when they lived together. She wanted to have a dog but it was not
approved for her apartment building.

Ashley had wanted to live near the ocean and had been to California
as a child many times. She loved the beach and Santa Monica was the
perfect place. Blair and Ashley shared the same California dreams.

Blake moved to Santa Monica before either of the two girls. He graduated from Fresno State University and planned to go to graduate school in Los Angeles. Blair met him when she was moving into her apartment. He lived in the same building and helped her and her dad move some of her things. His love of surfing brought him to Santa Monica. He often would go surfing in the morning before his classes. He tried to teach Blair how to surf but her fear of the ocean held her back from being able to learn the sport. He would make sure she was ok whenever Hunter was on a mission. Blake was a kind young man and always very thoughtful. His girlfriend was a massage therapist and often works odd hours.

Tears flowed as they hugged. Ashley and Blake were Blair's best friends. They had been there from the start and the three shared good times and bad. They both had gone Bridgeport for Hunter's funeral. Ashley had flown out with Blair's boss Olly and Blake arrived the day of the funeral. Some of Blair's friends from Alabama and Mississippi also made it to the funeral. Hunter was very popular in college. Many friends drove from Oxford, Mississippi to attend his funeral. So many of their friends made it to the funeral.

The bags were gathered by them as Blair clutched the American flag. They walked toward the parking lot in silence, just holding hands, the three of them. Good friends are so important and now more than ever.

Blair's parents were also great during the funeral but they had to return home to Alabama. Her dad had to go back to work and her mom was hoping to travel out to California in a few weeks. Knowing that Blair had so many friends made it much easier for them. Her mom promised to come to California but Blair wanted some time to figure out exactly what she should do next. Having such understanding parents made everything easier. Her mom and dad held her tight every moment. They were very close.

The three friends entered the parking deck across from the main terminal. Blake had his Honda Civic parked in the short term lot and they made there way toward it. Her bags were tucked into the trunk as she climbed into the back seat still clutching the American flag. No one would know what she was feeling at this time. Blair wasn't sure herself what she was feeling. They were married only three years but it seemed so much longer. Hunter played football for Ole Miss where they both went to school when they met. Blair was a sophomore and took the normal second year students schedule. Hunter was injured his senior year and it looked like he would not play again. His love for football and his dream of playing for the Dallas Cowboys were all lost.

Blair had dreams of Hollywood and the California dream had been shared with Hunter. They agreed that after they got married they would move to Los Angeles. Since Hunter no longer had his dream of a career in the NFL he wanted Blair to be able to chase her dream of Hollywood. Now she was in the back seat of a friends car holding his flag. The funeral was over on Friday, now it was Tuesday. Time seemed to be moving in slow motion since the visit from the three soldiers to her apartment that night. She could not put any of their conversation or words into reality until the actual day she claimed Hunter's body on the tarmac in Philadelphia with his dad. No one should have to do this she thought. Life seemed so unfair.

The drive along Lincoln Blvd. through Marina Del Ray and Venice toward Santa Monica seemed to be longer than most times. Traffic along the beaches was always a challenge but today it was very quiet. Tuesday's usually had a lot of tourist traffic headed to or from the airport or beaches. Blake turned off of Lincoln at Rose Avenue and drove down to Pacific Avenue. He could avoid some of the traffic back up that would be getting on the Santa Monica Freeway at the Lincoln entrance. They would pass the restaurants along Main Street that were always busy with locals and tourist. One of them was the small restaurant that Hunter worked at when he was home from one of his missions. He was a bouncer in a popular nightclub off of Main Street near the beaches. Blake slowed down as traffic backed up along Ocean Avenue. As they passed the Hotel California on Ocean Avenue Blair asked him to pull over.

"What's wrong?"

"I need to get out." Blake and Ashley looked at each other.

"Are you ok/" Ashley asked.

"This is all so hard. Hunter and I would walk down here many mornings. He loved the beach and so do I."

She wanted to walk the remainder of the way to her apartment. They were passing so many places where she had spent time with Hunter and she wanted to see them alone.

It seemed that every time Hunter would come home from one of his missions the beach would be his refuge. The sight of the Santa Monica pier and the Ferris wheel made her sad. They would rent bikes at the base of the walk under the pier and ride to Venice on many weekends. Blair had her roller blades in the trunk of their car and was always ready to skate along side of Hunter as he rode his bike. Pacific Park was a wonderful place full of memories that caused Blair to think how her life had changed.

"I just want to walk the rest of the way."

"I'll walk with you," Ashley said.

"I just want to walk alone for a little bit."

Blake pulled over in front of The Santa Monica Pier. Blair got out of the car. "Please be careful Blair. I wish you would let Ashley walk with you."

"I'm really ok, just need a little alone time."

"We will park and meet you."

It was only a few blocks to the Santa Monica Promenade from the Pier and her apartment on Arizona. The Santa Monica Pier was a popular place for tourist and locals. They had stopped near The Lobster House. It was a very nice restaurant on the Pacific Coast Highway just before you walked onto the Pier. You could look down on the beach and see the tourist renting bikes to ride along the beach. When Blair's parents would come for a visit she would convince them to rent bikes and ride along the path to Venice.

The Pier was Santa Monica's version of an amusement park and State Fair all wrapped into one. You could see the sights from the sun rise or setting to the palm trees blowing in the wind. There were places to get funnel cakes, hot dogs or ride the famous Merry-go-round. The Pier was full of vendor carts and gift counters. It offered dining and shopping plus some great sightseeing. It seemed like all the homeless also found the Pier a good place to spend time. They could panhandle or find a nice spot on the manicured lawn to rest. Blair always had a soft spot for the homeless. When she was eight her parents took her to Washington, D.C. to see the White House, Washington Monument and other famous sites. She saw a homeless man begging near the Lincoln Monument and cried for her dad to give her some money to help him. Her dad took her to a food stand and they bought a nice meal for the man and his other friends. That gave Blair a good feeling. She would often talk Hunter into doing the same thing when they went down to the Pier. She was a soft touch.

The walk along Ocean Avenue took her past so many places that she would take friends and family to when they came to visit. It was good that she had the time alone to gather her thoughts. She had so many memories that she had to see them for the first time alone. She always knew that Hunter would be back and they both loved the California way of life. Once you were out there you would understand this love. Many times she would have her friends from Alabama and Mississippi come to visit and they would see the California that Blair saw. Even Blair's parents knew that it was a great place for their daughter. Her dad would often say maybe when we retire we'll move out here too. That was Blair's mothers dream. She so missed her daughter.

Blair stopped at Coffee Bean for a latte'. She would always stop there every morning before going to work. The walk gave her time to think about the past few days. She had met so many new people at the funeral. Many of whom she had met for the first time.

One of Hunter's friends, Brian, was special. He and Hunter had gone to high school together and Brian was the one with him on the roof top. She wished that she could have spent more time with Brian and hear more stories about Hunter growing up but there was no time for that. Brian had been in the army special forces for over eight years when he was rejoined with his friend in Iraq. It was odd that they would be in the same command after not seeing each other for years. Brian made sure that he could spend some time with both Thomas and Blair when he was home. He knew that Hunter would have wanted him to do that. When Thomas, Hunter's dad, took Brian and Blair to the Philadelphia airport, Brian promised to keep in touch. He seemed like such a nice person and was so close to Hunter and his Dad. Blair gave Brian her address and got his from him. She wanted to stay in contact with Hunter's buddy. His address made her especially sad because it was the same as Hunter's when he was in Iraq.

The California sun was high overhead and watching people head down to the Santa Monica Pier brought back a rush of memories. Hunter loved the beach. When he came home from a mission he would want to spend days just going to the beach. The sidewalk stretched from Malibu to Venice and everyday you would see rollerbladers, bikers and walkers making their daily trek along the path. This was one of the reasons she picked Santa Monica as a place to move to. She had made two trips out to California to scout out an apartment and fell in love with the area. You could find every type of restaurant or activity within a few blocks. The Third Street Promenade was always busy with activity. You would see struggling musicians playing their instruments and hoping to sell CD's that they had placed in open guitar cases. People passing by would often drop a dollar or two in while stopping to listen to a few songs. On most Sunday nights a local dance studio held their lessons in the street. It was also the place for activist to promote their cause. Blair loved helping any cause that protected the environment. She would stop and pick up their literature and always donated to them.

When they moved Hunter had to stay behind in Oxford, Mississippi so Blair was responsible for finding a place to live. She liked it that way because he didn't seem to care and Blair like making the decision for them. She picked out the apartment, the city and most of the furniture.

The walk was good. It gave her time to think. Blair arrived at her apartment. The apartment was across the street from a large movie theater and next to Brookstones. There were always people waiting in line to get into the show. Today was no different. Blake and Ashley were waiting for her with her suitcases.

"I'll take them up for you," Blake said.

"I just want to go up by myself", she said.

"That's not a good idea" Ashley said. "Let me go with you."

Blake wasn't sure what to say. "Blair you know we love you. Let Ashley go up to the apartment with you."

She met Blake when she was moving in. Hunter was still in Mississippi transferring from the Mississippi National Guard to the U.S. Army. It would take a few weeks but she wanted to get into their apartment. Blake lived on the first floor and held the door for her and her dad when they carried a load of boxes up. She didn't have too much to move. Most of the stuff belonged to her. Hunter always said he traveled light. Blake helped her move some of the items and they became immediate friends. Blake was a few years older than Blair. He had moved to Santa Monica from upstate. He loved surfing and he could do it every day in Santa Monica. He was attending UCLA and working on his Masters degree. Blair would often get him to do small projects for her when Hunter was overseas. They both loved sushi and Hunter did not so Blake was her sushi partner.

"I'm going to be ok", she told her friends.

They believed her. She seemed fine. Blair told them that she would be ok and agreed to meet them at The Pub on Santa Monica Boulevard in two hours. She entered the elevator and pushed the button for the second floor. Her apartment number was 21 A. It was a small apartment but perfect for her and Hunter. Blair stood at the apartment door entrance. Memories flooded her mind. It would be the first time back home after Hunter's death. When she opened the door to their apartment she dropped her bag. There was furniture turned upside down and everything was a mess. Blair stated to cry. Someone had broken into the apartment and ransacked everything. She could not figure out why or who but things were tossed all over. They did not have a television but Hunter had bought her a retro stereo and it was on its side but still there. Hunter's Ole Miss Football helmet and the football signed by Archie Manning were in the corner. The apartment was in a safe building and that was one of the things her parents really liked when they saw it. Nothing seemed to be missing at first glance.

What happened, who would have done this? She had been gone for close to two weeks to Philadelphia but Blake lived in the same building and would have told her if they had any break-ins. This was the last straw. Blair sat in the middle of the floor and broke down. Her door was still open when Ashley came in.

"I could not leave you alone, my God what happened!"

They held each other and cried. Ashley helped Blair up and they both dried their tears.

"Where do I start?" Blair said.

"Let's call the police", Ashley told her.

The Santa Monica police showed up in about ten minutes because the station was located across the street on the Promenade. Ashley answered the knock. They were very efficient. Not many problems outside of the homeless issue came up. The officers were always present on the Promenade. It made the locals feel pretty safe. Officer Tuttle was the one to come to her apartment. Officer Bill Tuttle knew the girls and had often eaten in the pub where they both worked. He had also heard about Hunter's death and offered his sympathy to Blair.

"I know you've been gone for a while. Did you have anyone check on your apartment while you were gone?"

Blair said no one had been there that she knew of.

"I don't have any pets or plants so it wasn't necessary to have someone check my apartment", she said.

"You just got home today, I take it," officer Tuttle said looking at her luggage on the floor.

Ashley answered for Blair stating that they just picked her up from the airport and came straight to the apartment to put her bags away.

"Was the door open when you got here? Did it appear to be broken? Is anything missing that you can tell?"

The girls nodded no to each of the questions.

"Do you think that there was something special that someone would have been after?"

Office Tuttle remarked that it appeared that someone was searching for something. Blair had no idea why this would have happened. Officer Tuttle filled out a police report and left Blair with a copy. He told her to inventory the apartment and change the lock. She said she would come by the station when she had gone through everything.

The girls felt comfortable with Officer Tuttle. They would see him and his partner at The Pub. The Pub was a popular gathering place for locals. It was not very big and it was located on the corner of Santa Monica Boulevard and the start of the Third street Promenade. The location made it a great spot for lunch or dinner and to watch the activity on the street. The owners were from England and Ireland and had fashioned the bar like an old English Pub. The bar was made of beautiful long dark mahogany wood with many intricate carvings. There was a large population of English and Scottish people that had moved to Southern California and places like The Pub were like a piece of home. Locals would gather there daily and enjoy each others company and stories from home. Often you would see Allen or Chris joking with Nate and Joe about a recent soccer match. Soccer was always a big event at The Pub. Karaoke night also drew large crowds.

Blair had found a job at The Pub soon after moving to California. She was working at The California Kitchen and stopped into The Pub with Ashley for a drink one night. She met one of the owners and they became friends. She could work flexible schedules while trying to get into the film industry. She promised herself that she would work legitimate jobs only, not like the stories of girls that ended up in the porn industry. Her dad made her a promise that if she ever needed anything they would be there for her.

Olly was one of the owners of the Pub and treated Blair like a sister. They would often plan trips to Las Vegas or Mexico together when Hunter was on a mission. Olly went to Bridgewater for the funeral. She loved Blair and saw a lot of herself in Blair. Olly also moved to Santa Monica at a young age. Olly came to Santa Monica from Ireland when she was twenty years old. She was a beautiful petite blond. Olly had two young children and lived in a house along the ridge that overlooked the ocean. Her house was off the Pacific Coast Highway that ran toward Malibu. She would often have Blair meet her at one of the chic restaurants along the coast after work. They would have a drink and order meals that they would share. She was great fun to be with. She had planned a trip with Blair to Puerto Vallarta, Mexico. Olly and Blair liked traveling together. Hunter had been on a few short missions to South and Central America before the deployment to Iraq. Many of the patrons knew of Hunter's death and had sent flowers and cards to the funeral home. Blair was one of the favorites of the regulars that came to The Pub. Nate always asked about Blair whenever he came in. Nate was a famous barber that often would stop in when he had finished cutting the hair of a prominent Hollywood star. Allen, Chris and Joe also asked Olly about Blair and hoped that they would see her soon. Olly had not talked to Blair since returning from the funeral.

Blake came into The Pub and ordered a beer. His favorite was Pacifico, a Mexican beer that was very popular. When he told Olly that Blair would be coming to The Pub she could not wait to see her. Blake waited at an outside table. There were about six small tables that

went around the front of the Pub. The Pub had a large overhang that
protected the patrons from the afternoon sun. Blake saw Blair and
Ashley headed his way and knew that something was wrong. He got
up and met them part of the way.

"What's wrong?" Blake asked.

Ashley told him about the break-in which made no sense to any of
them. Blake felt guilty because he lived on the floor below and should
have checked the apartment for her.

"Blair, I'm so sorry that this has happened. What can I do?" Blake
asked.

"I'm going to stay with Ashley tonight. I just can't go back now."

Blake wanted the girls to sit down and talk. Maybe they should
have a drink and some dinner.

"I can't eat," Blair said.

Olly came running over and hugged Blair.

"I missed being with you the last few days. Olly had to return right
after the funeral and wished that she could have stayed to help Blair
after the luncheon. Are you ok?" she asked.

Blair told her about the break in and that she was glad Office
Tuttle was the one to come to her apartment. "You need to change the
locks."

"That's what Officer Tuttle said. I can't go back tonight. Ashley said
that I should stay with her."

Blair remembered that they left her suitcase in her apartment.

"I need some clothes."

"We're the same size, you can wear my things," Ashley said.

It was settled. Blair would walk home with Ashley and the three
of them would meet tomorrow to fix the apartment and get new locks
installed.

Blake made the girls sit at the table so they could calm Blair down.
Olly brought some appetizers over and a round of drinks.

"Did Officer Tuttle have any leads on the break-in?"

"No he said that it seemed strange that nothing looked like it was
missing. He is going to have me check everything out and call him back
with an inventory list. He said there had not been any other reported
break ins in the past few weeks."

They sat quiet and all three wondered why had someone broken in to her apartment and what were they looking for?

TWO

Baghdad was again filled with street bombs and Brian said that it would never change. The constant struggle for power between the Sunnis, Shiite's and Muslim factions tore the country apart. Iraqis wondered if a recent meeting in the highly fortified Green Zone would resolve the remaining disputes. Although they had a National Assembly, the struggle for power continued to exist. Brian had just returned that morning from his friend's funeral and now he watched them haul away bodies of innocent people that came to register for a spot in the Iraq police department.

Brian's driver, Al Azawi, was a Shiite who had worried that assisting the Americans would endanger his family. The American troops were the country's hope for a peaceful resolution while the Iraq National Assembly worked out the new order. Al Azawi had sent his family to the Southern City of Basra hoping to protect them from the constant upheaval in Baghdad. Although the regime of Saddam had been overthrown there were daily street bombings and gunfire always seemed to come out of nowhere.

Brian thought that it was hard to believe that just a few days ago he escorted Hunter's body back to the States and helped carry his friends casket from the church to the cemetery. They had been friends from high school and now his friend was gone. Brian was part of the Army's Special Forces that often guarded both American and Iraq officials. He was on the roof top with Hunter when he had been shot by a sniper. They had not seen each other for years before they were both sent to Baghdad. Brian thought it was funny that they would serve in the same outfit but having his high school buddy with him sure made the

13

duty much better. Hunter and Brian always traveled with a German Sheppard guard dog. They used them for bomb sniffing details. Brian looked forward to seeing his guard dog Xavier.

Hunter was a specialist in the Army's premiere unit and often was sent on special missions. He would often be gone for weeks on one of these missions. He had been deployed to the northern city of Tikrit, the home of Saddam. Brian had heard that Hunter had just returned from the mission to Tikrit that had a goal of searching one of Saddam's Castles. Hunter seemed very excited when his search team returned. Brian knew that Hunter had to report the findings to the head of his command in Riyadh, Saudi Arabia. He had wanted to ask him about it and what they found but they never had a chance to discuss it.

It was often the case with this unit that the missions were top secret. Hunter never seemed to open up since that time in San Salvador when his unit was charged with a special mission that included finding gold that was ear marked for the drug traffic bosses. He had detailed the mission findings to one of the men in the company only to learn that the man leaked the information to the news media. The information that was found was of no use since the drug lord had been exposed in the newspapers and he was able to go into hiding. Hunter became very private after that incident with information regarding his mission activities.

Baghdad was hot and the temperature reached 103 degree's. The sun seemed to be higher and sand never quit blowing. The trip back to his unit was long and Brian wasn't too anxious to get there. Brian knew he would get requests from the troops regarding the funeral, the weather in the States, and most of them would want some bits and pieces of home. They were all dedicated but lonely. He really needed to be alone.

Upon arrival to the camp Brian went to his barracks. He was glad to see his dog Xavier waiting for him. Life in Iraq was hard and having Xavier to look after was a release from the reality of war. Even though Xavier was a bomb sniffing dog Brian looked after him like anyone would treat their pet.

Although Brian and Hunter were good high school friends they lost track of each other for many years. Brian stayed in Philadelphia and Hunter had moved to Mississippi on a football scholarship. Brian had joined the Army and was certain that it would be his career. Brian heard that Hunter had got injured his senior year and that he joined the National guard soon after that. Brian always knew that his friend would be a football star. He figured that the football injury had to be tough on him. He also had since found out that Hunter had gotten married and moved to Los Angeles. He had not met Blair until the funeral, although she and Hunter had made a few trips to Bridgewater to see his Dad. Brian was glad to meet her but so sad it was under these circumstances.

The funeral was still in his mind. It was hard to shake it off. He went home for only a week but to bury his friend. The Army was gracious enough that they allowed Brian to accompany his friend's body back home for the funeral. After all they were high school friends and he had been on the roof top when Hunter was shot.

The barracks were highly protected due to recent car bombings throughout Baghdad. The use of German Sheppard dogs was important and they never entered until the dogs made sure all was clear. The U.S. troops were always a target of snipers and car bombers. How could such a noble cause turn sour? It had been two years since the start of the conflict with a strong resolve but now it seemed more like an occupation of a country that did not want you. When he was home Brian felt a sense of pride. The friends and family members that were at the funeral all expressed gratitude for what he and Hunter were doing. He also sensed an underlying question in people's conversation. Why are we still there? It seemed with each service man or woman lost the country grew more restless with the outcome and hoped for an end to the struggle.

Captain Montgomery came into Brian's barracks. He inquired about the funeral.

"It was a tough one," Brian said.

Captain Montgomery was the commander of their unit. He was always quiet and seemed deep in thought. It was his decision to continue the mission that came under fire while protecting diplomats. Captain Montgomery was only in his late twenties but had seen enough action in his nine months in Iraq to fill a lifetime. This was his second tour of duty in Iraq. He was from Georgia and like most of his men he missed home and his family. Captain Montgomery was a tall thin man and had leathery skin after being in the hot sun for so long. The men always thought it was strange that after missions Hunter and Captain Montgomery would meet to strategize.

Captain Montgomery often talked about fishing. He and his wife lived on Lake Lanier, north of Atlanta. It was a man made lake and had great fishing and boating. In recent years the State of Georgia had added a large Hotel and water park close to Buford, Georgia on the southern end on the lake. There was plenty of wildlife and two championship golf courses. The Captain didn't talk about family, just fishing, baseball and his love of the lake back home. He was also a big fan of the Atlanta Braves. If he wasn't talking about fishing he was talking about the Braves. He never seemed to have any conversation that seemed personal. He seemed distant to some of his men. It was rumored that he had been the tank driver that helped local Iraqi's topple the statue of Saddam in the Baghdad square that CNN had sent pictures of across the world. He had been Brian and Hunter's commander for about six months.

Both soldiers sat quietly for a while and reflected on the day Hunter was killed. The mission seemed simple enough. Guard two high ranking U.S officials as they met with key Iraqi officials. It was to be a short meeting not more than one hour. Something must have gone wrong because the meeting lasted more than three hours. The security guards were stationed on the roof and around the perimeter of the building for the whole time and became concerned about how long the meeting was taking. Anytime they had to guard officials they knew that word would get out and the chance of gun fire would increase.

Terrorist took pleasure in this sort of attacks. Hide and shoot from cover. Send a suicide bomber into the fray and wreak havoc. The length of the meeting made it very difficult to protect the officials and not lose any of the men. The decision to stay and let the meeting continue rested with Captain Montgomery. After the meeting had passed the two hour mark he tried to get the officials attention. That's when the gunfire started. Two soldiers were injured on the outside of the gate when a car bomber crashed into it. Then the gunfire struck a target. One dead, two injured and nothing accomplished. Hunter was strong and always alert but when the car bomber hit the gate he stood up on the roof. It was too late as Brian yelled to him.

They had a helicopter fly in to help quell the uprising but it was too late. They loaded the injured into a Suburban that they used to transport the officials. The helicopter took Hunter and Brian back to the base. Captain Montgomery ordered a second helicopter to fly in and after all was clear they flew the officials back to their headquarters.

Brian did not want to talk about the funeral or anything else. The men had seen too many of their friends injured or die. Iraq had been a tough battlefield. Many of the soldiers wanted to help the Iraqi people. There were so many sad sights. Children left without parents. Wives without husbands, so many without homes. It was hard to reason what they had accomplished when the devastation was so great.

"I know you are tired Brian but we do have some things to complete here. I received a request to box Hunter's personal belongings and forward them to the FBI."

Brian had a puzzled look on his face.

"Why the FBI?"

Brian was not sure why the items should go through them.

"Guess they have to inspect everything before it goes stateside," the Captain said. "I've looked around and found some of his stuff in the foot locker but thought you might know where more of his things were. Can you to help me go through his stuff?"

It was never anything that was easy to do but wives; parents and children back home needed closure. Getting personal belongings often helped with that process. Brian said, "I will need some time."

"Ok," Captain Montgomery said.

Brian met Captain Montgomery after mess and they went to Hunter's barracks. He had his trunk at the foot of his cot like everyone. He often said he traveled light and thus never seemed to have very many personal things. Like everyone's trunk there were pictures and a few items that never made sense to others except the individual. Captain Montgomery said "I've looked through that stuff in the trunk."

Brian was surprised that Captain Montgomery had already gone through some of Hunter's stuff. Brian knew that Blair or Hunter's dad would want anything they found. He knew that he had some of Hunter's letters and a package in his trunk. Hunter said that he was planning on sending some things to his wife and asked Brian to keep them for him. It was a difficult task and hard to look at the items.

The body armor that had arrived too late sat at the end of the bunk and just was a reminder of how little protection each soldier had. Brian went to his locker and took some items out.

"These were Hunter's, Captain."

There was a bulky envelope with something in it. Brian opened it and it was letters with some trinkets. Maybe letters from Blair he thought.

"Where did you get that package?"

"He gave it to me and he said if anything happened to him he would want Blair to have it. They are just letters, probably letters they sent to each other."

Captain Montgomery said, "We should inspect them."

Brian thought that the Captain was overly interested in the package.

"I just think that it doesn't seem right," he said and re-sealed the envelope. Brian said he would address it and send the package as instructed in the morning to the FBI.

"I'll put the letters with all the other stuff and send them to the FBI."

"I'll do it for you Brian."

"That's Ok Captain. I want to do this last thing for him."

Captain Montgomery insisted but Brian held his ground.

"This is all that I have left to do for him Captain."

Brian put the package in his footlocker and lay on his bunk. He knew that he had to send the package the next day to Riyadh. He wondered why Captain Montgomery was so anxious to get the items off to the FBI. It seemed to him that the Captain was overly anxious. Brian got up the next morning and had cleared his thoughts regarding Hunter's items. He would get the package ready for shipment to the FBI but first he wanted to remove the letters that he felt should go to Blair. The box was sealed and taken to be dispatched to Riyadh for inspection. The second package would also be given to the clerk. Once it was cleared it would be forwarded to Blair.

It was on the way to the mail area that Brian took out the package and addressed it to Blair. After all that's what Hunter asked him to do. It was probably some love letters Blair had sent to her husband he thought.

"I'll just send these direct to Blair. She would want them."

It seemed like the right thing to do. Even though he had just met her she seemed fragile and these might help her in her time of grief. It's a good thing I was here to do this he thought.

Captain Montgomery met Brian at the dispatcher's office. Brian was surprised to see him there.

"I'm sending the package as instructed sir."

"Brian you don't know how important this may be."

"It's important to me too sir."

Captain Montgomery was glad that he had asked Brian to help box Hunter's things up. He would not have known that Hunter had given Brian a package to hold for him.

When Brian left the dispatchers office Captain Montgomery asked to use the computer. He said that he had to forward some important information to Washington. The Captain waited until Brian left and asked to see the package going to Riyadh.

"Sorry I can't do that Sir."

"That's a command."

"Federal law Sir."

Captain Montgomery left but was not through.

Brain went back to the barracks alone. He didn't tell the Captain that he sent Blair some items that did not go in the package for inspection. He just wanted to do one last thing for his friend.

THREE

Thomas Adams was walking back to his car. The funeral was over and all the friends had gone back home. He remembered what his brother had said that the hardest part was after everyone was gone. Thomas was an ex Marine and proud of his son. The funeral was with a full military guard. The whole town seemed to come to the funeral. Thomas knew that visiting the cemetery was the only way he could make himself believe that his son was really dead. Thomas spent much of Hunter's childhood overseas and had missed seeing his son grow up. By the time he was out of the service Hunter was in high school and a football star. Thomas wanted to make up for lost time with his son. Now that was not to be.

The small town outside of Philadelphia ran along the Delaware River. Bridgewater was a great place to live. It had a population of about 15,000 people and most of them had lived there their whole life. You could walk down the street and know just about everyone. It was centrally located. You could cross the Burlington Toll Bridge into New Jersey and head for the Jersey shore in a few minutes. Downtown Philadelphia was less than an hours ride. Although many comedians made fun of New Jersey, the shore line offered a paradise of fun. Thomas and Hunter had gone to Atlantic City on his last visit home. Blair did not like to gamble but knew that Hunter and his dad did. Also, it was good for them to be together. A bonding thing she told him.

Many thoughts entered Thomas's mind as he walked to his car. Thomas thought that so many friends had come to honor his son but yet he felt so alone. Like so many parents he felt like so much went unsaid and he wished he had it to do over. You never know what life had in store for you. Parents should not bury their children he thought. He thought back that seeing Brian, his son's old high school friend in his dress uniform at the airport made him more aware of how much he missed the time when Brian and Hunter were playing football for Bridgewater High.

Hunter was a local sports star. It seemed that some schools were interested in Hunter but none of them made him the offer he was looking for. Scholarship offers came in and when he got the one from The University of Mississippi he knew that was the one. He told his Dad that although he would be far from home, the opportunity to play for a Southeast Conference school may be the ticket to the NFL. Hunter loved the Dallas Cowboys and always dreamed of playing for them some day. Many SEC players made it to the NFL and scouts from teams like the Cowboys would visit these schools because of their location and reputation.

Blair was not a football fan but she loved fall days on the Grove, the campus center and staging area for tailgate parties. That is where she met Hunter for the first time. It was a warm football Saturday, about 9:00 a.m., and she had sat with some friends in the grove, near the walk of fame, where the football team would pass on the way to the stadium. She saw a tall strong young man with the number 10 jersey draped over his arms walking by and asked who that was. That's Hunter Adams, he's the star running back and is he ever cute. She made sure she would run into that running back first chance she got. She often would tell Thomas that story. It made him feel good.

Thomas made Blair promise to call him when she got home. He had hoped to hear from her and that she had made it back safely. He got into his blue Chevrolet Impala and headed toward his house. The car was not new but very reliable. It got good fuel mileage and with the recent rising cost of fuel that was important. The ride from the cemetery to his house was about four miles. It was a sunny day and the May flowers were coming up along the roadside.

May was always a good month on the east coast. The weather was getting warmer and the flowers were popping out everywhere. Mother Nature had created a bouquet of colors that filled the woods with nature's beauty. You could always spot a raccoon or beaver along the creek side rebuilding their fortress for the summer ahead. It had been an unusually hard winter. Over thirty inches of snow had fallen and there were numerous ice storms. But now the flowers were in bloom and the Cherry trees were full of beautiful pink flowers. The ride along highway 13 was teaming with spring life. The Neshaminy River crossed highway 13 between Croydon and Bridgewater. You had to be careful because at times the river overflowed onto the highway. A line of Bradford Pear trees full of white flowers sprang into view as he drove along the highway. Almost there he said to himself. Spring meant the beginning but Thomas felt more like this was the end. He wondered how he could go on. Hunter was his only child and now he was gone. As he rounded the next curve he saw his driveway coming into view. It was just a couple of days ago that many friends filled the drive and street after the funeral. He parked in his circle driveway and entered into his house. It was still a mess but most everything had been put back into its place.

The phone rang.

"Hello," he said.

"Hi, it's me, Blair."

"I'm so glad to hear from you honey. How was your flight home?"

"I'm sorry I didn't call right away but I wanted to let you know that I was home safe."

"Are you ok?"

"I guess so."

"I miss you already. Bet it was difficult going into your apartment."

"Well it became more difficult because someone broke in while I was gone."

"Oh no!" Thomas said. "Are you ok Blair?"

"Yes, but it was so hard seeing our stuff turned over and messed up. I'm glad that Hunter's football helmet and trophies were ok. I want to send you his football things."

"You should keep them Blair."

"No, I want you to have them she said. I know how much they mean to you and Hunter would have wanted you to have them."

"Ok, he said. I will cherish them always."

Thomas thought his son sure made a good choice. Blair is very thoughtful and sweet. He wished that he and Hunter were closer when Hunter was growing up. After he married Blair, it seemed that Blair brought them back together. She was big on family and wanted to make sure that Hunter kept close with his dad.

"Have you called the police Blair?"

"Yes, they made a report, Ashley one of my friends here, will help me go through our stuff to see if anything is missing. It appears that all the big things are there." Thomas hesitated to tell Blair.

"Blair, I'm not sure what to make of this but my house was broken into the day I took you back to the Philadelphia airport."

"You can't be serious. Why would someone want to do this to us?"

Blair started to cry. Thomas tried to comfort her.

"Nothing was missing, just looked like kids looking for something. Maybe they were looking for liquor or money. Anyway I called the Bridgewater police and Captain Douglas made a report of the incident. I have thought it had to be kids."

Blair tried to regain her composure but it was tough.

"I am going to stay with my friend Ashley tonight."

"That's a good idea," Thomas said.

"You should be with someone."

"Are you ok," Blair asked.

"I guess," said Thomas.

"I'll call you in a couple of days," Blair said. Thomas remembered the story of how Blair and his son met. He did love that story and it made him feel good to think about his son and things that he had done.

"Blair, just be careful," he said.

Thomas hung up the phone and wondered what were the odds of both of them having a break-in. He still had a lot of things to pick up but Thomas just wasn't in the mood. It had been a few days since his break in and most everything had been put back in its place. He grabbed a cold beer and headed outside.

The weather had been nice every day except the day of the funeral. It rained so hard that they had to have the graveyard service under a shelter. It must have dropped 20 degree's that day he thought to himself as he walked outside. The military funeral was impressive to the small town's folks. There must have been over 500 people in attendance. As taps were played and the American flag was folded over the coffin a 21 gun salute rang out. Thomas remembered that the sound of the gunfire startled Blair. The Army guard folded the flag and handed it to her. The site of such a young widow was hard to understand. Blair had just turned 23 and although Hunter was a few years older than her, it seemed like she was more mature.

Thomas and Blair had to go to the Philadelphia airport to claim his son's body a few days earlier. Blair was the strength that Thomas needed. She held him tight as the honor guard approached. When Hunter's body arrived at the Philadelphia airport they also had a flag folding ceremony. Blair insisted that Thomas have that flag. It was the flag that had draped the coffin from Iraq to home.

Thomas walked around outside and gazed into the woods behind his house. The birds were having a feeding frenzy around the berry bush in his backyard. His yard was very large. He had not been in the yard since the night of the funeral. He had sat at a small table on the porch with some friends that night. The house was sort of a renovated Farm house that was in his family for years. The sky was very clear and you could see the moon overhead, although it was still daylight. That's odd, Thomas thought, as he looked at the back of his property. He walked to the end of his lot and saw that the fence had been broken. It was a split rail fence that he had put up about 10 years ago around the whole yard. There was over 150 feet of fence along the back of the house. As he walked closer he saw that there were tire tracks in the woods where the fence had been broken. Thomas inspected the tracks and headed back inside. Better call Captain Douglas he thought. None of this made any sense to Thomas. It appears that there is nothing missing. My house and Blair's apartment ransacked. He knew it was strange but there was no answer to the puzzle.

Captain Douglas was an old Marine friend and would know what to look for Thomas thought. He knew most of the families in the neighborhood but some new people had moved in and the whole town was growing. He called Captain Douglas to let him know about the tire tracks and the fence being broken. Maybe this would lead to the people who broke into his home. He didn't know how they missed seeing the broken fence after the initial report was completed.

Thomas went back into the living room after he called Captain Douglas and sat in his recliner. He looked at the triangle folded American flag and sighed. Thomas was very sad. He had so many hopes now all those were gone. The Captain said that he would be over in a little bit to survey the yard. Thomas didn't know what to do. He just sat in the chair and looked out the front window.

FOUR

Ahmad looked at the sky as if he had never seen it before. The nightmare of being in Abu Ghraid prison for the past two months was finally over. He had been picked up in a daily round-up of Iraqis by the Local Police. He was suspected as being a terrorist.

The Abu Ghraib prison was located in Abu Ghraib, an Iraq city about 32 km west of Baghdad. It had become internationally known as a place where Saddam Hussein tortured and executed dissidents. The prison came to the notice of the world when American television publicized several graphic and disturbing photos of Coalition prisoner abuse there. The Coalition changed the name to Camp Redemption and actually located its prisoners in a tent area on the outside of the prison walls. It was also used by the Coalition as a forward operation base.

Ahmad was detained and questioned many times. He knew that the American and British troops that questioned the prisoners would get information from some of them but not him. He was strong of will and would never give them any information. The coalition troops had under estimated Ahmad. They thought he was just a poor farmer caught in the round up of suspected terrorist. Ahmad was cunning and had learned many western tactics while attending University in London. He was also aware that the coalition troops had names and descriptions of suspected Saddam loyalist so he changed his name and disguised himself. It was easy to pick up the identification of another citizen who had been killed in the fighting. It was important to stay free.

He was driven back to the center of the city with another released prisoner, close to where the American troops had helped the uprising of

Iraqis pull down the statue of Saddam. The driver zigzagged through
underpasses to make sure that they could avoid anyone that may drop
a grenade on them. They passed a Humvee that had soldiers on top of
it. Their gunners were going side to side to make sure that they would
protect the men that traveled in their group. Iraq had forced the Army
to change its tactics. It was more of a plan on the go type of operation
than the conventional warfare that most of the men had been trained
for. Ahmad told them, "I want out. I will walk the rest of the way."
He got out of the back of the Jeep and started walking. The soldiers
watched him for a few minutes and headed back to their camp.

After the Jeep was out of view he changed direction and headed
toward a Mosque. He entered and headed to a side room where he
met his friend El Hassen. Hassen was also a Saddam loyalist that had
eluded the coalition troops although he had been picked up and spent
time in Abu Ghraib prison. During the early occupation many Iraqis
had been detained at Abu Ghraib before being let free. It was a difficult
time for both the American and British troops. The Iraqi arm had
been scattered throughout the region and there was no local authority
to seek assistance from. The identification of the men that were taken
into custody was almost impossible to verify.

Ahmad and Hassen went into the small room off the side of the
Mosque where a group of men had been talking.

"You are free my brother. Praise Allah! We have much to do."

The two men were happy to be reunited. They were both loyalist
to the regime of Saddam Hussein and had unfinished business. They
had not seen each other for months but were aware of recent issues that
would change their mission.

Iraq's economy was dominated by the oil sector, which had provided
about 95% of its economy. The eight year war with Iran and now the
fall of the Ba'ath party has led these influential men to plot together.
They needed the western influence out of Iraq so they could regain
some of their power. Ahmad and Hassen entered another room off the
mosque. They were greeted by a small group of men. Among them
was Muhammad Assar.

"Praise Allah," they said. "Our brother's are free!"

"We have been chosen by Allah for a great task."

"We have been chosen for this mission by our Brother, Commander Muhammad. He knows our discipline is strong. We will be strong for the mission ahead."

Iraq was a nation that had a long history of strife and its factions were dedicated to their cause. From Iraq's early beginning to the current State of Iraq that saw a nation with a population of over 26 million people trying to assimilate into a democracy.

Ahmad and Hassen would be the catalyst to lead the group in their plans to get back into power. It would take a critical turn of events and they felt that they knew where it could be found. Muhammad had details of importance that would send Ahmad and Hassen on a search. The search would gather important documents that they needed to regain a foothold in the country. The coalition forces had steered clear of the activity in local Mosque because of religious implications. It was a time when they had hoped to earn the support from the Iraqi people and by honoring their right to worship was just one way to show them the respect that would help to further the coalition's goals.

In another meeting Afghan rebels met in the southern city of Kandahar, Afghanistan. This was a largely unsettled area long a strong hold of Taliban support. The Taliban had largely unskilled but highly motivated followers. They had another mission in mind. That of creating havoc on the American troops. Their leader was now enlisting men for suicide attacks on the American troops that occupied their province.

Afghanistan was torn with the al-Qaida and Taliban terrorist taking refuge there.

The insurgents would continue to use guerrilla tactics. This group was headed by El Jaafi. He was a direct lieutenant of Osama bin Laden. His band of cut throats had no morals and he was a blood thirsty terrorist.

El Jaafi was planning to take a small group of his men who were more highly trained on the special mission. Some of these men had lived in the States and found a way to assimilate into normal American lives. They attended Universities and some had gone to pilot schools to learn how to fly. These men made up the core of supporters. Al Yawer was a pivotal member of this group. He was a certified pilot and knew his way around.

Al Yawer was a very smart man and El Jaafi counted heavily on his knowledge. He knew that all the men would trust his instincts and

orders. Al Yawer had a special relationship to El Jaafi. It all went back to
the war with Iran. Although El Jaafi was older he and Al Yawer would
act as one when it came to planning a mission of this magnitude.

The men would never question any commands and Al Yawer offered
them the ability to infiltrate and keep their disguise until the time was
ready to strike.

El Jaafi knew that with this group of men they could travel to the
United States and meet without much suspicion. They made their plans
to travel separately so as not to have a problem with the new security
that had been put into place at all the United States airports.

Back in Baghdad the meeting in the mosque was coming to a close.
Ahmad and Hassen had both spent time in Abu Ghraid prison and were
lucky enough to be let free. They appeared to their captors, as meager
farmers, that had been taken into custody. In the opinion of the men
who questioned them at Abu Ghraid they were not very smart and
harmless. Ahmad had been able to take the identification of another
Iraqi who had been killed in the invasion. He kept that on him and
was thought to be that man when he was at Abu Ghraib prison. It
was critical for the entire Saddam loyalist to either go into hiding or to
protect their real identification with a false one.

The coalition troops were at a strong disadvantage because so many
Iraqi men were without identification and there was no longer any
central authority to provide verification for those with identification.

Ahmad had been an integral part of Saddam's inner circle. He was
highly motivated to protect the Iraq that Saddam had built. He was a
Saddam loyalist. He had been one of the key figures in helping Saddam hide
his gold and critical weapons. He had attended University in London and
had spent a great deal of time on the West Coast of the United States.

The news of Saddam's capture and possible trial upset him greatly.
The thought that Saddam could appear before a special tribunal and
that he may face the death penalty saddened Ahmad. The Americans
and British, he felt had forced the new Iraq government to deal this
fate to Saddam. The charges of killing rival politicians, gassing Kurds,
invading Kuwait and suppressing Shiite uprisings were preposterous.
Ahmad knew that the death sentence was part of the Iraq legal system
before the U.S. led invasion two years ago. But he felt that the U.S.

and British were putting pressure on the new Iraq government to carry out this deed.

This group of Saddam supporters met in the mosque to plan their mission. They knew from information they received that they must travel to the United States. The group included three men who had lived in Southern California and would be able to gain entrance to the United States. Another key man along with Ahmad and Hassen was Jasim Muhammad. Jasim had been born in Long Beach, California. His father was involved in the early development of computer chips. Jasim and his family returned to Iraq when his father's employer outsourced his job. Many Iraqi men had been to Universities in the west. It would help them when they traveled because they understood American culture. When he returned to Iraq, Jasim met Ahmad Aswar and became involved in the Ba'ath party. He became a Saddam loyalist. He never was able to understand why his father had lost his job in the United States and blamed the United States for their fate. Jasim would be a key into the Southern California landscape. It was once his home and he was a U.S. citizen. He would be the first one to travel and would set-up their headquarters. Jasim was a pilot and his training would come in handy. The west coast offered unusual terrain and a small airplane could help scout it out.

Ahmad would want Jasim to prepare a safe place for them in the Long Beach area. He figured that they could travel up the coast to Santa Monica from Long Beach and have easy access to either planes or ships in the event that they had to escape. The men made their plans with the mission clear. Ahmad was the group's leader and he would travel last to the United States through London. Because he had attended University in London he knew that it would be easy to get there and be able to travel to California. He would detail the plans to the group of men and tell Muhammad Assar what their plans were. They would find the key documents and help their group regain the power that they were seeking.

International travel had changed greatly since 9/11. The United States had employed many airport screeners and required that other countries that had flights coming into the U.S. do the same thing. New documents would be prepared for some of these men. Ahmad would make sure they would get to their destination.

FIVE

Blair walked into the living room of Ashley's apartment.

"Wow I guess I was more tired than I thought. Ashley thank you so much for letting me spend the night. I think it was the first real sleep I've gotten in weeks." Ashley's cat Clark rubbed himself along Blair's legs.

"No problem Blair. After we get dressed we will go to your place and see what we can pick up. Together we will be able to get a lot done."

"We also have to fill out that report for Officer Tuttle."

"We should call a locksmith to change your door lock."

"I guess that's a good idea. Maybe one can come out when we are there later today."

The two girls walked down Santa Monica Blvd. toward the Promenade. They were going to meet Blake, he said he wanted to help put Blair's apartment back together. The three friends met in the Promenade at the corner of third and Santa Monica Blvd. It was a short walk to Arizona Avenue and Blair's apartment. There was a cool breeze over the Promenade from the Pacific Ocean. This was normal for the month of May. It made for a refreshing walk as the three strolled down toward Blair's apartment.

They went up the elevator to the second floor. Apartment 21A was the fourth one on the right side of the hallway. Blair opened the door and they all walked in.

"I just don't understand how they got in. Nothing seems to be damaged around the door."

"People who break into homes have tools that help them open your locks. Bet that's what they did Blair."

The three looked around for a place to start.

"Things are not too bad," Ashley said.

"I can move some of the bigger things," Blake added, as he turned the table back on its legs. There were three chairs that he put around the table. He looked around to see what he should do next.

"I will get a trash bag so you can put anything broken in there."

He looked around but was surprised to see that most of the items were just turned over on the floor. Only a few items were actually damaged.

"I might have to keep those items for insurance."

"Your right," said Ashley.

They had been at it for about an hour and half and were making great progress when the phone rang.

"Hi, I'm looking for Mrs. Blair Adams," said the voice.

"I'm Mrs. Adams" Blair answered.

"I'm Allisa Jones with the Federal Bureau of Investigation."

"The FBI? What do you want with me?"

"I'm so sorry to bother you at this time, and we want to offer our condolence for the loss of your husband. I would like to meet with you to go over some details that are necessary regarding Mr. Adams and his time in the military."

Why would the FBI be concerned?

"Mrs. Adams, your husband like many other American soldiers may have had details that our department is responsible to close. This is normal and part of the new homeland security effort."

"I'm still not sure why the FBI would be involved. I don't know anything."

"Ms. Adams I can give you those details when we meet."

"I would like some idea of what you are talking about before we meet," Blair said. "Mrs. Adams we have to ask you some questions because you have been out of the country with Mr. Adams several times during his time in the military."

Blair thought back about the time that Hunter had been wounded in Afghanistan and was sent to Germany. She was so concerned that she got approval from the Army to fly there and see him. He had been shot in the shoulder and also had damaged his teeth while diving over a barricade. Blair started thinking about that trip and some unusual things came to mind.

"If I agree to meet you Ms. Jones can I bring one of my friends with me?"

"We would prefer that you met with us alone Mrs. Adams." "Us?"

"Of course I will have a person from our office with me to record any information that you may provide that can help close our file."

"Mrs. Adams, I can assure you that we just want to clear up a few questions and than you will be free to do what you need to."

"Can I call you back Ms. Jones."

"How about if I call you back later Mrs. Adams, we can set the time for our meeting then."

Blair agreed to be home later for that call and said goodbye.

"Who was that on the phone?" Blake asked.

"I'm really not sure. She said she was from the FBI."

"What the hell does the FBI want with you?"

"I'm not sure but I have to think. Blake, can you stay with me?"

"Sure."

Blair was more confused than ever and had no idea what to do next. She knew that Ashley would have to go to work and she needed someone to keep her company. Blake could give her some ideas if she only knew the questions to ask. Ashley listened to their conversation. Once they stopped talking, her and Blake went back to straightening the apartment. Blair sat at the table and was deep in thought. Her mind raced back to Germany and her trip there. Hunter had been in a hospital, his arm was in a cast and they had made a mold so they could make him a bridge for his missing teeth. He was feeling much better when Blair arrived and he arranged to take them on a trip to Switzerland. He wanted to show her the Matterhorn and the beautiful scenery. He told her they would have to travel as students so as not to create any question as to why an American soldier was traveling around Switzerland. His right arm was in a cast and he had a partial plate so that he could chew until his new bridge would be ready.

It seemed odd to Blair at the time but Hunter had multiple passports. He said it was to protect him as he traveled out of uniform. Why multiple passports? Why pretend they were students? Now the FBI is involved.

"Oh Hunter, what am I to do."

Hunter was 6 foot 4 and he had a rugged build. He had been in great shape his whole life. With the hope of a career in football and his time in the U.S. Army he was always running, lifting weights and eating right. He had the most beautiful eyes Blair had ever seen. He could look right through you with those blue eyes. People would stare at them when they walked by. What a beautiful couple. Blair counted on him. His strength was reassuring to her. Now when she needed him, he wasn't there.

Blair's mind went back to Switzerland. It was so beautiful. She had just looked at the pictures they took at the Matterhorn. They stayed in a small bed and breakfast type of place. The bedroom they had overlooked a wonderland of snow. It was a scene out of a motion picture she thought. Hunter so loved their time together on that trip. He made sure that they had breakfast in bed and filled the room with flowers and candles. Blair loved fresh flowers and the scent of candles burning. They made love that day like it was their honeymoon all over again. He loved her blond hair and the way it curled around the side of her cheeks. She was his movie star.

There was no question. Blair was beautiful. She had won a few beauty pageants back in Alabama but most people would say it was her personality that set her apart from the other contestants. She also had appeared in a few local productions back home in Alabama. Although her hometown of Trussville, Alabama, was small the local ACTA Theater was well known, and produced some very good plays. Her work in the local theater won her recognition and gave her the idea of moving to Hollywood. It was at the University of Mississippi after meeting Hunter that this dream became a reality. Like many young women that hoped to make it in Hollywood she ended up taking a job in the restaurant industry.

Blair wondered why her husband had passports with different names. She never thought about that when they were together.

Was he working with the FBI?

She could not stop her train of thought until Blake said, "Ashley do you want us to walk you to work?"

"No, it's only a few blocks."

"I'm so sorry Ashley. I'm just a ball of nerves. Please let us walk with you."

"Blair we are almost done here. You and Blake could finish up in about a half hour. I'll be ok."

"We will come in to The Pub and eat dinner after while," she said to Ashley.

"That sounds good. I know a lot of people would be glad to see you."

Ms. Jones told her colleague that it wasn't going to be as easy as they hoped.

"If she agrees to meet me tomorrow I might get her away from that apartment so you can go back. It has to be there. We must find the document before anyone else does."

"This time search her place but don't do any damage. We can't afford any more suspicion. I don't want her to know that anyone has been in that apartment again."

Ms. Jones colleague, Tony Baxter, had been in the Washington Bureau and had recently been transferred to Southern California. Tony was a veteran of the Bureau and had received many accommodations for his work. He could accomplish the task handed to him, although he felt that he should be in charge. That he had to take orders from a woman bothered him. He would let Ms. Jones set up the meeting with Blair Adams but he would handle the apartment search.

Ms. Jones had received an email from Hunter's unit in Baghdad. It was forwarded from the Washington Bureau. Baxter knew she received the email but she did not share it with him.

"Damn female boss."

He wondered what was the information that she had and why not share it with him.

Blake and Blair had finished their work at the apartment and decided to head to The Pub to meet Ashley for dinner. Everything had been pretty much put back into place and Blair didn't know of anything missing. She would call Officer Tuttle after they ate.

Blair and Blake made there way down Third and through the tourist in the Promenade. One of her friends was playing his guitar on the corner of Third and Broadway. Blair stopped and said "hi." She always supported all her friends, and he was close to finishing his first CD. She dropped a ten dollar bill into his guitar case and they continued their walk. The Pub was ahead on the corner of Santa Monica Blvd. and Third. It was so nice to be greeted by so many people and well wishers. Allen and Joe came over to say hello. Allen was a famous chef and often made special dinners and dropped them off at Blair's apartment. He had moved to the States from England and he and his wife loved the California coast. Their daughter had just made her First Communion and Allen was a proud father. Joe had worked on many movie and television projects including Star Wars. He always had interesting stories that he shared with Blair when she was tending bar. So many of The Pub's regulars had Hollywood connections. You would often see directors dining outside and discussing their next project.

Blake and Blair had a seat at an outside table and Olly came over and hugged Blair.

"I just want to help you honey," Olly said.

"You take as much time off as necessary. We'll help you with everything."

Olly and Sonia were partners in The Pub. Sonia was from Liverpool and had dedicated an entire wall of The Pub to the Beatles. She had seen them play when she lived in Liverpool and loved their work. Her father, Mike, would often help the two women with operation issues at The Pub. Both owners were great and supported their employee's that were trying to make it in the motion picture industry. Sonia's husband Paul was a lot of fun. He would make you laugh doing the simplest of things. His British accent was still pretty strong especially when he starting talking fast. Everyone just loved them.

Olly sat down with Blair and Blake. Blair told her about the conversation with the FBI agent Ms. Jones. Like Blair, Olly wasn't sure what to make of it but said, "you have to meet her and see what she wants."

"I guess your right Olly. Maybe I'll arrange the meeting here so you can make sure everything is ok."

"Good idea," Olly said. Blake agreed.

"You could even meet her upstairs where it is quiet if she wants."

The Pub had an upstairs that had video games and pool tables for patrons. There were about five dining tables upstairs and it was usually quiet there during the daytime. Most of the patrons during the day would either want to eat outside or along the windows in the front of The Pub. The glass windows would often be slid open during the day to let the cool breeze in. Blair felt better about the possible meeting and knew that having her friends close would be the protection she needed. She would suggest The Pub to Ms. Jones as their meeting place when she called back.

Ms. Jones told Tony Baxter that he needed to be close to Blair's apartment when she called. "I will call your cell phone Baxter so that you can watch to see when she leaves. Make sure she doesn't leave someone behind."

"I know what to do," Baxter said, "just set the meeting up. I'll do the rest."

Baxter did not like Ms. Jones. The fact that they did not find the documents that they were seeking made their relationship even more strained. Ms. Jones wished that Baxter was more cooperative but knew that he had the experience needed for this assignment.

Blair was pleased that nothing was missing when she gave Officer Tuttle the report and had only found some dishes and a few small items off her coffee table broken. Not enough for an insurance report she thought. Her dad made sure that they had insurance for an event just like this.

Blair and Blake finished their dinner at The Pub and knew that they needed to head back to Blair's apartment so that when Allisa Jones called Blair would be there.

The walk back to her apartment was good. Things felt more normal after dinner. They went up to her apartment and waited for Ms. Jones to call. It was just about a half an hour when the phone rang and Blair answered.

"Good afternoon Mrs. Adams this is Allisa Jones."

"Hi, Ms. Jones."

"I hope that you are doing ok," Ms. Jones said.

"Mrs. Adams our meeting won't be very long and I won't bring anyone else with me if that makes you feel better."

"Yes it does. Please call me Blair."

Blair was now feeling a little better about the meeting with Ms. Jones and the FBI involvement. She knew that the location at The

Pub would be safe and with just her and Ms. Jones it should not be too threatening.

"Ms. Jones I was thinking. I work here in Santa Monica and it would be easiest for me if you met me where I work."

"That's not a problem as long as we can have about an hour to talk Mrs. Adams. It would be best if there is a quiet place to sit."

"Yes that can be arranged. Call me Blair please; it makes it seem not so formal."

"Sure, and you can call me Allisa if it helps you."

"Thanks, how about meeting tomorrow around 3:00 p.m. at The Pub. It's on the corner of Santa Monica Blvd. and the Promenade."

"Blair that sounds good. You're sure there is quiet place where we won't be disturbed?"

"Yes, they have a large upstairs room that is used for meetings and overflow crowds especially during the Soccer tournaments."

The 3:00 p.m. time would also be good because the lunch crowd would be gone and it would be a little quieter. The Pub was a gathering place for the local European crowd that loved soccer.

The British and Irish crowd would often overflow onto the patio outside the pub during tournament time. Soccer was very popular in Europe and the local British, Scottish and Irish crowd would carry on into the late evening when it was tourney time. Because of the time difference most of the matches ran very late or were on delayed broadcast.

The meeting was set. Blair called Olly at The Pub to tell her what she and Ms. Jones agreed to.

"Sounds good to me," Olly said.

"We will make sure everything is set up for you, and we know the only way out is through the downstairs exit so it should be safe."

Blair trusted her friends, and appreciated their suggestions.

"Were you able to finish up your apartment?"

"Yes we got everything picked up in my apartment and I have to stop by the post office for a special delivery package before I come to The Pub tomorrow. Blake and Ashley were the greatest help."

She had found a special delivery notice on her door when she had returned home. Probably something from my dad she thought. He often sent things UPS but guess he sent this regular mail. Wonder why they didn't leave it at the door, she thought.

SIX

The plane flight to New York LaGuardia Airport was without event. Al Yawer made it through security checks both at his layover in London and when he departed Iraq. Having two separate tickets with different destinations would stop anyone who was watching him travel. His final destination was easy to plan from London. He exited the London Airport where he met another operative with a second set of travel documents and identification.

London had a vast terrorist cell that had started to make plans for bombings in the city. Their plans were to cause local unrest and political upheaval for Tony Blair's government's involvement in Iraq. The new set of identification was pivotal. This helped him went he boarded his next flight for New York. He would travel to New York under the new set of identification.

Once he retrieved his luggage at LaGuardia Yawer walked through the airport and stopped at a local sports bar along the Spirit Airline concourse. He ordered a sandwich and sat at a small table along the windows. Another traveler sat behind him and put his small bag next to Yawer's suitcase. Yawer ate half of his food and gathered his suitcase plus the small bag that the traveler behind him had left. Yawer left the airport and waited for a taxi cab. Traveling in and out of LaGuardia was always a task unless you used local taxi service. While waiting for his cab, Yawer opened the small bag left for him and found details with a location for him to travel to. He would ask the cab driver to take him to an address in the Bronx near Yankee Stadium.

El Jaafi waited in the house for Yawer. He knew from calls he received that the transfer in London went well and that Yawer would soon be meeting his contact in the LaGuardia Airport. The house was on the lower Bronx not too far from Yankee Stadium and the subway. Once they were together in the Bronx, travel through New York would be easy with the subway system. You could transfer from one line to another and get anywhere in the Metro area in a flash. The plan was set. Yawer and El Jaafi would travel to Bridgewater, Pennsylvania and check out the home of Thomas Adams. They would look for the documents that they knew had to exist.

It was ironic that while in London Yawer passed another traveler. El Hassen waiting for his plane flight to the Los Angeles LAX Airport. Hassen was familiar with the London Airport because he and Ahmad had spent time in London at the University.

The flight to LAX was tedious due to the many short flights taken to get to his final destination. While in London Hassen stayed with friends that had attended University with him and Ahmad. They were also operatives and helped him set up the plans for the rest of the group. Ahmad had traveled a few days earlier than Hassen. When he got to California he found the place that Jasim had rented for them in Long Beach. Once he was settled in they would start their plan to find the documents. He and Jasim had gone to a local airport and rented a plane to canvass the area by air. The coast line along the shore from Long Beach to Santa Monica was beautiful. It was not unusual to see small aircraft in flight daily along this route. Most were tourist that hoped to get a glimpse of homes of the rich and famous movie stars. Homes would sometimes look like they were on stilts on the mountain sides overlooking the ocean.

You could always find a flier announcing that there was an airplane or helicopter flight available for sight seeing along the California coast. Many ex-airline pilots would find it financially rewarding to enter into this sort of business. The California experience was different than anywhere else in the world. You could be in a local restaurant eating lunch or dinner and be sitting next to Julia Roberts or Dick Van Dyke. Locals found this normal and part of everyday life. But the tourist from Kentucky or Michigan that came to this area would search for just one celebrity finding. They would buy maps that would lead them through Malibu, Brentwood and Beverly Hills to the homes of the stars.

The men found a spot that would let them land and take off after they returned to Long Beach. It was not too far from where the Queen Mary was docked. Ahmad would wait for his friend Hassen, and they would travel together to Santa Monica, while the remainder of his group would plan their exit by small plane to a safe haven in the Northwest before returning to Iraq. Hassen and Ahmad were the key to this operation.

El Jaafi set the plans with his men and waited for Al Yawer to arrive. The lower Bronx was a virtual mix of ethnic people and they would not seem to be out of place there. Jaafi had been in New York many times and was there when the Trade Center was attacked on September 11th, 2001. He had done some local reconnaissance for a group of men that had planned to drive a car bomb into the financial district. They were still in the planning stages when they turned on their television and saw what had transpired. They had thought up a plan that would have caused much concern and some damage but never did they think anyone could have created such devastating results. They all cheered in their apartment when they saw the damage the plane's caused at the World Trade center and knew that they must leave the area before a round up of suspects took place.

El Jaafi and his group separated so that they could leave the area and possibly make it back to Afghanistan safely. He found it a little more difficult due to almost all the airports on the East coast being closed after the damage in New York, and the Pentagon. They had to lay low for months until travel relaxed and they were able to return home.

Al Yawer came by taxi to the safe house in the Bronx. He found the group had set up plans for the trip to Bridgewater and their exit back to Afghanistan if they found the information they were seeking. Yawer was the key to this operation. Jaafi knew that he could set the plans for travel to and from Bridgewater but the actual attempt to get the document that they were looking for would be the plan the Yawer would devise. The group knew that Yawer would lead them to Bridgewater. He was a cunning person and had been pivotal in similar action. He was also one to take the lead and would direct the men as to what their part of the plan would be. No one would stand in Yawer's way and if they did they would not live to tell of it.

Yawer studied the document in the bag left for him at the LaGuardia airport. It detailed Thomas Adams address and that it was his son that had been to the Castle of Saddam that held the secret that they were seeking. The plan would be put into place and he would lead the group.

The safe house in the Bronx was an old two story duplex that was on a quiet street. It was just a few blocks from Yankee Stadium. Yawer found that the group had rented a Chevrolet Malibu. They had reserved rooms at the Day's Inn outside of Bridgewater. He would study the lay of the land and make sure that they had access to leave the area in case they had to use force to complete their goal. This group of Afghan travelers would meet for a few days to plan their deed and then leave to return home after hopefully finding the documents. If the documents were not there, they would have to travel to Southern California, and search the home of Blair Adams.

When Yawer arrived at the safe house in the Bronx he and Jaafi planned their next move. Jaafi suggested that he and Yawer should travel to Bridgewater prior to their plan taking place to check out the area. They decided to go to Bridgewater early the next day. The drive from the Bronx through New York took them along highway 278 and over the Verrazano Narrows Bridge. They would follow highway 278 to the interstate highway 95 that would take them south toward Philadelphia.

They had to travel through a few toll roads as they made their way through Staten Island. When they got to Elizabeth, New Jersey they got on highway 95 south. The trip would take about 3 to 4 hours depending on traffic. There was a lot of construction along the highway but traffic was light. They stopped in Mansfield Square, New Jersey to review the areas map and have lunch.

Al Yawer said this would be a better place to stay and he and El Jaafi rented a room at the Day's Inn just off the highway. They would return to Mansfield Square after checking out the Bridgewater home of Thomas Adams. The ride to Bridgewater from Mansfield Square took less then 45 minutes. They traveled down highway 95 to highway 276. Thomas Adam's house was just off highway 13 close to the bridge that crossed the Neshaminy River. Yawer drove their Malibu down the street in front of Thomas Adams' home and was concerned when he saw a local police car in the circular drive. He drove past slowly and tried to observe what was going on. There was another police car in the back yard of the Adam's home. It seemed that some men were looking into the woods but Al Yawer and El Jaafi could not make out what was going on from the street. They decided to return to Mansfield Square and advise their group in the Bronx that they would remain in Mansfield Square. This would have to be their headquarters and due to the police at the Adam's home they must accelerate their plans.

Back in California, Hassen made it to Long Beach and met Ahmad. They knew that they may have to make another trip across to Philadelphia if their search in California did not pan out. They felt that the documents they were searching for would be the key to help their coalition of conspirators gain the power that they were seeking. Hassen was brought up to speed about the coast line. They had rented a Ford Focus and would drive up from Long Beach on highway 405 toward Highway 10 and Santa Monica. Ahmad had seen the area from the air and now was seeing it for the first time from the ground.

They found a parking lot on 4th Street and walked toward the Promenade. They knew that Blair Adams lived in an apartment on Arizona Blvd. and that she worked in a Pub a few blocks away. They hoped that they could find an easy access to her apartment and if so maybe do a quick search of the place. Hassen held a picture of Blair that they had downloaded from the internet. They found it when they searched the Hollywood catalog of members of the screen actor's guild. She was blond and very beautiful he thought. They had picked up a map of Santa Monica and were happy that most everything was in walking distance. They reached the corner of 3rd and Santa Monica Blvd. They saw The Pub where Blair Adams worked. They noted that it was small but it appeared that it had a second story. There were windows that overlooked the Promenade from the second floor. They also noted that The Pub wrapped around the corner and had about six tables on the street. If things didn't pan out at her apartment they would make a search of The Pub after hours.

Hassen suggested they walk the rest of the way toward her apartment. It was only a couple of blocks to Arizona and they saw the address they were looking for. It was a three story building that appeared to be relatively new. There was a movie theater across the street and many

restaurants and gift shops on both sides. They sat down at a small table
kitty corner from the apartment and ordered coffee. They noticed that
the residents that came and went from the apartment building were
using a key card at the door to enter. They also noted that there was
a small police sub station that looked into the front of the apartment
building. They drank their coffee and watched for about an hour.

Ahmad nodded to Hassen when they saw a young blond leaving
the apartment building. They looked at the picture that Hassen held,
and it was Blair Adams. She was talking to a young man that came
out of the building with her. The two walked along the Promenade in
the direction of The Pub they had seen earlier. Ahmad said, "Hassen
this may be our best opportunity to seek entrance to her apartment."
They paid for their coffee's and walked across the street toward the
apartment building.

A young couple carrying a lot of bags and a large box were also
just coming to the door. Hassen offered to help and they were very
appreciative. The couple had just returned from a shopping trip to the
Ikea store in Los Angeles, and purchased items for their new apartment.
The couple did not know many people in their building but thought
that these two young men were very nice to help them. Ahmad and
Hassen held the door and helped the young man carry a box that
appeared to be a piece of furniture that you had to assemble. They
asked if the young couple needed help getting the items to their floor,
but they said no thanks they were on the first floor. As the two men
helped the young couple another guest had also entered the apartment.
He didn't talk to anyone but just looked down as the others carried the
bags and a large box. The man was a tall individual who was wearing
a suit and seemed all business. He got into the elevator and headed
toward the second floor.

Tony Baxter thought to himself, what a lucky break finding that
group with all their stuff. He had been watching the apartment when
he saw Mrs. Adams and a friend leave. Baxter did not want to use the
tools of his trade and create any suspicion. He thought I will just enter
with them while they struggle with their stuff. He got into the elevator
and went directly to the second floor. Apartment 21A was the forth one
on the right and entry was easy for Baxter. To be cautious he knocked
first to insure no one was still in the apartment. His skill was getting

into places he didn't belong. He put his sharp tool into the door lock and was able to gain entrance to the apartment. He noted that the apartment had been put back in place and figured that he would have at least an hour for this search. He figured that he didn't need too long since he had already checked most of it out. Baxter wanted to check the top of the closet and go through the refrigerator. Sometimes people would hide things in the fridge. He noticed that a small bag was on the side of the table. Baxter checked it out and found that there were only a few broken dishes in it.

The young couple thanked Ahmad and Hassen for their help. "You're welcome," they said, and they entered the elevator. They noticed at the door it had a list of tenants and their apartment numbers. They would look for the apartment with Blair Adams name on it. They saw it was listed as 21A. How lucky they thought. It was easy access to the apartment building and now they can search the place. They knew that Ms. Adams had gone out so they moved toward apartment 21A. Hassen and Ahmad looked down the hall to make sure no one was coming. Ahmad put his hand into his pocket and slid a tool out that he carried to gain entrance into the apartment.

Baxter looked surprised as he heard noise at the door and it began to open. He had no where to hide. He stepped back toward the small bathroom and drew his gun. Ahmad entered the apartment followed by Hassen. They started speaking in Arabic and moved fast through the apartment entrance and closed the door behind them. They looked around and could see that it was one large room with a short wall separating the bedroom from the rest of the apartment. Ahmad turned to Hassen when Baxter flew out of the bathroom gun drawn, "Put your hands up, I'm with the FBI." He did not see that Ahmad had held a knife in his right hand. Ahmad reared back and threw the knife at Baxter. The knife hit Baxter, he was stabbed in the left shoulder. Baxter fell to the ground but got off two shots. His first shot entered through the skull of Hassen scattering brains and blood all over the bedroom wall. The second shot went through the ceiling as Baxter was falling backwards. Ahmad drew his weapon and shot at Baxter as he was falling to the floor. His shots hit Baxter in the leg and the other shoulder when Baxter rolled over and fired back. His only shot hit Ahmad in the chest. Ahmad fell to the floor clutching his chest as blood puddle on the carpet. Baxter passed out with blood flowing from his leg and shoulder wounds.

Baxter lay on Blair's apartment floor bleeding. He had been there for about fifteen minutes when Officer Tuttle came in with two other officers. They had been called by residents who had heard the gunfire. Officer Tuttle could not believe his eyes. He saw that there were possibly three dead bodies in the apartment. This is the same apartment that he had been to a day ago for a break-in. Who were these men and why in Blair's apartment. Where was Blair he thought? He made a call to the station and ordered an EMS unit and the medical examiner to the scene. He also hoped his Chief would send more help so that they could search the area for possible other suspects. They put an APB out for any suspicious looking individuals in the area.

Officer Tuttle looked around the room and he and his two officers inspected the three men on the ground. Two were dead and one wounded and bleeding. They searched the men for identification. The wounded man had an FBI identification badge and his identification said he was Tony Baxter, special agent out of the Los Angeles bureau. Officer Tuttle knew that the small police force in Santa Monica may have handled a few cases but never anything of this magnitude. He also wondered what was going on and how was Blair Adams involved. He waited for the EMS unit to take the wounded FBI man to the hospital. He also wanted to start a search for Blair Adams.

SEVEN

Blair Adams had entered The Pub and was acknowledged by Olly who was behind the bar. Regular patrons waved hello as she approached Olly.

Olly said, "Your guest is upstairs waiting for you. She is the only one up there Blair. Would you like something to drink?"

"Just some ice water please."

Blair never drank any soft drinks. She was a health nut and always ate organic foods and drank bottled water. Her only vise was an occasional alcoholic drink. She loved different wines. Blair gave Olly a package that she had picked up at the Santa Monica Post office. What's in the package Olly asked.

"Not sure, Blair said but I'm afraid to open it. It came from Iraq, Hunter's old command address. It may be something he sent me before he died. I'm not ready to open it."

Olly put the package behind the bar and said "when you're ready, I'll be there for you."

Blair went upstairs and saw Agent Jones. Ms. Jones was obviously a very good looking woman who hid her features. Early in her career she had been assigned to the New York bureau and did some uncover work. She had some great success. She had been re-assigned to the Philadelphia bureau and worked as a special agent for a few years before being promoted to the Washington Bureau. One of her early task involved following leads after the planes hit the Pentagon during the September 11th, attacks. She was pivotal in finding a terror cell that had set up its operation in Maryland not too far out of the Capitol. She also worked with the head of the Philadelphia bureau and they had found an individual who was about to sell state secrets. Ms. Jones was given many high awards for her work in this search. She was promoted to special agent in Los Angeles, California. Her main job was to continue a watch for possible terror cells along the west coast from Long Beach to Malibu. She had two special agents that reported to her. One agent was Tony Baxter, a man in his mid forties the other was Justin Wallace a younger man in his early 30's. She reported to Dean Curry the bureau chief in the Los Angeles FBI office. Allisa Jones had Tony Baxter watching Blair's apartment so he could search it when she left for the meeting. Justin Wallace was positioned across from The Pub at Hooter's watching as Blair entered. He was her lookout to make sure that Blair was alone when she entered The Pub. Allisa Jones was very thorough. She did not want anything to go wrong. Ms. Jones felt that Blair may not be aware that her husband had found what could be very critical information in a recent search of one of Saddam's castles. Often family members were unaware of what missions their spouse was involved in.

That was the way it was suppose to be. Ms. Jones knew that after Captain Montgomery helped search through Hunter's belongings and found nothing, that the documents must be somewhere. She had received a copy of his email the day before. It was her hope that Blair may know something to help in this search. How could she get that information without alerting Blair as to the reason for the meeting was the key? Ms. Jones was the only person sitting upstairs. Blair walked toward the small table and introduced herself.

"I'm Blair Adams and I guess you are Ms. Jones."

"Yes Blair, thank you for meeting me and please call me Allisa. Have a seat please."

"I'm not sure why you want to meet with me Ms. Jones?"

"I understand," answered Allisa. "Many times we do this and most times it is just a formality to close our files. First of all Blair I want again to offer our condolence for your loss. I'm sure that this has been a trying time for you and if there is any way we can help make it easier we would be happy to help."

"It has been very difficult," said Blair.

"Not all of it has sunk in yet. I did find out that the FBI will be forwarding a death certificate which is confusing because I figured it would come from the Army."

"It comes from the FBI in certain events Blair. Due to the Office of Homeland Security overseeing all the agencies they forward certain documents through the FBI."

Agent Jones saw that Blair was a bit tense but hoped that by answering some of her questions she could gain Blair's confidence and eventually she would answer some of the her questions.

Olly came to the top of the stairs and asked," Can I bring you a menu?"

She wanted to make sure that Blair was ok and figured by doing a normal restaurant thing no one would suspect that she was protecting Blair. Ms. Jones knew that Blair was employed at The Pub and that Olly was her friend. She wasn't concerned with the location of the meeting she just needed all the information that she could gather. She also wanted to get Blair out of her apartment so that Tony Baxter could make one more search. His first effort brought no answers and was cut short when there was a fire alarm in the building.

"Ms. Jones," said Blair "would you like some lunch."

"Not now but thank you."

Agent Justin Wallace continued his watch of The Pub from across the street. He also waited to hear from Tony Baxter that the search had been completed. He would phone Ms. Jones with the results but was not to call her unless they had urgent information. She did not want to alert Blair to anything that was happening.

This meeting would be a time to gather information and maybe if necessary set the stage for a second meeting. Blair and Allisa continued to talk about the role of the FBI in events like this. Agent Jones was explaining the role of her office while getting to know Blair. Although Ms. Jones had a complete file on Blair Adams she hoped that having her talk about herself that she would put her at ease and could get the information she was seeking.

Officer Tuttle entered The Pub and said, "hello," to Olly. It was not unusual to see him during the day. He and his partner would often eat lunch there. It was convenient to sit at an outside table and keep an eye on the promenade while eating lunch. The Santa Monica police kept in close touch with all the business owners.

Officer Tuttle asked Olly, "Do you know where Blair might be?"

"She's upstairs meeting with someone." Olly asked, "Is everything ok?"

"I have to talk to her, it's important."

Before Olly could say anything else he turned toward the stairway. Olly called back to him but he didn't answer. Officer Tuttle continued up the stairs and saw Blair and another young woman talking.

"Blair, I'm sorry to bother you but it's very important." Blair turned and looked startled. "What is it Officer?"

"Your apartment has had another break-in."

"Oh no!" Blair said "I can't believe that my apartment has been broken into again." Ms. Jones looked around like someone had just dropped a bomb.

"Yes but this time it is much worse. There were three men in your apartment and two of them are dead and one is seriously wounded."

"What?"

"We got a call from a neighbor on the third floor that some bullets were fired into their apartment from below. We started over right away when there were more calls about numerous shots on the second floor. We went down the hall and saw your door ajar and when we walked in there were three men lying on the floor and blood everywhere."

Ms. Jones found herself asking about the one man still alive. Both Officer Tuttle and Blair looked back toward her. She knew that she should not have entered the conversation. The shock of this event and having Tony Baxter at the apartment caused the slip up.

Officer Tuttle asked, "Who are you?"

"I'm a friend of Blair's," she answered.

Blair turned back toward Officer Tuttle and asked about the men and her apartment.

Officer Tuttle said, "We did not see any evidence of damage except for the blood everywhere. The other thing that is so unusual Blair is one of the men that had been shot is an FBI agent."

Blair turned and looked at Ms. Jones.

Ms. Jones said, "Blair I will explain everything."

Officer Tuttle looked at both women.

"What is going on?" he said.

Before Blair could answer Ms. Jones introduced herself to Officer Tuttle.

"I'm Agent Allisa Jones of the FBI," she said.

Officer Tuttle looked bewildered.

"What do you have to do with this?"

Blair sat back down and tears started to form around her eyes.

Ms. Jones said, "I can explain everything Blair."

Officer Tuttle said, "I want to hear this too!"

"First, Ms. Jones said, what about the FBI agent that was shot?"

"He was bleeding badly and we rushed him to the Hospital. Multiple wounds to the leg and both shoulders but it looks like he will make it," Officer Tuttle said.

"What Hospital is he being taken to?"

"Los Angeles Memorial on Washington Blvd." Officer Tuttle answered. "But before you go anywhere I have some questions that I need answered."

"Officer this is an FBI matter," Ms. Jones answered.

"Not so quick, Officer Tuttle said, the murder of two men and shooting of another happened in Santa Monica and it is in our jurisdiction."

"I need to call one of my men to tend to Baxter," Ms. Jones said and she started to dial Justin Wallace who was still stationed across the street.

"Wallace, you need to get to Los Angeles Memorial on Washington Blvd. Baxter has been shot. I'll call headquarters and meet you there in a little bit."

Officer Tuttle and Blair looked at Ms. Jones and wondered what was going on. Ms. Jones said, "Everyone needs to sit and I will explain."

Olly came up the stairs to see what was going on and saw the three starting to sit at the table. She also saw that Blair had been crying. Olly came over and tried to comfort Blair and to see what had happened.

"What's going on?" Olly said. Officer Tuttle answered.

"Blair's apartment has been broken into again but this time three men were found and it appears that they had a shoot out."

"A shoot out!"

"Yes, and two of them are dead and one is in serious condition."

Blair tried to answer but she was still in a state of shock.

Olly said "I'll get you a drink honey."

Olly hurried downstairs and got Blair a glass of wine and a cold bottle of water.

"Here honey take some of this," she said.

Officer Tuttle told Ms. Jones, "It's time for you to explain."

Ms. Jones said, "Really, Blair and I need to talk first."

"Not so fast," Officer Tuttle said. "We have two dead men and another in serious condition and I think you set the whole thing up."

"I did not set it up. I did know that one of my men, Tony Baxter, would be in Blair's apartment but I have no idea who the other two men are."

"I would like some answers," Blair said. Everyone turned to look at her. She still had tears in her eyes but she had a determined look on her face. One that had not been there for a long time. If you knew Blair, and saw this look you knew she was serious.

"My apartment has been broken into twice. My things have been scattered and now you tell me that there are dead men on the floor. My husband has been killed and I'm not sure of anything. I want answers and I want them now."

Ms. Jones knew that she was in a tight situation. How much information should she provide and what about the local police and the owner of The Pub.

"Blair, I want to level with you."

"You better go back to calling me Mrs. Adams," Blair said.

"Mrs. Adams, we did have an agent go to your apartment to look for a document that is critical in an on-going investigation of National Security. I cannot tell you any more about that. I am sorry that my agent damaged some of your things when he went into your apartment. We will pay for any damage and cover the cost of repairs to your apartment."

"What in the hell are you looking for in my apartment?"

"I told you all that I can for now. I really have to take care of my injured agent and I will call you back to set up a meeting to answer your other questions."

"I'm going to the Hospital with you Ms. Jones," Officer Tuttle said.

She was not pleased with that but knew that she had no choice.

"Ok, you can come along but this is an FBI investigation. We will share all the details with the local police as we get them but we will take the lead on this."

Blair said, "Not so fast. I need some answers before anyone goes anyplace. I have had it with all this crap. I came here to meet you and get some answers but instead you have someone in my apartment searching through my stuff. I need to know why and I want to know now."

"Blair, I'll be able to give you that information but really I need to attend to my agent that has been shot. How about if I call you and we can set up another meeting. I'll give you all the information you want."

"I can't go back home with dead bodies and blood all over my apartment. I'm not sure where I will go. I need your number to contact you for this explanation meeting."

"Your right, here's my card with my number on it. Call me to let me know where you will be. We want to help protect you."

"Now I need protection. What's next?"

Olly said, "You'll stay with me honey."

"I don't want to put you and the kids in danger Olly."

"You're like my sister Blair. You're coming home with me."

Officer Tuttle and Ms. Jones walked downstairs and would go to Los Angeles Memorial Hospital.

Olly sat in the upstairs room with Blair.

"Olly I'm so confused. Why is the FBI searching my apartment? What is going on? Did Hunter do something wrong? I just don't know what is going on."

"I'll call Blake and let him know where you will be. I'll take you home with me and Ashley will be here in a few minutes to work the bar. I have some things that you can change into and you need to relax."

Blair was understandably shook up. She wanted to stay upstairs at The Pub while Olly waited for Ashley. She needed to gather her composure. When Ashley arrived Olly told her that Blair had another break in and that there had been a shoot out this time.

"I'm going to take her home with me," Olly told Ashley.

Blair and Olly left the bar and headed to Olly's car.

Ashley was behind the bar and talking to Chris one of the locals who always came in around lunch time.

"Where did Blair and Olly go?" he asked.

"I'm not sure why but she took Blair back to her place."

Ashley didn't want to tell Chris about the second break in because she didn't really know what had transpired. It was best to just let Blair's friends know that Blair was going to be with Olly. It was not unusual for Blair to go home with Olly. She often would help her with the kids when Olly needed.

Ashley was clearing the back of the bar and found a package on the lower shelf.

Ashley thought, I wonder whose package this is. She saw that it had Blair's name on it. She probably forgot it here. I'll just leave it in the back room office for her.

Ashley knew that Blair was always leaving stuff behind. She took the package from under the bar and put it on the desk in the office. Ashley looked at the return address and saw that it was from Iraq. Guess that it was from Hunter and Blair didn't want to open it yet. Ashley figured that she would tell Blair where she put the package tomorrow.

EIGHT

Both Jaafi and Al Yawer felt that staying in Mansfield Square was a good idea. They called back to the men who were waiting for orders in the Bronx.

"We will be staying here," Yawer said.

The local police seem to be staking out Mr. Adams house. They had two cars out there, one in the back yard and the other in the driveway. Jaafi told Omar that he should come to Mansfield Square and to bring some of their equipment with him. Omar was told to check into the Days Inn at Mansfield Square. It is the first Mansfield Square exit and the hotel is one mile from highway 95 on the right hand side of the road.

"Just two of you need to come, and bring weapons. We are in room 201," Jaafi told them.

Mansfield Square was a quiet little town in New Jersey a few miles east from Trenton. It was also a few miles from a Six Flags Amusement Park. This often caused the hotels to fill up on weekends. Like a lot of small towns in this area there was a lot of Civil War history. Monuments to lost soldiers and great Generals were all over town. The downtown was very quaint with shops lining both sides of the street. It was the perfect place to raise a family. No one would suspect that the local Days Inn was harboring a group of terrorists. This made it a perfect hiding place.

Although Jaafi was the head of this group Yawer would be in charge of the planning. Jaafi didn't mind. Yawer had saved Jaafi's life during the long war with Iran. Jaafi was a young lieutenant in the Iraqi army and had led his men in an attack on a small town on the Iranian and

Iraqi border. Yawer had been taken in by Jaafi and his men and was on the mission with them. Yawer was grateful to Jaafi for saving him and always followed Jaafi in camp and tried to learn all that he could. The attack took place during the day and had been successful. The group that Jaafi led split into two so that they could protect their position. Jaafi felt he had everything secured when a group of Iranian guerrilla's made a sneak attack. Jaafi lost many men in the struggle and he was taken captive. He was being tortured by the Iranian soldiers when Yawer appeared with the rest of the men to save Jaafi. Everyone knew of this and Yawer was praised for his leadership and rose through the ranks of the army. Yawer was a fierce fighter and killed many soldiers himself. He carried his friend Jaafi to safety. Jaafi was in his debt and would always remember what Yawer did for him. After that long war ended Jaafi felt that Saddam did not support his troops and he went to Afghanistan and fell in with Osama bin Laden. He convinced his friend Yawer to join him in this venture.

Jaafi and Yawer were together in Islamabad, Pakistan with Osama when he organized the Taliban and master minded his terrorist organization. Osama sent Jaafi, one of his lieutenants to Afghanistan. They would hold regular meetings along with Malta Usman, a key member of Osama's, and a suspected minister in the Taliban. El Jaafi was with Osama bin Laden and Malta Usman in Afghanistan when he was given the task of finding key documents that were said to exist. The information that they held would give their cause great strength. They also found that a U.S. team that searched one of Saddam's castles had been reported to have found the information needed. El Jaafi quickly put together his team and would not consider the task without his loyal supporter and friend Yawer.

Yawer told Omar, one of his trusted men who had great knowledge about the area, to make sure they were careful when registering at the hotel. The Days Inn was a favorite place for U.S. military to stay while training in the region. McGuire Air Force base was located to the southeast of Mansfield Square. Omar had attended school at the College of New Jersey located in Trenton and knew the area well. Jaafi and Yawer made their plans while waiting for Omar and Abdullah to arrive at the Days Inn. They would all travel the next day to Bridgewater and start the surveillance of Thomas Adams home. The group of Taliban men were organizing the search for the documents and planning a trip to California if necessary. They knew through their investigation that the lead U.S. soldier was Hunter Adams. He was in charge of the search. After capturing and torturing one of the U.S. men involved they found out that Hunter Adams had found some documents at the castle.

Hunter Adams must have been killed before he got the documents to his superiors. This was thought to be known due to the fact that Adams was sent on another mission the next morning after the search of the castle. They also knew that Mr. Adams was from Bridgewater and that he and his wife lived in Southern California. Because this group was very familiar with the East Coast it made sense to start there. Yawer said, "If this takes too long we will split up and one group will go to California."

Omar registered at the desk of the Days Inn and asked for a room on the lower level. When he was at the desk a group of Air Force soldiers came into the lobby. They were headed toward the small bar located to the right of the registration desk.

Omar casually said, "Hello" and thought he would ask about a local restaurant he had been to in the past.

The clerk said, "oh yes, it's still there."

Omar mentioned their famous desserts and breads.

The clerk said, "My girlfriend and I love that place."

Omar took his key and headed toward his room. He was given 204 on the lower level and three rooms from Jaafi and Yawer. He and Abdullah moved their bags into the room and called Yawer. The group met in Yawer's room and planned their trip to Bridgewater. Jaafi and Yawer wanted to make sure that they did not have a run in with the local or State police. They did not care if they caused harm to Thomas Adams. They were just interested in finding the document or eliminating Bridgewater and heading to Southern California.

Captain Douglas told Thomas that the tire tracks were very strange. He said kids would not have gone to that much trouble in a break-in.

"This was a planned break-in," Captain Douglas said.

"Thomas you must have something that is valuable to someone. You have to think and look around. Are you sure nothing is missing?"

Thomas again searched his mind as he walked through the house with Captain Douglas. He had a few items that were broken but could not place any missing items.

He said, "Hunter had some baseball cards but they are all here and I have a few things from Viet Nam but they have been accounted for."

Captain Douglas said, "My men made a mold of the tire tracks but they were standard tracks for an off road vehicle like a Jeep Wrangler with 17 inch knobby tires. The wheel base was short like that of a Jeep Wrangler or an older Ford Ranger. We tried to see if your house had any finger prints but came up with nothing."

"Thomas, we will have a squad car drive by on a regular basis for the next few days. Either they were scared away or decided that what they were looking for wasn't here."

Dino Tuchy was mad as hell.

"Steve, I can't believe two of my best agents made such a mess and came up empty. What the hell were you thinking of by parking behind the house."

Steve Watkins, special agent out of the Philadelphia bureau had his head down. "Boss we knew that so many friends had been coming to the Adams house after the funeral bringing food and all, that coming through the woods offered a perfect hiding spot in case someone came by."

"You and Frank better figure out how to get one more shot of getting in that house. I have to report to the Washington Bureau and they're not going to be happy. It should have been a one trip venture."

Dino Tuchy was the number one field agent for the Bureau and was heading this task force. He also had heard that Allisa Jones, special agent in Southern California, had not found anything in the search of Mrs. Adams apartment in California. He would call the Director and report but wanted to get his men into the Adams house one more time.

"Steve, you and Frank should give the search another try tonight. Both of you need to case the property and get in and out as quick as possible. I understand the dumb shit local police are snooping around. We need to resolve this."

Frank Walker and Steve Watkins would head off to Bridgewater and try to get into the Adams home later that evening.

Al Yawer told El Jaafi that time was critical. He felt that he and Omar should go to Bridgewater that evening and scout out the Adam's house.

"If we can make our move we will settle this or head to California."

Jaafi agreed that the plan made sense.

He said, "We should all go."

Yawer said, "That would be too many people for this sort of mission. Omar and I can get in and out without much fuss. If Adams is home we will do away with him. He does not cause me concern, the local police are my only concern."

Yawer and Omar took two boxes from Omar's trunk and put them in the Malibu. We will call you after the deed has been done, he told Jaafi and Abdullah. They headed for Bridgewater and the Adams house.

Steve Watkins and Frank Walker were competent agents and both had been with the bureau for over fifteen years. They did not want their boss Dino Tuchy upset with them. They also were not used to failure. They decided to head for Bridgewater after gathering a few tools in case they needed them.

Thomas Adams thought it was tough being in the home alone. He had been alone for quite a few years but the knowledge that his son or daughter-in-law might come to visit or at least call made it seem like someone was always there. He decided to call his brother to see if they were in. Thomas's brother Bill was retired and he and his wife did a lot of traveling. Bill was great during the past few weeks and helped with the funeral.

"Hi Thomas, glad you called. Martha is making one of your favorite dishes. Why don't you come over and eat with us."

"I don't want to bother you," Thomas said.

"You're no bother, your family and we would love to have you come eat with us tonight."

Thomas didn't want to butt in but he wanted to get Bill's opinion of the events of the past few days. It was only 5:30 and Thomas knew that Bill and Martha always ate around 7:00pm.

"Thanks," Thomas said, "how about if I stop at our favorite place and bring dessert."

"That sounds good," Bill said. "See you in a little bit."

Steve looked at his watch and told Frank that they should be at the Adams residents about 7:00 pm.

"We should be able to park down the street after we pass by to make sure the coast is clear. Let's get this done as soon as possible so Dino doesn't eat our ass out again."

Yawer wanted to get to Bridgewater and start the search. He said to Omar, "If we get there about 7:30pm we can be done in less than an hour."

NINE

Allisa Jones sat in the small waiting room outside the emergency entrance. Justin Wallace said, "The doctor will talk to us in about a half an hour. I'm sure the surgery went ok."

Allisa felt guilty because she wasn't thinking about Baxter's surgery, just how was she going to explain all of this to the Director.

The team of surgeons at Los Angeles Memorial were very highly rated. They took care of the knife wound in the right shoulder very quickly and moved on to Baxter's other wounds. The gunshot in the other shoulder was superficial and only grazed the skin. The wound in the leg was more serious. It had hit close to an artery and Baxter had lost a lot of blood. When he arrived at the E.R. they put a temporary suture in it. This took a little more time to clean and suture but it had been successful. Baxter should recover without any complications.

Officer Tuttle joined Agent Jones in the waiting room and inquired about Baxter's condition.

"We should hear from the operating team soon," she answered.

He sat down and thought about the line of questions that he wanted to ask.

"Agent Jones I need to ask you a couple of questions."

"This isn't the best time Officer Tuttle."

"I know but we must act on this incident so that we can start our investigation."

The Doctor came into the waiting room and asked who was with the Baxter family. Allisa Jones said, "I'm waiting to hear about Mr. Baxter."

"Are you family?" the doctor asked.

"Tony Baxter doesn't have any family here. I'm Allisa Jones and we work together."

"We normally would want to respond to a family member."

"I can assure you that he has no family and that you can give me the details."

Allisa showed the doctor her FBI identification.

"Ms. Jones, our surgery went good. His shoulders wounds were taken care of and the only complication was his leg wound."

"What kind of complications?"

"The wound was close to an artery and caused a lot of bleeding. After we sutured it we had to give him two pints of blood. It looks like his wounds should heal just fine.

He will be in recovery for about an hour, then we will get him into a room."

After the doctor left Officer Tuttle resumed his line of questions. "Agent Jones, I must ask you to either come down to the station or answer my questions now."

"Officer Tuttle, I'm not leaving the hospital until I talk to Agent Baxter. As far as going to your station this is an FBI matter and we'll deal with it. I will promise to keep you in the loop but we're going to take the lead in this investigation."

Officer Tuttle was very aggravated and wanted to proceed but he also understood the issue of talking to the wounded agent. He also wanted to know what Agent Baxter had to tell. His office called to update him on the men in Blair's apartment. He did not share this with Allisa Jones.

While Officer Tuttle had been with Ms. Jones and Blair at The Pub his men were completing the investigation. They had found identification on the men who were shot and killed in Blair's apartment. It showed that they were of possible Arabic decent. They checked this out but so far nothing seemed to pan out. The identification they carried was false. The Santa Monica Police would want to run finger print analysis at the morgue.

This information was also given to the Los Angeles County Task Force that handled matters for the department of Homeland Security. The head of the FBI Los Angeles bureau Dean Curry had also received a copy of the report from The Homeland Security Office. The Santa

Monica Police were hoping to get some help in tracing the identification of the two dead men.

"I will agree with you Agent Jones about waiting to talk to Agent Baxter. I will also share the investigation with you but I want to know what your agent has to say," officer Tuttle said. Agent Jones reluctantly agreed but also said that she needed to make a call. Officer Tuttle waited with Justin Wallace in the E.R. waiting room. Allisa Jones walked outside and called The Washington Bureau.

"Hi, this is agent Jones, is the Director in."

John Martin was the head of the FBI in Washington D. C. and had been placed in his job by the President. John was a no nonsense sort of person and agent Jones had not wanted to make this call. John Franklin Martin was in his early 40's and was rumored to be in line for the post of Head of Homeland Security. He was also one of the most eligible bachelors in Washington. The Office of Homeland Security had been the new post that handled most issues that other agencies like FEMA or the FBI would handle on their own.

"Yes, he's in I'll transfer the call for you."

"John Martin."

"Hi, Mr. Martin this is agent Allisa Jones reporting in."

"Yes agent Jones what have you got?" Martin did not waste time with small talk, he would go straight to the jest of the issue.

"Well we have made some headway in our case, sir."

"What do you mean by headway agent Jones?"

"We have searched through Mrs. Adams apartment and did not find any sign of documents that we are looking for."

"That doesn't seem like headway to me agent Jones. What the hell have you got?"

"Our agent Tony Baxter was in the process of completing the apartment search when two men also came into the apartment."

"And?"

"Agent Baxter was able to shoot both men although he was wounded in the action. Both men were dead at the scene, Sir."

"That is just great! What the hell kind of headway do you think you've made agent Jones. You haven't found anything, you killed two possible leads in the investigation, and now we don't have any more than we did when you started."

"Agent Jones who were these two men in Mrs. Adams apartment?"

"We are working on that sir."

"Well while you're working on that the local police are ahead of you Jones. Those two men are believed to be possible Arabs and we need to know more about them."

Agent Jones could not believe that officer Tuttle and the Santa Monica Police were already into the investigation and she was not in the loop.

Agent Jones thought she would try to re-direct the conversation.

"If the documents are not in California they must be in Philadelphia."

"We haven't found anything there yet but our team is making a check as we speak," Martin said.

"I'm not happy with your results agent Jones. I suggest we send in a few more people to help you."

"Sir, I don't think I need any help."

"Well I do because there is a new wrinkle to the plot. Who are these two men that Baxter killed. Are they Arab's? If so what are they after? Where are they from?

We have to find out their identity. I've called Dean in the Los Angeles office to apprise him of the situation. I will forward a message to him to take over the lead and you are to assist him in this matter."

"Yes Sir."

Agent Jones was mad but understood that she didn't have anything positive to say. She did not tell the Director about the local police and their involvement and now they had the lead on the investigation. The Director already knew that they had more information than she did.

She re-entered the waiting room and agent Walker and Office Tuttle said, "Baxter is being moved into room 605 B."

"We can go up to his room in five minutes," Walker added.

"Officer Tuttle, I have talked to my Director and he is sending more FBI agents from the Los Angeles bureau. We will take the lead in this investigation and I will question my agent," Ms. Jones said.

She was still thinking about the fact that Officer Tuttle knew some key things about the men killed by her agent but hasn't said a thing. "I would like five minutes alone with Baxter and then you will have the opportunity to ask him anything you want."

"I want to be there the whole time," officer Tuttle said.

"This is an FBI matter," Ms. Jones reiterated.

"Bullshit," officer Tuttle answered. "I've called my Captain and he's on his way. It happened in our jurisdiction and it is our case."

They were at an impasse when the Captain of the Santa Monica Police entered.

Officer Tuttle saw Captain Parker and called out to him.

"We're over here Captain."

"I'm Captain Henry Parker with the Santa Monica Police."

Captain Parker was a veteran of the Santa Monica Police Force. He had been a Los Angeles detective for over fifteen years before taking the post of Captain in Santa Monica. Captain Parker was a strong individual and would not take any crap from anyone including the FBI. He had been involved with a joint task force with the FBI on gang crime and they soon found out that he would not be second fiddle. The Captain would make sure that this FBI agent knew he was not working for her.

"I'm agent Allisa Jones and this is agent Justin Wallace. Captain I was just telling your officer that our wounded agent must be interviewed by the FBI alone."

"Not a problem," Captain Parker said.

"I just came here to get with officer Tuttle. Bill, we have some information that will help us in the case. We need to go. Agent Jones, I will expect you to be available later."

Agent Jones looked confused and was caught off guard.

"I've explained to your officer that we will handle this investigation."

"Agent Jones this is our investigation, period. Don't be confused about that fact. This is Santa Monica and my turf. You are my guest. If you withhold any information I'll have your ass."

Ms. Jones was stunned.

"Let's go Bill," he said to officer Tuttle.

Agent Jones just stood there with agent Walker wondering what had happened.

TEN

Blair went home with Olly and she was more confused than ever. What was going on? There had been two break-ins, and now she had been told that two men were killed in her apartment. The FBI was involved with the Santa Monica Police Department. Who does she trust? What should she do now?

They were sitting in the living room when the phone rang.

Olly answered the phone. "Blair it's for you."

"Who is it?"

"She said it was the FBI agent you met with at the Pub."

"Agent Jones? Why should I talk to her? I think she's been lying the whole time."

"Honey, you better talk to her. She obviously knows something more and maybe now you might get some real information."

Blair doubted that Allisa Jones would reveal anything. She felt that the only reason Ms. Jones wanted to talk to her in the first place was to get her out of the apartment. But why? Guess I have to know that, Blair thought. Although she did not want to talk to Ms. Jones, she took the phone.

"Hi, this is Mrs. Adams."

"Blair, I know that you may be upset and I can explain everything."

"I'm more than upset! Remember my husband is dead, my apartment is being used as a shooting gallery by your men, which by the way; why in the hell are they in my apartment?"

"Blair, we need to meet, I will explain everything. I will be able to help you and I have some information for you."

"This time I want to have a friend with me agent Jones."

"That not a problem, but Blair this is critical to the FBI's investigation so I must get your reassurance that nothing I tell you will be repeated to anyone."

Blair agreed to meet with agent Jones tomorrow at noon. They planned to meet along the Pacific Coast Highway near the Santa Monica Pier. Blair told Agent Jones that there was a series of park benches before the bus stop at the entrance to the Pier, and no one would really notice them. It was a real tourist gathering area. Agent Jones agreed and said she would be alone. Blair felt that by being outside she would be able to talk to Agent Jones and if things got emotional she could better deal with it than being at The Pub.

"Blair, I will be meeting you with information that the FBI has and I'm not suppose to share it with you. I feel you deserve to know what it is."

Blair got off the phone and was glad that she had Olly to talk this over with. Agent Jones had given Blair the feeling that this may be more bad news. How much more bad news could there be Blair thought. Olly agreed to accompany Blair to talk to agent Jones. It was late and the two of them sat and talked for a couple of hours before either of them was ready to go to sleep. Olly told her that they should try to get some rest. They both headed off to bed. Blair slept in the kid's room. It had a great view of the ocean and she loved watching the moons reflection on the water. Blair's sleep was disturbed. She kept having dreams that made her question so much. She remembered the trips that Hunter had been on. The time he spent in South America and he was never able to tell her exactly where he was and what his assignment was about. She thought again about the trip to Switzerland when he got injured. The passport issue did not make sense. Hunter, what were you doing? She could not get those questions out of her mind.

Blair got up about 5:00 a.m., which was very unusual. She was usually up late and often slept in till noon. She liked working the late shift at The Pub. The tips were great and most of her friends came in late. She went to the kitchen and made a cup of tea and looked out of the window that faced the Pacific Ocean. It was a beautiful home. The upper level had three bedrooms and looked over the cliffs westward toward the ocean. Often tourist would drive down the street looking at these homes hoping a movie star would appear. You could see all the way down the canyon to the Pacific Coast Highway. Sitting in the big chair looking at the moon over the ocean Blair thought back about the trip that Hunter had taken her on in Central America. They went to Belize, and she thought it was just beautiful. They both loved mountain climbing and they were able to do a lot of it there. One of the funny things she remembered, is that he seemed to be familiar with the area and was able to show Blair sights as if he had seen them before. She hadn't thought about it then, but now everything seemed suspicious to her.

The meeting at noon would maybe hold some answers. Blair wished she could have slept more but sleep was not in the cards. She could not turn her mind off to rest. Olly was fast asleep. Blair envied her and loved her. Olly was a great friend and Blair felt so lucky to have her. I should call Hunter's dad she thought. Three hours different for the east coast. It's only a little after 8:00 am there. I'll wait another hour she thought.

Olly called out to her.

"Blair, are you ok? Guess you can't sleep!"

"Not really," she answered.

"I'm going to get up and sit with you."

"Please try to go back to sleep. I am sorry if I woke you."

Olly usually opened The Pub, and was use to getting up early.

"Don't be silly, I'm going to take a shower and go to The Pub, then I'll be back with breakfast for us."

"Ok," Blair said. "Can I help with anything around here while you're gone?"

"Nope, everything is good. The kids are staying with me mum this week and I have everything done around the house."

Blair continued to stare out the big window as the sun began to rise. She could see its rays coming up over the roof tops. Sunsets were the best from this view but the early morning light coming in the window to wake up the city seemed special. Blair was rarely up at this time so she really didn't get to see many sunrises. This was the California she loved. People back east always referred to California as a nut house. So many crazy's out here dad would say when they visited. The Promenade always had its share of people carrying signs proclaiming the end of the world or some other future shock. On one visit a man carried a sign saying the world would end on October 21st. Blair's dad would stop by him daily and count off the number of days left and laugh. On October 22nd Blair took a picture of the man and emailed it to her dad. The new sign proclaimed January 15th as the end of the world. Her dad thought that was great. He called back to laugh with her about the date change on the sign. They had a special relationship. Like some father's and daughters and they shared the same level of humor. He always called her his little kid.

Olly left the house and told Blair to make sure everything was locked.

"I'll be back in a few hours," she said.

Blair looked at the clock and said it should be 9:00 a.m. in Bridgewater.

Blair went to the phone and dialed Thomas Adams. The phone rang and Thomas answered.

"Hi, I'm so glad to hear from you Blair. How is everything going?"

"Things are really strange here. I had a call from the FBI wanting to talk to me about Hunter. When I went to meet the special agent they had another person in my apartment who ending up shooting two other men."

"What? In your apartment? Are you sure you're ok?"

"Yes, I'm at my friend house. It's all so confusing."

"I can't believe that this isn't somehow related," Thomas told her.

"What about this shooting in your apartment?"

"I'm not really sure but I have a meeting with a special agent of the FBI today at noon and hope to get some answers. I do feel that having the Santa Monica police involved is good because I know the officer and trust him. I think he doesn't like the FBI person."

"Be careful," Thomas told her. "Is someone going with you?"

"Yes, Olly is going with me and we are meeting the agent at noon in the park. I'll be careful but I am also worried about you. Did you call about your break-in?"

"Yes, I don't know if you remember Captain Douglas but he came over and he has his men watching my place."

"Did you tell Captain Douglas about my break-in?"

"No, I didn't think it was related at the time."

"Maybe you should tell him. You never know especially with the FBI involved."

Being an ex-marine Thomas heard so many stories of espionage and the FBI or CIA undercover involvement that he never thought that he would actually be involved in one. What would prompt the FBI to be in his daughter-in-laws apartment? What about the two men in the shooting? Could his break-in be part of this? Now there were so many questions in his mind that were not there before.

Blair said, "I'm not sure about where I will stay. I just don't know what to do. I'm hoping to go to my apartment after meeting with the FBI to see what shape it is in."

"Don't go by yourself."

"I'll be ok; if Olly can't go with me I'll ask Blake or Ashley to go. Guess I can call Officer Tuttle and he will meet us there."

"Call me after your meeting," Thomas said.

"Ok, I'll call you after I meet with the FBI person. I'm going to ask if she knows anything about your break-in too. Seems like something is going on and I think she knows what it is."

Olly came in just as Blair was hanging up.

"Are you ok?" she asked.

"I just wanted to talk to Hunter's dad. He should know about the FBI."

"I agree the more information everyone has the better off you'll both be. Is he doing ok?"

"I didn't tell you that he had a break-in before but now I'm wondering if it is related. I will ask Agent Jones about that."

"Maybe you should write down some questions because there are so many loose ends you might forget something. I wish I had a small tape recorder for you."

Blair's mind was in a state of total confusion. Every thought was a question. Writing some of them down made a lot of sense.

"I brought some coffee and croissants from the Coffee Bean. I know that is one of your favorite places," Olly said.

"You are so sweet," Blair told her.

"I like the idea of writing down questions to ask. Will you help me organize them?"

"Of course, I'll do anything to help. I'll go get a pen and some paper, you can get plates."

Where do I start Blair thought? They sat at a little table overlooking the Pacific Ocean and wrote down questions and talked. Talking was good medicine for Blair. So much had happened that she needed someone who could listen and help her stay on track. Olly was the perfect person for that. She was a smart business woman who had found her way to the United States at a young age and became successful in the restaurant business. Blair looked up to Olly and would listen to suggestions she made. Olly and Blair shared so many things in common.

They looked up at the clock. They would be meeting Agent Jones in a few hours. It seemed like time was moving slow.

"I can't wait to get this over," Blair said. "I hope that I can find out what is going on and why."

They ate their breakfast and Blair wrote down some notes. They were suggestions that she and Olly had come up with. Blair said, "she was going to take the lead on questioning Agent Jones and wanted some answers." There was that determined look on her face as she looked at the waves crashing on the cliff below. The ocean had a calming effect on her as she studied the paper in her hands. Maybe the upcoming meeting would resolve the questions. The two women planned their meeting with Agent Jones and ate their breakfast.

ELEVEN

Thomas turned on some lights in the house so it would look like someone was home. He locked the front door and called Captain Douglas as instructed to let him know that he was going out. Bill and Martha love cheesecake he thought. I'll stop by and get one.

Al Yawer told Omar that the trip would not take too long and he suggested that they should park on the street behind the Adams house and walk through the woods to the house. It looked like a long ranch home he told Omar and the woods would offer cover for their mission. Yawer was a very organized individual that thought things out to a finite measure. He liked having Omar with him because Omar followed directions without improvising on his own. The drive to Bridgewater in the Malibu was smooth. They traveled down highway 13 across the Neshamine River toward the Adams house. They should be at their destination in about 10 minutes Yawer said.

Steve Watkins told Frank Walker that they should enter the house through the woods. He said that would be the best way to stay out of sight. They had parked down the street from the Adams house and walked through the woods. Steve was making final plans when he saw Thomas Adams get in his car and leave. They noticed a local police car slowing down in front of the home and waited for it to pass.

"It looks like they are coming by pretty regular," Frank said.

"The good thing is when Adams left he kept lights on so we can go through the house pretty quick."

Steve suggested that on the last search the upstairs had been gone through pretty good but they did not check the basement or garage.

Frank said, "I will take the garage."

"Ok," said Steve.

The two agents quickly ran from their cover in the woods to the back of the Adams home. There was a door in the back of the garage that Steve was able to jimmy open and he and Frank made their way into the garage. It was dark but the street light outside helped to illuminate the interior of the garage. Steve said he would head down into the basement.

"Once you've finished go back to our spot in the woods," Steve said. "I will meet you there."

Omar asked Al Yawer, "do you think I should take the sawed off shotgun just in case?"

"No it would cause too much noise."

Yawer gave him a glock with a silencer on it.

"If you see something that does not belong, shoot it. We must do this quick."

Yawer and Omar made their way through the woods and stopped at the edge of the tree line to case the back of the home. There were lights on in most every room.

"Someone might be in there," Yawer said, "I will go first and then once I am at the back of the home you follow."

Omar knew that Yawer would signal to him once it was clear. Yawer ran in a crossing pattern through the yard to the back of the home. He noticed that the garage had a door that faced the woods and would make a great entrance. He signaled to Omar that it was clear.

Frank Walker finished his search of the garage and knew that Steve would not take too long in the basement. The garage produced nothing but Frank was thorough in his search. He looked through the two cabinets and made sure that everything was back in place as he had found it. He did not want to face the wrath of Dino Tuchy when they got back to the bureau.

Omar ran to the back of the home and joined Yawer. A bright light appeared to be coming down the street. Both men ducked down so that they would not be seen but so they could watch the lights. It was the local Bridgewater police making a pass in front of the Adams home. They should be gone in a few minutes Yawer told Omar.

Frank saw the lights from the street and crouched behind the lawn mower. He felt that his get away would be safe as soon as the car passed.

The police car stopped in front of the Adams home and an officer got out. He grabbed his flashlight and started to walk toward the home. Officer Douglas told his men to make sure that on some of their trips to walk around the back of the house. He stressed that, due to the tire tracks found on the previous break-in.

The officer, Andy Emery, had been new to the force. He spent 4 years in the U.S. Army before coming home and joining the Bridgewater police force. He was always happy to get an assignment that may offer a chance for action. During his time in the Army he had been to Afghanistan and had trained for action. Bridgewater was a quiet town and anything more than a traffic violation would be action for them.

Frank Walker wondered why the police car had stopped for so long. He wanted to look out the window but saw a flashlight headed his way. He crawled along the floor toward the corner where a large work bench was built. He could crawl under it if necessary he thought.

Yawer whispered to Omar that they should make their way around the side of the house away from the garage. It appeared that the officer was coming around to the garage side.

"We can hide in the shrubs behind the kitchen," he whispered.

They moved near the kitchen and under the shrubs. There were three very large pine bushes that ran along the back of the house. They were about five feet tall and over ten feet long. They would be great cover for the two men.

"The officer should not pose any problem, Yawer said, but if he does shoot him."

Andy Emery was almost to the side of the garage when his radio went off. He pulled it off his shoulder and answered. It was Captain Douglas.

"Yes sir, I'm checking the yard and back of the house right now. Ok, I'll check the woods too."

He returned the radio to its shoulder holster and continued around the side of the garage.

He flashed his light into the garage window and then along the walk toward a back door. No sign of anything wrong he said to himself.

Andy walked toward the woods. It was a clear night and the full moon made it easy to see along the edge of the tree lined yard. Andy was a few years younger than Hunter Adams but knew about Hunter's football legend well. Everyone in Bridgewater knew Hunter Adams the local football star and now a war hero. Like everyone his age Andy came to the funeral home to pay his respects. He was glad that he could help by keeping an eye on Mr. Adams house. Why would anyone want to break-in to a home after someone had died he thought?

The tree line looked clear and as he walked toward the split rail fence, everything looked ok. He turned and walked toward the back of the house shining his flashlight along the perimeter. He looked up at the moon and thought how full and bright it was. Andy shined his light near the shrubs by the kitchen. A muffled sound was heard as he felt a sharp pain in his right shoulder. He had been shot! Andy fell to the ground clutching his shoulder. Omar crawled from under the shrub and headed toward the wounded officer.

Frank Walker came out from under the work bench when he saw the officer headed toward the woods. He watched him search the tree line and then turn around toward the house. The officer seemed to fall to the ground all of a sudden. Then Frank saw a figure headed toward the officer. Frank made his way to the garage door and caught sight of Omar in the shadow of the house. Omar had a gun extended and it appeared that he was moving in for the kill. Frank burst out of the garage and shot at the shadow going toward the officer. Omar clutched at his side and turned and shot back as he fell to the ground.

Al Yawer had just come out from under the shrub when he saw the garage door open. He saw Frank appear and shoot at Omar. Yawer blasted two shots toward Frank and one hit him in the chest. Blood exploded all over the garage door as Frank fell backwards into the wall.

Steve was coming up from the basement when he heard the noise from outside. He ran to see what was going on.

Omar had been shot and Yawer saw him go down. He headed toward the figure that came out of the garage that he shot at and saw Frank lying against the garage wall. Yawer put another bullet in Frank's head. Blood spattered all over the garage wall as Frank lay in the pool of brain matter. Yawer was going to make sure no one would be alive to tell of this. He went to Omar's side when another figure came from the house and started shooting. Yawer went down and started to crawl toward his friend.

Steve had seen Omar and Yawer in the yard and also saw a figure lying in the grass and thought it was Frank. He did not see that Frank had been shot at the back of the garage door. Yawer shot back at the figure from the house. Steve was able to take cover and called to his friend to see if he was ok. There was no answer. Yawer saw that Omar had been shot but seemed to be able to crawl. Neither man saw that the officer had turned over on his stomach and took his pistol out of its holster. Andy shot at the figures on the grass crawling toward the woods. Steve was happy that the man lying on the grass was alive and shooting back. He still thought that it was his partner. Steve shot toward the woods where the two men were crawling. Andy heard where the next round of shots was coming from and he shot at Steve. Now Steve was confused. Who in the hell is that lying in the grass? Why were they were shooting at him? Steve stayed down to think for a minute. Andy called out. "I'm Officer Andy Emery, of the Bridgewater police, toss your gun out or I'll shoot again."

Steve called back. "Steve Watkins, United States Federal Bureau of Investigation. Stop shooting!"

Steve jumped off the porch and crawled toward the wounded officer.

Andy Emery yelled, "Stop or I'll shoot. Toss me your identification." Steve saw the uniform and knew that it was a local cop. Now where was Frank he thought?

Yawer dragged Omar into the woods and they made their way to the parked car. The mission failed and now they would have more problems here in Bridgewater. Steve told the officer who he was again.

"I have a partner out here somewhere," Steve said.

Andy answered back, "They were shooting at someone near the garage."

While Steve headed toward the garage Andy took his radio off his shoulder and called in to Captain Douglas.

"Captain this is Andy, there was some shooting at the Adams house and I've been hit. There is also a man who is identifying himself as an FBI agent," Andy said.

"How bad are you hit son," said Captain Douglas?

"Just shot in the shoulder. I think I got one of the other men though."

"What other men," Captain Douglas said?

Andy said, "There were two other men shooting but I'm not sure who they were."

"Where are they now?"

"Crawled into the woods," Andy answered.

"We are on our way Andy."

Two squad cars were dispatched to the scene plus Captain Douglas had one car sent to the perimeter of the neighborhood. He was sure that there would be a fast car trying to get away from the scene. Steve saw Frank lying in a pool of blood. His head had been blown apart and he had a large hole in his chest. Steve was sick. What had happened here? The quiet town came alive with sirens. Locals came rushing to their doors to see what had happened. Must have been a bad traffic accident most of them thought. Bridgewater did not have a murder in over thirty years and most incidents were traffic related. Two squad cars pulled up in front of Thomas Adams home. Captain Douglas came running around the back with his gun drawn. He saw Steve standing over the body of Frank Walker. He called out to Steve to drop his gun. Steve called back that he was FBI and was under the direction of the Philadelphia Bureau. Captain Douglas asked for his identification. He took it out and showed it to Captain Douglas.

Three other officers ran into the woods to follow the trail of the men who got away. They could see a trail of blood and broken tree limbs where one man must have dragged the other. Captain Douglas told them to follow the trail and call to the squad car that was circling the neighborhood.

Captain Douglas went over to help Andy. The local EMS unit had arrived and headed to help the two men on the ground. They stopped at the back of the garage first.

Steve said there's no hope here, as he stood over Frank's body. They went to take care of the officer on the ground. Andy's wound was bleeding but the bullet went through the shoulder. They were able to bandage him and put him on a stretcher. Andy gave Captain Douglas a recap before he was taken to the local hospital.

Captain Douglas sat Steve Watkins down, he appeared to be shaken. Steve did not respond to Captain Douglas line of questions.

"What were you two doing here?" Captain Douglas asked?

Finally Steve turned toward the Captain.

"I have to report to my Bureau chief."

"You need to answer my questions first or I will have you taken and put in jail for breaking and entering Mr. Adams home."

"I'll answer your questions sir, but I have to call in first."

Captain Douglas agreed to let Steve contact his office, but he sat with Steve when he called.

Dino's cell phone rang.

"Hi Steve, what have you found?"

Steve didn't know where to start. Dino was probably going to blow up when he heard the news. He didn't need his two experienced agents involved in an altercation that would get the press and local police involved. Dino knew that the Washington Bureau had this mission as top priority.

"Sir, we ran into some problems."

"What kind of problems?"

"When we were coming out of the Adams house we were ambushed by two gunmen."

Steve was surprised when Dino asked if they were ok.

"Actually sir," he paused, "Frank was shot, and he's dead!"

Dino was silent on the other end of the phone for it seemed like an eternity to Steve. "How did it happen?"

"Looks like he was surprised, and they murdered him sir. They blew his head apart!"

Steve and Frank were two very experienced agents and Dino had worked with both of them for over 10 years. Dino asked who else is involved.

"The local police are here sir, and one of their men has also been shot."

"How much do they know?"

"I'm sitting with the Captain of the Bridgewater police," Steve said. Steve handed his phone to Captain Douglas.

"I'm Captain Douglas of the Bridgewater police." Steve had only heard the other officers call him Captain, he did not know his name.

"Captain Douglas, my name is Dino Tuchy of the Federal Bureau of Investigation.

I am the head of the Philadelphia Bureau and report to the director in Washington. It is very important that the local news media not be involved in this investigation."

"That may be a problem," Captain Douglas told him.

"This is a small town and a shoot out of this magnitude will cause quite a stir."   "I understand," Dino said, "but they can't know the details. I am demanding that you and your staff insure that until I arrive that no one will give the reporters any details. They can't know the FBI is involved or why we're involved."

"That may be easy Mr. Tuchy because I don't know why the FBI is involved but if you want my cooperation you'll fill me in when you get here."

"Deal," said Dino.

TWELVE

Blair told Olly that she was very nervous about the meeting with Allisa Jones.

"I just know that she has some bad news for me. Why else would she want to meet with me and she did say that she would let me know what was going on."

Olly tried to convince her that it was probably just some information regarding the apartment shoot out and had nothing to do with bad news. Deep down Olly wasn't sure why the FBI agent wanted to meet with Blair and also feared the news she would bring.

Allisa Jones had been taken off the case by the FBI director John Martin and she was suppose to give all her information to the Los Angeles office and the bureau head Dean Curry. Now she would be expected to assist Curry. Allisa did not feel that she failed; she also had no use for Dean Curry. He was a male chauvinist and made no bones about it. When Allisa was promoted to her new position she heard from the grape vine that Dean said she was sleeping with someone in Washington. She was determined to solve this case even if it was in an unofficial position. Allisa Jones was a beautiful woman. She tried to hide her beauty by dressing very conservatively and kept her hair tied back all the time. She never wanted people to get to close to her. She was from the Bronx and a poor family background. She entered the agency in New York and worked in many slums, sometimes as an undercover agent.

On a cold night in Manhattan she was working a case that involved a corporate officer selling critical information to a foreign source. She had been placed as a secretary in the corporate office and was feeding the local agents the inside information that she gathered. She also found a way to get the suspect to trust her and he became romantically involved with her. She was able to get the key information through this involvement to close the case. She got the information and had to escape the apartment almost naked. It had to be below 30 degrees and she made her way through the blowing wind to turn the information over to the New York Office. She was rewarded with an assignment in the Washington Bureau. Many other agents did not like the fact that she did not give them the information and took all the glory herself. She never told anyone how she got the information.

In the Washington assignment she worked with some of the outlying agents. One agent, Dino Tuchy in the Philadelphia Bureau had her helping to work on an International case of espionage. Together they were instrumental in breaking the case. This case got Allisa the attention of the new FBI Director, John Franklin Martin. She was promoted to the Los Angeles Bureau and given the task of working with the Department of Homeland Security.

Allisa Jones was very proud and was not going to give up on this case. She knew that she would be taking a big chance by giving Blair Adams some key information but she was used to taking chances. She took chances in New York, and was not going to be stopped now.

Blair got dressed and called out to Olly in the other room.

"Do you mind if I wear one of your tops with my Jeans?"

"No, go ahead honey."

"I just love your clothes."

Blair had this thing about shoes like a lot of girls her age. She could wear almost anything and decide in minutes, except for the shoes. Today she was at a loss because she didn't have her shoes to pick from.

"Can I wear one of your pair of shoes?"

"Sure," Olly called out as she dressed in her room.

Olly came into the room where Blair was finishing getting dressed. Blair was sitting on the floor with four pair of shoes all lined up.

"Not sure which one to choose," she said.

Olly could see that Blair was very nervous and tried to joke with her.

"Why wear any shoes, you've got great feet." Ollie knew that Blair hated her feet. "Yeah, sure! I look like a bare footed duck", Blair said.

The two women finished dressing and left the house. Blair told Olly that she wanted her to stay with her the whole time regardless of what Agent Jones would say.

"I'll be with you as long as you want," Ollie answered.

They left the house in Olly's Suburban and headed down the Pacific Coast Highway toward the Santa Monica Pier.

Blair was very quiet as they passed Wilshire Blvd. Wilshire was the first street from San Vicente Blvd. where they entered the Pacific Coast Highway from Olly's house. Soon they would be at Santa Monica Place then find a parking spot to walk to the Pier. Olly wanted to say something to break the ice but didn't know what to say. She was relieved when Blair asked her about stopping at The Pub for a bottle of water before they head to the Pier.

Sure she said, "do you want to get a sandwich too?"

"No just something to drink."

Olly parked the Suburban in her usual parking spot behind The Pub. The women walked to The Pub and both grabbed a bottle of water and headed toward the Santa Monica Pier. It was a beautiful day with hardly a cloud in the sky. It was about 75 degrees and a gentle breeze came off the ocean. The sky was steely blue and the palm trees moved ever so lightly in the breeze. The weather in Santa Monica was always a bit cooler than that of Los Angeles. There was often fog that would roll in early in the morning but the sun would burn it off, and the gentle breeze that came off the Pacific Ocean was always welcomed. They crossed the Pacific Coast Highway at Santa Monica Blvd. They walked along the grassy park toward the Pier. Blair could see a woman sitting on the park benches that she had suggested as a meeting place to Agent Jones. It did not look like Agent Jones but they moved toward the meeting spot. Agent Jones got up from her spot and waved to Blair and Olly. Both women were surprised to see that it was indeed agent Jones. Allisa Jones was wearing jeans and a sweater. Her hair was a light auburn with blond streaks and hung shoulder length. The only time they had met her she looked a little older and had a suit on with her hair pulled back off her face. They both looked at each other with a bit of a surprised look on their face.

"Hi Agent Jones," Blair said.

"Glad you agreed to meet me Blair."

Blair introduced Olly to agent Jones. All three women sat on the park bench and Agent Jones began to talk.

"Blair, I have been working with the FBI for a long time, and we in the Bureau often use people outside of our organization to help us in some of the cases we have. I would like to offer you and your friend the chance to help the FBI in this case."

Blair looked at Agent Jones and said, "What case? I'm so confused that I really don't know what you're even talking about. I want to know about Hunter and the information you have regarding the break-in at my apartment."

"I'm going to get to that, but first I want to have you involved in more then just giving you information. Blair, I'm offering you the opportunity to work with me to solve this case."

"I'm not sure, what do you want me to do?"

"I am going to tell you everything we know about this case. If I don't find the answers here I will continue by going to Bridgewater and talking to Hunter's dad. The answer is somewhere, and I have to find it."

Blair felt her heart beating a thousand times a minute. She could hardly breathe let alone answer this request. What did Bridgewater have to do with this? Agent Jones knew so much, this startled Blair. "If you decide to come with me to Bridgewater you could be of great help. Hunter's dad will know that we are on a mission and that he will cooperate with us if he knows anything. I'll pay for everything if you decide to come along and I will be with you the whole time."

"First I want to know about my husband and why my apartment has been broken into."

"I'll get to that and again want you to know that I need your help in this investigation. If I give you the information you need, do you think you would be willing to help me?" Agent Jones asked.

"Yes, if it gives me the answers that I need to go on," she said.

"Blair, I'm going to detail the case we are working on. It will give you the answers you are looking for and it may give me the answers that we need to solve this case. Your husband was working for the FBI in Iraq. He was a special agent and had been one for many years."

Blair almost blacked out at this revelation. She was too stunned to say anything. Olly started to say something but Agent Jones gave her a signal to be quiet as she continued.

"Hunter was recruited while he was going to school at the University of Mississippi. It was rumored that there was a cult of men that were storing weapons outside of Tupelo. Your husband was injured but still on the football team. This would be the perfect cover. He would be able to get into places we would never get into. He was an Ole Miss football player and that was the key we needed. It took some time to convince him that he could do this. He worried about you and how this might affect your relationship."

Blair almost cried out when she heard this news. She had tears in her eyes and Olly held onto her.

"Blair, please don't be mad because he didn't tell you about his work. He could not because it may have put you into danger. You can see already what danger has come your way now."

"We found out that there was a local chapter of separatist that planned to blow up the court house in Tupelo. They wanted to kill two prominent politicians that had helped to end racial segregation in the Mississippi schools. Hunter was able to get introduced into the group and earned their trust. He needed to be able to assimilate into their organization while keeping the façade of playing football and being a student. He was responsible for us breaking the group up and we were able to arrest most of the leaders. He was also able to keep his identity in tack without being found out as the informant. Because of his success and the importance that he saw in this work he agreed to continue full time with the FBI."

Blair sat on the edge of the park bench as Allisa Jones continued the story.

"We had him join the Mississippi National Guard as a cover. He was transferred to the United States Army Special Forces. He had missions to South and Central America and was one of the highest regarded agents we ever had. The war in Afghanistan and Iraq offered us many opportunities."

This information left both Blair and Olly silent.

"We have many agents like Hunter stationed with the armed forces helping the FBI and Homeland Security protect the interest of the United States. The U.S forces have their mission, but we feel that our mission is broader. We plan the future, the military plans for the present. We have to make sure that our country is safe for today and tomorrow. We have our people in key places to protect America's interest. Our government knows that the Middle East and the possible oil crisis that comes with our involvement there will affect our future. The issue of oil and it's importance to our economy will effect everyone in the world."

Blair was not a fan of the United States stand in Iraq and often felt that we had overstayed our presence. She also was not a fan of the current administration. Blair had become more politically involved with Hunter in the military. She was an avid reader of political articles and books. She often was outspoken about her views and very knowledgeable when discussing them.

"Agent Jones, I can't hardly believe that Hunter was an agent in the FBI. I have had so many questions lately about events in the past and maybe this answers some of them. If he was with the FBI some of those things make sense. But why if he was undercover is everyone breaking into my apartment? Is this also why Hunter's dad has had his house broken into?"

"Yes Blair, the break-ins must be linked to all of this. I am telling you things that our agency has kept secret and not all the agents involved know the whole story. You have to understand that I would get fired and could face jail time for telling you all of this."

Blair was grateful to Agent Jones and felt she could be trusted.

"I am willing to help you Ms. Jones but I'm not sure what I could do."

"Blair, before you get too involved you better think this out," Olly said. "You're not trained for this."

"Blair you probably have information that everyone is looking for and don't even know that you have it, Agent Jones said. The break-ins are due to everyone seeking that information."

"I don't know what you mean Ms. Jones."

"Blair, think about it! Had your husband sent you something and told you to keep it until he gets home? Maybe you received a letter with a map or information regarding one of his missions!"

"I don't have anything like that Ms. Jones," Blair said.

"What would this information be about?"

"Blair I have been told that on one of his last missions he was in charge of a search party that may have found important documents in a castle that belonged to Saddam Hussein. The information would be critical to our efforts. The President wants to have this information, that's how important it is."

Blair was thinking when her cell phone rang. She looked at the screen to see who it was and saw it was Hunter's dad. I'll call him back later she thought.

"I'm still not sure Agent Jones. I need some time to think this out. Olly is right.

I don't know anything about this type of investigative work. Can I have some time before I give you my final answer?"

"Blair I'm not trying to rush you but before tomorrow I may have to leave here to continue the investigation. You have to decide by tonight. Even if you only decide to go through all your things to see if you have something that may seem suspicious. I want your help and you must keep your promise not to tell anyone what I have told you."

Both Blair and Olly agreed to keep the information secret. Blair said she would call agent Jones by 7:00 p.m. with her decision. Agent Jones said, "My cell phone number is 555-678-2315. It isn't on my card that I gave you earlier."

Blair felt grateful and confused.

"Olly I'm not sure what to do."

"I can't tell you what to do Blair but I will support any decision you make."

The two women left Agent Jones at the Pier and walked together back toward The Pub. Agent Jones was hoping that she may have triggered some thoughts in Blair's mind that would have her search through items that Hunter had sent. If nothing else this would eliminate the need for searching the apartment a third time. She was sure with the revelation about Hunter being in the FBI that Blair would be more willing to share information with Agent Jones. In either case Agent Jones was going to continue with the investigation.

THIRTEEN

Blair and Olly walked back toward Olly's car.

"I'm starved," Blair said.

"Let's stop in at The Pub and have Manual make us some lunch," Olly said.

"That sounds good."

"I need to call Hunter's dad back. I'll wait until we get to The Pub."

The noise on the street in the Promenade was always loud. There were people standing on corners playing guitars or other musical instruments. You always had the occasional preacher barking out his message to those passing by. They crossed Second Avenue and headed toward Santa Monica Blvd. They got to Santa Monica and Second and headed up toward 3rd Street. A man carrying a sign that read the end of the world is at hand. Blair looked at Olly and said he might be right. The temperature had gone up about 5 degrees since they first sat down at the Pier with Agent Jones.

"I need a cold drink."

They got to The Pub and Blair decided to sit at an outside table. She loved the scenery and often would enjoy people watching from those tables. Olly went inside and came out with two bottles of water.

Ashley was working that day and walked outside to say "hello." She hugged Blair and asked, "How are you doing?"

"I'm still in a state of shock. The break-in was one thing but the second time was more than I can handle."

"Olly filled me in about the shoot out. Have they found out who those men were yet?"

Blair wasn't sure how to answer that.

"I really don't know. Officer Tuttle hasn't gotten back to me. I spent the night at Olly's and he might not know where I was."

"He was here a little while ago," Ashley said.

"Did he ask about me," Blair said?

"Yes, and I said that you had stayed at Olly's last night. Manual said that Olly had come by to open up and she said you were still at her house. Can I do anything to help you", Ashley asked?

"Thanks, I'm ok now." They hugged again.

Ashley asked Blair what she wanted to eat.

"Tell Manual to make me one of his famous omelets with spinach, cilantro and cheese." Ashley went back into The Pub and Olly came back out.

"I have to go to the market for Manual," she said.

"You go ahead and eat and I'll be back in a about a half an hour."

Blair decided that this was a good time to return the call to Thomas Adams. She dialed his home number and the phone rang but there wasn't any answer.

She left him a message.

"Hi, this is Blair, sorry I missed you but if you get a chance just call me back. Hope everything is ok."

The sun was high over the top of the buildings on the corner and Blair was glad that there was an awning over the outside tables. She was watching the people on the corner waiting for a bus. The usual array of kooks stood in line with the normal work force. Blair chuckled when she saw a man wearing shorts and a lady's bra standing in the bus line. This is my California she thought to herself. Her cell phone rang.

"Hello, this is Blair."

She never knew if it could be a possible audition or a friend wanting to check on her.

"Hi, it's Blake, how are you doing?"

She hadn't talked to Blake in a while and wanted to update him on so much. She also remembered the promise to Agent Jones and was a bit cautious. She knew that he had an early class and probably just got out of it.

"Not really great but I'm making it."

She had a great relationship with her friends and Blake had been there from the first day that she moved into her apartment.

"Blake it appears that the FBI knows more than they had told me and I want to try to get agent Jones to trust me with some of that information."

"You better be careful, Blair. The FBI is no one to fool with. Do you want me along for protection?"

Blair laughed. She thought that must have been the first time she laughed in a long time.

"What kind of protection do you think you can offer?" she said.

This caused both of them to laugh. Blake was about one of the nicest people she knew but he was not someone you would think of for protection.

"Well I guess protection was a bad choice of words," Blake said.

They both laughed again.

"I could at least go with you when you meet with her if you wanted."

"I think it would be easier for me to get her to tell me something if I was alone. I appreciate your offer and once I know more I will need your help."

She felt guilty not telling Blake what she had already found out. He would understand she said to herself because there is so much more she needed to know. She detailed the events about the second break-in and the shoot out but left out the fact that Agent Jones told her that Hunter was a member of the FBI. She wanted Blake to know what Olly and Ashley knew and she wanted him to hear it from her. She promised to call him when he got home from school. It was his late night class and he would not be back until after ten.

Ashley came out with Blair's breakfast and Manual also came out to see his prized creation and make sure Blair was happy with it.

"You're the best Manual," she said.

"You too Senora Blair."

She always loved working her shift at The Pub when he was cooking. He would make sure all the customers that were regulars had a little special touch to their order.

"Can I do anything else for you?" he asked.

"This is perfect! I hope to be back working in a few days," she answered.

As she started eating her omelet her thoughts took her in so many directions. What was next? Maybe I should call Hunter's dad again before I decide on what to do. She enjoyed the time eating alone on the patio of The Pub. It was almost as nothing had happened.

"Hello," came a voice from the street.

It startled her. It was Officer Tuttle.

"Sorry I didn't mean to scare you," he said.

"I was just in a dream world. Sit down officer."

"I don't want to disturb your lunch," he said, "but I have some important information for you."

"Please tell me what it is. I'm done anyway. Manual makes these omelets so big I can never eat the whole thing."

"We have been trying to find out the identification of the men that were in your apartment. Our office seemed to find a road block with every move until Captain Parker got a call from the FBI office in Los Angeles."

Blair almost dropped her fork.

"Well, it appears that we will be working on this investigation with their office, and the head man, a Mr. Dean Curry. He called back and told us their identification. Not exactly sure why they were in your apartment, but both men are Iraqi Nationals. Their ID did not help but it was through a fingerprint analysis search that their true identification was discovered."

Blair didn't know exactly what to say but the look on her face must have said a lot.

"Are you ok?" officer Tuttle asked.

"Yes, I just get more confused with every piece of this puzzle."

"I know," he said. "We're pretty confused also. Captain Parker has gone to the FBI's Los Angeles Bureau office to meet with Dean Curry. I wanted to see if I could find you to let you know what we have found out."

"Do you know what these men were looking for?" Blair asked.

"No maybe that's why the FBI agreed to meet with Captain Parker today. I think they have an idea of what is going on but won't tell anyone. We have part of the puzzle and they have the other part. They usually are not willing to share information. If you think of something Blair, please let us know as soon as possible. I will try to keep you informed."

"When you say they were Iraqi Nationals, just what do you mean?"

"That's kind of a crazy thing. It appears that one of them may be on the Army's list of Saddam supporters."

"You mean the men that were on the deck of cards list that the Army put out?"

"Yes, it appears that one of them may be a close confidant of Saddam."

"This really does not make any sense. Thanks for giving me the information."

Officer Tuttle got up from the table and again asked if she was ok before he left.

This new information helped her make up her mind. I will call Agent Jones and help her. I need to know what is going on and I want to make sure whatever Hunter was doing was ok. I have to protect his name.

Olly returned from the market. Blair filled her in on what officer Tuttle had to say. She also told Olly of her decision to help Agent Jones.

"I just have to make sure that the information they think Hunter had gets to the right people. I know he was always very loyal to the Army, and our country and I don't want anything bad said of him."

Olly understood. "I don't blame you. I am just worried that this might be too dangerous for someone not trained in this sort of thing."

"Agent Jones said she would make sure that I was safe. I'm going to give her a call."

Blair dialed Agent Jones cell phone number. Agent Jones answered and seemed pleased that Blair called her so soon.

"Hi Blair, I'm glad that you called."

"Agent Jones, I know a little more about this situation and want to help if I can. I also want you to level with me before I commit to assisting you."

"What kind of information are you looking for Blair?"

"How about some information about the men in my apartment. When we met you didn't say anything about them. Have you found out any more?"

Blair felt that officer Tuttle gave her the details freely and had no reason to hold back the truth. She wanted to see what Agent Jones would tell her.

"Blair, I'll level with you. Like I told you before the FBI Director wasn't too pleased with my performance on the search of your apartment. The shooting caused him to take the case away from me and put it in the hands of Dean Curry and the L.A. office. I have the opportunity to solve this case with your help and clear both your husband and myself."

"That doesn't answer my question about the men in my apartment."

"I understand. I have found out from our L.A. office that they were both Iraqi Nationals and one of them has been on the Homeland Security watch list. How he got into this country we're not sure. His name was Ahmad, and had recently been under investigation by the U.S. Army and held at the Abu Ghraib prison in Baghdad. We're still investigating the identification of the second man."

Blair listened as Allisa continued.

"Blair I have told you everything that I know. I have told Dean Curry that you have been very cooperative to the investigation. I'm sure he will want to talk to you but unless I get more information I can't help you with your questions. I feel that you have some information that you haven't shared with me. This may be information that you don't even realize that you have."

"The only information that I had was that the two men were Iraqi's. I found this out just minutes ago from officer Tuttle. I don't know anything else."

"Blair, I think your telling me the truth. I still want your help."

"I want to help you agent Jones."

"We'll be a good team Blair. I'm packing for the trip to Philadelphia. Come with me and together we can get some answers."

"I'm not sure what value I would be but I will come along."

"Pack lightly; we'll be on the move a lot until we find out the answer to this mystery."

"We will fly out to the Philadelphia airport this evening."

"I'll meet you at the airport. What airline are we leaving on?"

"I can get us on United real easy."

"What time should I be there?"

"Make it close to nine tonight. Meet me at the United Ticket Counter."

"I'll see you there," Blair said.

Blair felt Agent Jones had leveled with her and was excited about the prospect of working on this mystery verses being part of it. She told Olly that she had to get some things together and would keep in touch with her.

"Tell Ashley and Blake that I had to go to Philadelphia to see Hunter's dad, they'll understand and not ask too many questions."

Blair left the table at The Pub and headed down the Promenade toward her apartment. Olly wanted to do something but just watched and hoped that this was a good move.

Ashley came out and asked where Blair had gone to.

"She is going back to Philly," Olly said.

"Guess Hunter's dad needed her. She just felt she came home too soon."

"I understand, Ashley said, especially with the break-in and everything else. I forgot to remind her about the package she left here yesterday. I put it in the office for her."

"She will be back soon and we can give it to her then," Olly answered.

"It's probably nothing important."

FOURTEEN

Al Yawer helped Omar to his feet when they got into the woods.

"Are you ok, can you make it back to the car?"

Omar just nodded but it was obvious he was in a lot of pain. It was too dark to tell exactly where he had been hit and how serious. Shots were still coming from the yard of Thomas Adams' home and Yawer knew that they had to move quickly.

The night was very dark but there was a full moon that shown down on the clearing ahead. The tree line shielded the two fugitives from the back of the Adams home. The woods were thick with large maple trees that helped hide both of them but the sound of sirens rang out in the night. The dew was heavy on the grass and Omar was wet from crawling into the woods. Yawer could not tell what was blood and what was wet from the dew. They had to get to their car and get there soon. The sirens seemed to surround them as they made their way through the thickest part of the tree line. The car was still a block away and Omar slumped as they came out of the woods. Yawer lifted him back on his shoulders. Yawer would have to carry him the rest of the way. Omar was close to comatose. Yawer could not leave him there.

Captain Douglas stood over Andy as the paramedics helped him onto a stretcher.

"You did real good kid," Captain Douglas said. "Did you see the men that went into the woods?"

Andy was pretty clear of the events, but said he only saw the man who identified himself as an FBI agent.

"I know that when I got to the area by the split rail fence that the shots came from under the large shrub behind the house. I was knocked

99

down by one of the shots and lost it for a minute or so. There were many shots after that along the back of the house. Not all of them seemed to be coming at me," he said.

Captain Douglas got on his radio and called to the two cars that he had circling the neighborhood.

"Do you see anything suspicious?" he asked.

"No sir, but we are moving to Bloom Bird Street that is right behind the woods and Mr. Adams home."

"Fan out and make sure you cover every inch," Captain Douglas said.

Steve asked Captain Douglas how he could help.

"You and I need to head into the woods to see if those men are still hiding. You also need to fill me in on what in the hell is going on here."

Steve wasn't exactly sure himself. The objective seemed so easy. Get into the Adams home, search it one more time and get out. Where had it gone wrong? Steve told Captain Douglas that his bureau chief Dino Tuchy would fill him in on the details. The only thing he could tell Captain Douglas is that he and his partner were ambushed on the way out of the Adams home.

The moon gave the two men entering the woods a clear view of the exterior of the tree line ahead. They decided that the safest move was to stick together and fan out when they got half way through. Neither man knew what they were dealing with nor if there were more fugitives in the woods waiting for the original two that were escaping.

Yawer had Omar over his right shoulder and moved along the tree line for cover. The plan to leave the car a few blocks away was a good plan but now it made for a hard retreat. Omar had passed out and Yawer was carrying dead weight. He wanted to get to their car and escape the sirens that seemed to get closer. The car was in sight and Yawer felt a bit of relief. He just had got Omar into the back seat when a squad car with a bright light came toward them. He jumped over the front seat and started the car. Yawer had the element of surprise on his side. With the lights off he gunned the engine and headed right at the squad car. Yawer sideswiped the squad car spinning it around as he headed down Bloom Bird Street. He knew that the retreat out of town would not be easy. I must eliminate some of their men he thought. The police car lodged against a parked truck badly damaging the driver's side of the escaping vehicle. Captain Douglas heard a loud crash as he and Steve Watkins made their way into the woods.

"Sounds like it is over to our right," he said, Steve agreed. They moved in the direction of the crash they had heard.

Yawer headed down Bloom Bird Street and took the first left. He heard other sirens headed his way. The chase was on. He kept the lights off on his car so that he would not be seen from a distance. The scouting of the neighborhood before had helped. He knew that Bloom Bird Street did not go through to the highway. He also knew that there were many dead ends in the area and did not want to get stuck in one of them. More lights and sirens seemed to get closer. Yawer turned down Cannon street and sped up. Just when he turned to look back, a car from out of nowhere came out of a driveway. Yawer swerved to miss it.

Captain Douglas and Steve made their way out of the woods and saw two officers standing next to a badly damaged cop car.

"What the hell happened?"

"Someone driving without their headlights on hit us," they said.

"Shit, would you turn your lights on if you were trying to get away?"

He called out on his radio to the other squad car. They said they were in pursuit of a dark compact vehicle that was headed West on Cannon.

"Get a good description for us. I'll get the State Police on the horn and have them join the chase. They may be driving with their headlights off so be aware."

He called to the local office of the State Police and filled them in. They said they will cover Highway 13 in both directions. That was the only way out of town. Sounded like a good plan.

Captain Douglas told Steve, "We should get back to the squad car to join the chase." Steve said he should wait for Dino to get to Bridgewater. They both headed back through the woods to the Adams home.

Captain Douglas told Steve, "Have Mr. Tuchy meet me at our headquarters in Bridgewater."

Steve said he would give Dino the message.

Captain Douglas got into his squad car and took a short cut to Cannon street. He came to a car still in the middle of the street. Captain Douglas got out and asked the two people standing near the car if they were ok. Billy Bridges and his wife were shaken but said they were ok. They told the Captain that a dark car, a Chevrolet Malibu they thought, came down the street without headlights on and almost t-boned their car. Captain Douglas did not alert them to the fact that these were men being pursued. He took their information and headed back to his squad car. He got on his radio and alerted both his men and the State police that they were probably looking for a dark mid sized Chevrolet Malibu. He also said that the driver's side had been hit when it collided with the squad car.

Yawer kept driving through the neighborhood and looked for a spot to hide their car. He knew that by now the local police would have a description of the Chevrolet and that the damage to the driver's side would give them away. He knew that there was a large field a few blocks away. He again turned the headlights off and turned right on Apple Lane. He saw a perfect spot and pulled the Chevrolet over the curb and into the tree covered cove. They needed a new get-a-way vehicle. He drove into the brush and was able to cover the back of the vehicle from the street view. The woods were very thick in that area and he was more than two hundred yards off the street. Yawer crawled into the back to check on Omar. He had been bleeding very badly. Yawer tried to listen for a heartbeat but there was none. Omar was dead! I must hide his body so the police will not find it. Omar knew that this was a dangerous mission and Allah would be pleased that he gave his life for this cause.

Yawer left the vehicle in the woods as he started a search for another way out of town. He saw some lights from the corner and slowly walked toward them. It was a party store and a group of teens had gathered in front of the store. He just walked by and ventured down the street. He could come back to get Omar's body once he found new transportation. The group of teens had been playing loud music and never looked up as Yawer passed by. Yawer looked at the street signs as he turned the corner. He was at the corner of Apple Lane and Pine. He headed north on Pine and saw a line of cars parked along the side of the street. As he approached the line of vehicles it became evident that someone was having a party in the neighborhood. He scanned the line of cars and a group of motorcycles caught his eye. That could be the perfect get-a-way vehicle. Yawer pushed a Harley away from the group and toward the end of the line of cars. He was able to start it and headed around the corner of Pine back down Apple Lane. The group of teens was still standing outside the party store. They looked up when they saw a red Harley as it passed. They did not seem to take notice of the person riding it. One of them said that's a cool bike. "It's a Harley Dyna; only 1,500 of them were made. Billy Jamison has one just like it."

Yawer pulled the Harley into the woods next to the Chevrolet. He was able to get the gear out of the Chevrolet and put it into the side saddlebags on the Harley.

He would have to leave Omar. He pulled Omar out of the back seat and dragged his body deeper into the wooded area. He found a ditch, probably created by heavy spring rains or melting snow. It was about three or four feet deep. He laid Omar's body in the ditch and covered it with branches and dead leaves. He saw a tree limb and put it on top of Omar's body. He was able to push dirt on top of the body with the make shift shovel he had. Once Omar's body was covered he returned to the car and wiped all of it down. He did not want any evidence left. He put the documents that they had brought with them into the saddle bags on the bike. He wanted to make sure that the maps were not left in the Chevrolet. Yawer pushed the Harley out of the woods and started it. He headed down Apple Lane and knew that he had to get out of town before the Harley came up missing. The streets would lead him to Highway 13 and back to Mansfield Square. He did not feel that there would be a problem now that he found a new form of transportation.

Captain Douglas circled the streets of the neighborhood. He felt that the fugitives were still close by and that they would be looking for an escape route. He passed a group of teens standing in front of a party store. Captain Douglas stopped and asked the group if they saw a dark Chevrolet go by. They said that they did not.

"Did you see anyone driving really fast or without their headlights on?"

No was the answer. He headed down Apple Lane and turned onto Pine. Wow, cars everywhere he thought. This would be a good place to hide the Chevrolet; no one would notice it among this line of vehicles.

He drove down Pine slowly looking at every vehicle. He did not see any sign of the Chevrolet or any other vehicle that matched that description. With damage to the driver's side it would be easy to spot. The cars were lined up and down the street. There weren't any empty spots; nothing seemed out of the ordinary. There were about 4 motorcycles in the middle of the line of cars. Must be a party he thought.

Yawer turned off of Apple Lane and onto Main Street. That would lead him to Highway 13 and his escape route. He saw a State Police car headed his way. The first test was about to happen. Yawer had put the helmet on that was on the seat of the Harley and hoped that he would not cause any additional attention. The police car went by and Yawer kept his head down. He was driving at a normal speed so as to not cause any attention. Highway 13 was ahead and he would head north toward Mansfield Square. He did not feel that he should alert El Jaafi and Abdulla until he was safely out of Bridgewater. There was a traffic line on Highway 13 after he made his turn. The State Police had set-up a road block. They were stopping every vehicle. Yawer knew that they would be looking for two men and a car but he did not want to take any chances. He watched as the cars proceeded slowly to the check point. It appeared that the police were searching the cars and trucks. Two Officers were checking from each side. It also appeared that drivers were producing some sort of papers to be checked. He had to get out of this line.

Captain Douglas called to his squad cars to see where they were and if they had found anything. They had circled the area twice and also had heard from the State Police that the road blocks had been set-up on Highway 13 in both directions. Captain Douglas told them that they should continue to concentrate on the local area and the State Police could handle the Highway. He headed back toward Mr. Adams house to see if by any chance the fugitives headed back to the scene of the crime.

Yawer pulled the bike off to the side of the road. He got off the bike and made it appear that he had engine trouble. The vehicle behind him slowed down and asked if they could help.

"No thanks," he said, "just seems to have a miss and I don't want to get stranded."

"Do you know what is going on?" they asked him.

"I'm not sure, just traveling through town on my way to New York."

They waved goodbye and wished him good luck with the bike. He continued to act as if he was having problems as other cars passed by and he pushed the bike further off the road. When he was sure that he was far enough off the side of the road he got back on and headed into the woods. The ride through the woods would be easy as long as he did not make too much noise. When he felt that he was near the road block he turned the bike off and pushed it for about thirty feet. This was not an easy task. The Harley was very heavy and the ground was soft in spots. He was able to get past where he felt the police were and re-started the bike. He continued riding through the woods until he was about a ½ mile past the road block. Yawer returned to the highway and headed north toward Mansfield Square.

Steve Watkins called Dino Tuchy to find out how close Dino was to Bridgewater.

"We're just about to get off of highway 13," Dino said.

"I took a little longer because the State Police had a roadblock set-up on the highway."

Steve told him that it might be best to meet at the Adams home. The local police and State police are checking the area for the men that got away and we can check the home one more time if you want. Dino agreed and said we should contact Captain Douglas but not until I had one more look around. Captain Douglas circled the Adams home but there was no sign of the fugitive. I have to try to contact Thomas he thought. Maybe we should set-up a 24 hour watch here just in case they return. He figured that after a few hours of searching for the men that got away in the woods that he would re-direct a team to the Adams home. He continued down the street searching the next few blocks.

Yawer was an experienced motorcycle rider and the ride up highway 13 was a smooth trip. He thought the best route would be to head toward West Bristol and cross the Delaware River at the Burlington-Bristol Toll bridge. This would be less traveled than the bridge on highway 276. He would be in New Jersey after crossing the Delaware River and would contact El Jaafi to update him on what has happened. His escape was critical.

FIFTEEN

Dino Tuchy was with the Bureau for over 25 years and was one of the most decorated field agents. He was given the Philadelphia assignment after he helped break up a case where a man was about to sell state secrets. He was a tough boss and Steve knew that all hell would be raised when he arrived. Dino had been divorced for a long time, a by-product of the job. Many agents knew that the job would cause marital grief. It was once rumored that Dino had an affair with another Agent but no one knew for sure. Steve Watkins was still dealing with the sudden loss of his long time partner Frank Walker. How would he explain that to Dino?

Frank Walker was single and had been living in an apartment near the downtown area of Philadelphia that had seen a lot of renovation. Steve was glad that he didn't have to tell a wife with children that their dad had been killed on the job. Steve had been to Frank's place a few times when he and his wife would head to a concert or ballgame. Frank was a quiet guy who liked to play golf and ride his Harley on weekends. He was well liked by everyone. Steve and Frank had been partners for a long time but because Frank was single they did not socialize very much. Although many of their assignments were more investigative work, the reality of danger was always there. When it does happen it was always a shock. Steve was in shock.

Steve Watkins moved his car in front of the Adams home and would wait for Dino to arrive. After about ten minutes the black Chevrolet Suburban pulled up to the Adams' home. Steve got out of his car to greet Dino. Dino had brought one of his bureau men, Kevin Reese, with him.

"Hi boss."

Steve was surprised when Dino put his hand on Steve shoulder and offered his concern over Franks' death.

"Are you ok Steve?"

"I'm not really sure," he said.

"So much has happened so quickly that it hasn't quite set in yet."

"It's hard to lose anyone," Dino said, "especially your partner."

Steve almost broke down but held together. He felt that they needed to solve this and get the men who killed his partner.

"Fill me in," Dino said.

"Frank and I made our way into the home with no problem. We saw that the local police were passing by and watching the house from the street. I decided to go through the house and Frank was searching the garage. We would be in and out in less than fifteen minutes. I'm not exactly sure what happened but I was in the house when I heard a couple of shots. They were muffled like a silencer was used. I came out on the back porch and there were some shots fired from a man on the lawn toward the woods. I thought it was Frank shooting at someone until the same person shot at me. It took a few minutes to realize that it was a local cop shooting at me. I found Frank at the back door of the garage. They murdered him boss."

Dino felt sorry for Steve. He had never lost a partner and didn't quite know what to say. He thought it would be best to keep Steve thinking about the case.

"Did you complete your search?"

"I was about done but don't know what Frank had accomplished."

"You and Kevin go back into the house and I will call the local Captain to tell him that we will meet him here. It will give you both a few minutes to complete the search."

The two agents headed toward the Adams home as Dino called Captain Douglas.

Captain Douglas' phone rang. He thought that there were more calls to his phone and radio in the last hours than the last two years.

"This is Captain Douglas."

"Captain, this is Dino Tuchy of the FBI. I'm almost to the Adams home and would like to meet you there."

"Mr. Tuchy I am just completing the trip around the neighborhood," Captain Douglas told him. "I passed by the Adams home a few minutes ago and all seemed quiet. I will be there to meet you in about ten minutes."

Dino thought he would move to the front porch of the Adams home so that he could warn his men when the local police arrived. Steve had told him that a second EMS unit had taken Frank's body to the Bridgewater hospital. Dino knocked on the door and Steve came to see what was up. He informed them to complete the search quickly and look through the yard for clues to the shoot out. Captain Douglas pulled up to the Adams home and saw two cars parked in front. He did not see anyone in the cars so he pulled behind them and got out of his squad car. Dino called out to the Captain.

"We're up here!"

Captain Douglas walked toward the porch.

"Where are your men?"

Dino told him that we needed to check the area where our agent was killed.

"I sent them out back to where he was shot."

Captain Douglas thought that was a normal move. Although no one really knew what was normal for the FBI. Captain Douglas was about to find out. Dino was quick to point out to Captain Douglas that the FBI would be taking the lead in this investigation but would keep the local police involved.

"I need to know what's going on," Captain Douglas said.

"We have one of our citizen's homes being involved in multiple break-ins and now a shoot-out."

Dino agreed to give Captain Douglas a heads up. Captain Douglas said he still had to find Thomas Adams and let him know what had happened. Dino suggested that his men and Captain Douglas should search through the Adams home together to make sure that there wasn't any problem before Mr. Adams arrived. Dino said his men should be done searching the yard and back of the garage.

"Sorry for your loss," Captain Douglas said.

The two men walked around the garage to the back of the house to find the two FBI agents. By this time they had been through the home and were on the back porch.

"We need you two to accompany us through the Adams home," Dino said.

Steve looked a little confused knowing that they just finished going through the house a minute ago.

"I want to make sure everything is ok inside and Captain Douglas should be with us," he said.

It was obvious that Dino was making it seem that they were going to share everything with the local police. Steve knew if they found something in their search it would not be detailed to the local police.

Captain Douglas said, "I should lead the way."

"Sure," said Dino.

They entered the home through the back door of the garage. It was still opened from the earlier break-in. Captain Douglas had not asked why the FBI was there in the first place but Dino knew that would come up. The garage led to the kitchen door where all four men entered the home. They turned on the kitchen light and everything looked in place. Captain Douglas turned to Dino and asked the question. "Why are you here and what has the FBI so interested in a break-in here in Bridgewater?"

Dino said he would answer that question, "First we should complete the search of the Adams home."

Captain Douglas said, "I need to know what was going on, and need to know now."

"I can't tell you the whole story until I talk to the Director," Dino said, "but before the night is out I will fill you in. I will also need to know what you and Mr. Adams have to offer to the story."

"We will see," Captain Douglas said.

"Let's all split up and check the rooms."

Dino said that was a good idea.

"We're just making sure that there isn't someone still here or that they haven't left any evidence behind."

The four men walked through the kitchen and Dino suggested they not touch anything so the crime lab could do a finger print analysis. Captain Douglas said that they would have to have the State Police do that because he did not have that capability.

Dino said "I ordered a crime lab team to Bridgewater and they should be there any minute."

Captain Douglas knew now that the FBI wasn't going to let the local police handle much of the investigation.

The house seemed to be neat and did not appear that anything was out of place. Captain Douglas told Dino that in the first break-in there were tables and lamps turned over and papers tossed around.

"Looked like someone was looking for something," he said. "We thought it was kids because Mr. Adams son had a pretty good baseball card collection and a lot of trophies from his high school and college days."

"Did you find anything missing?" Dino asked.

"Mr. Adams said he had checked and everything seems to be here. That is what made me suspicious because the baseball cards were never touched and kids would have taken them."

"I agree," Dino said, "seemed like you had that detail covered."

"We still don't know who did the break-in," Captain Douglas said, "but maybe your crime lab will give us some answers."

"You know I will give you a copy of their report," Dino answered.

The search through the home produced nothing other than to confirm that it was empty and nothing had been disturbed. All four men walked out to the front porch and Dino said he wanted to wait for the Crime Lab to arrive. Captain Douglas called out to his squad cars on the radio to see where they were in their search.

"Captain we've gone up and down every street and cannot find anything suspicious."

He then called the local hospital to see how Andy was doing.

Dino told Steve, "Making it look like kids in the first break-in was a good idea but you should have taken something that kids would have wanted. You could have taken a television, radio or a few baseball cards."

Steve said, "We did not want to take anything due to the loss of Mr. Adams son, it would only cause him more grief."

"We would get them back to him," Dino said.

"I guess, but we thought it was best at the time to do it the way Frank and I planned."

Dino knew that Steve was still hurting so he dropped the line of questions and walked over to Captain Douglas.

"Our crime lab techs will be here soon. Do you want to wait with us for them or should we meet you back at your office."

"I still have fugitives on the loose in my town," Captain Douglas said, "Until that is resolved I will be on the search for them."

"I will call you and we can set-up a meeting place," Dino suggested.

Captain Douglas reminded Dino that Mr. Adams did not know about the second incident at his home and may come back at any minute.

"I will keep a lookout for him," Dino said.

Captain Douglas said, "Mr. Adams brother lived just outside of Bridgewater near Croydon. I am going to send a man over to his brother's house to see if Thomas is there."

"Good idea," Dino said. "Call me if you need our help."

Captain Douglas walked to his squad car and when he got inside he called the State Police to see if there road block had come up with anything. The vehicle searches both north and south on highway 13 had not brought any results. They decided that they would keep their position until midnight. He informed the State Police Captain that the FBI had sent a team headed by a Dino Tuchy to Bridgewater. The State Police had the same reaction that the local police did. Why the FBI? What was going on and what was the FBI not telling them? Captain Douglas called to Croydon to get the local police to see if Mr. Adams was at his brother's home. He talked to an officer and did not want to cause any more concern than necessary.

"We have a small problem here in Bridgewater and one of our citizens may be visiting his brothers home just outside of Croydon. If you could send a car out to check on him and ask him to call me I would appreciate it. His brother is Bill Adams and lives off highway 13 on Columbia Drive."

The Croydon Officer said they would be happy to help and said they would send a squad car over to the Adams home on Columbia Drive. They knew who Bill Adams was and where he lived. Captain Douglas gave the Officer his cell phone number. "If he's not at his brother's house let me know."

The officer agreed to call Captain Douglas once they visited the Adams home.

Yawer headed up highway 13 through Croydon when he spotted a local police car headed toward him. He made sure that he was doing the speed limit and tried not to look suspicious. The car passed him by and Yawer breathed a sigh of relief. He would soon be at West Bristol and out of Pennsylvania. The Officer turned to look at the red Harley as it passed. Wow, that's the first Harley Dyna I've ever seen. Being a motorcycle enthusiast he had seen one in a recent article about bikes. I would love to drive one he thought.

Dino sat on the porch of the Adams home and he and Kevin talked about the best way to keep critical information from the local police.

"They have to know that it's something big but what should we tell them" Kevin said.

"We will let them know that there is a possibility of a group of anti-war activist that is causing a disturbance at the home of military personnel that have been killed in Iraq. We could say it has happened in other cities and the FBI wants to make sure that we can protect our citizens from them."

"Great idea," Kevin said "it may cover both break-ins and this incident. We'll have to tell them that this is the first sign of violence and that is why they haven't heard about this."

The search for the men continued both through Bridgewater and on highway 13 in and out of town. The two squad cars continued to drive around the neighborhood near the Adams home. When they came in contact with local citizens they said they were looking for kids that may have broken into a home. They did not want to cause concern especially since they had not found the men that caused all the shooting.

As he drove back down Apple Lane Captain Douglas got a call from his office. "Captain we just got a call from the Dietlin's house. Seems they were having a graduation party and someone stole a motorcycle parked in front of their house."

He was only a block away from there and said he was on his way. He turned down Pine Street off of Apple Lane where he had seen a line of cars and four motorcycles parked on an earlier search of the neighborhood. Mr. Dietlin came out and said one of the men attending his son's graduation party had his Harley Davidson missing. Captain Douglas wanted to get a full description of the bike. The owner said it was a new red Dyna model Harley Davidson. There were only a few of them made the man said. The bike is worth over $20,000. Captain Douglas now knew that the fugitives must have ditched their car in favor of the Harley. He went back to his squad car and immediately called the State Police to alert them to look for a red Harley with one or two men aboard. He doubled back around the corner and again saw the group of teens that he questioned earlier.

"Have any of you seen a Harley come by in the past hour?"

"Yes said Perry White. It was headed down Apple Lane toward highway 13."

"How many people were riding on it?"

"One, said Perry, it looked just like the one that Billy Jamison owns."

"What color was the Harley?"

"Red," said Perry.

Captain Douglas called back to the State Police. We need to send information north and south to be on the lookout for a new red Harley with one rider.

"Seems to be a special bike" he told them.

Captain Douglas felt that the men or man must be out of town on the highway by now. He wasn't going to share the information with the FBI yet but needed to know more about why they were involved.

"I will put an All Points Bulletin out for the man and the bike. The APB would get to every local authority in Pennsylvania in a matter of minutes."

The APB was sent by the State Police and should be to every police office in the State so that they can be on the lookout for the red Harley. Captain Douglas called to his men to inform them about the red Harley. He also said we need to search the wooded areas by foot because they must have ditched the dark Chevrolet. This would be no easy task. Bridgewater like many small towns was heavily covered with wooded areas. That was part of the small town charm.

The search began with all the local officers in Bridgewater searching the woods. Because of the location of the missing Harley they decided that they should start the search around that area. They were told to tell anyone that asked that a fox was spotted and could be rabid. People should report it to the main police office if they spotted it. Captain Douglas knew if the story got out that they had shootings and fugitives on the loose it would cause a panic. The fox story would make sense especially in the spring. Because there were so many wooded lots around Bridgewater the local residents would often see fox, rabbits and beavers in the spring building their nest and homes.

The cell phone rang and Captain Douglas answered.

"Glad you called Thomas. I sent the local Croydon police to make sure you were ok. Thought you might be at Bill's house but being safe I just had to know."

Thomas said he was sorry that he did not inform Captain Douglas that he would be going out for the whole night.

"I plan to spend the night here and return home in the morning" he told the Captain.

"Probably a good idea, when you get back to town call me because I would like to go over a few things with you. It's not urgent but I just want to make sure you're kept in the loop."

Thomas figured that there must be some new information regarding his break in. Thomas hung up and told Bill and Martha that Captain Douglas just wanted to make sure he was ok.

"Nice to have the authorities looking out for you" Bill said.

The Croydon Officer went back to his car and headed back on his normal route. When he got in the squad car his radio buzzed him. He got the information that an APB had been put out to be on the lookout for a red Harley with one rider possibly going north or south on Highway 13. Has to be the red Harley he saw before on Highway 13 when he was going to Bill Adams house. The officer got on the radio and informed the State Police that he spotted one rider going north on highway 13 on a red Harley Dyna about fifteen minutes ago. When the news came in the State Police ordered all state patrol cars to travel north of Croydon and be on the lookout for the biker. They asked the officer how he knew what kind of bike it was.

"I love Harley's and the Dyna was featured in an article this month in a local magazine."

The chase was on and so much lay in balance. No one really knew how critical this information would be.

SIXTEEN

Blair got out of the airport limo. She used this service whenever she was going out of town. She paid the driver the eleven dollars and grabbed her bag. She headed across the street to the LAX terminal. She looked at her watch, nine o'clock, can't believe I'm early. Allisa Jones had told her that they had the red eye flight to Philadelphia and that they should meet at the United Ticket Counter around 10:00 p.m. She thought that she should call Olly and let her know that everything was ok. She grabbed her cell phone and dialed Olly's number.

"I'm at LAX and everything is going good she told her. I will call you when we get to Philly."

Olly was still uncertain that this was a good idea, but when Blair made up her mind there was no changing it.

"I feel bad that I didn't talk to Blake and Ashley" she said. "They have been so great to me."

"They will understand" Olly told her.

"I'll just say that Hunter's dad was having some problems and you needed to help him. They understood and wish they could help more."

Olly made her promise that she would call every day.

"You know that I will" Blair said. Olly also said you probably should call your parents.

"I haven't told them about the first break-in let alone all the other things. Maybe I'll wait to see what happens in the next few days. I talked to my Mom yesterday, just to let her know that I was ok, and didn't want to get them upset about the problems here. You know I've talked to them every day but until I know what's going on for sure I don't want to have them come out here."

Blair walked to the United Ticket Counter and saw Allisa Jones by the ticket booth talking to a gate agent.

"Hi Allisa," Blair said.

"Hi Blair, I was hoping that you would be a little early. This is Steven, he works for United Airlines and we went to school together in New York."

Blair said "hello" and seemed unsure as to why they were talking to a gate agent instead of going to the ticket counter.

"Steven said he will get us on the next flight to Philadelphia so we can make our meeting at headquarters."

Blair was even more confused but went along with the conversation.

"You know the meeting is very important Allisa," Blair added.

"Yeah you're right about that," she answered.

When Steven walked away Allisa filled her in.

"We are flying stand-by as government agents. I showed them my security clearance and have a set for you." Blair looked at the packet that Allisa handed her and saw it had her picture and a description with the FBI logo on it. Her name was inscribed across the documents with the FBI seal in the lower right corner, it looked very official.

"Blair you're an FBI Agent according to these documents. Just be cool and no one will suspect."

Blair thought this would be like rehearsing for a play. I can do this, no problem Allisa.

"I just don't know how you got all this and so quick."

"I'm FBI, that's what we do. I have my contacts and your picture was on file from your Screen Actor's Guild Card. I've had a lot of time from our noon meeting to plan this."

"What if I said, I wasn't going to go with you?"

"Then, I would burn these and go myself. But I knew that you needed to know the answer and felt you would be here."

"It looks like you packed very light. How did you get your stuff into one large duffle bag?"

"It's something Hunter showed me. He traveled so much and always said he traveled light. You just roll all your clothes like a newspaper and set them in your travel bag like logs. They stay real good and you can pack double the amount of clothes. You didn't tell me what we would need so I brought a suit and a lot of casual things. The tough part was shoes. I just love my shoes."

Steven came back and said everything was set. The plane had plenty of open seats and he would get them on before take off. He asked to see Blair's documents and after checking those out he said they looked fine. He told Allisa to meet back at gate 17 in about thirty minutes before takeoff and he would escort them onto the plane. He gave them both a boarding pass for security check-in. Allisa kissed him on the cheek.

"We'll have to get together when I get back" she said.

"Sure thing" Steven answered.

"Let's get a coffee and talk" Allisa told Blair.

They walked to the security check-in and handed their boarding passes and driver's license to the officer checking documents. Their bags came off the scanner and they collected them and headed for the coffee shop. Blair had more questions but knew that now was not the time to ask. This was the time to listen. Maybe Allisa would give her answers to some of her questions. She was committed to the trip and anyway she was an FBI Agent now.

Allisa got them two coffees and asked if Blair was hungry.

"Not really, I haven't been able to eat much for weeks. I had a large omelet earlier and that would hold me for a long time."

"We're going to be on the move so you will need your strength."

"I'll be ok" Blair said.

It was obvious that Blair was in good shape. She always watched what she ate and exercised a lot. Hiking and being on roller blades were two of her favorite things. The past few weeks had taken its toll on her. With the news of Hunter's death and the ordeal of the funeral she had lost a few pounds. Her mom made sure that she was getting some food and taking vitamins but this had been a tough time.

"Blair, I'm going to need your help on this mission. The FBI thinks that I blew it at your apartment. When Baxter got shot, and killed those two intruders they took me off your case. I plan to use my contacts in Philadelphia to get the information we need to solve this."

"I hope you have some good contacts," Blair told her.

"Well I have a real good old friend that is the head of the Philadelphia Bureau and I have alerted him to our arrival. He will help me because he is on the same case. This will make both of our careers or kill mine for good."

"What do you mean he is on the same case?"

"The Bureau figured that either the information we were looking for was with you or with Hunter's dad. He has been working to find the information in Bridgewater if it existed there."

"Does that mean that the FBI was involved in the break-in at his dads place?" "Yes," Allisa answered. "They didn't find anything there either."

"I'm not about to help do anything that will hurt his dad," Blair said. "I promise that I don't want you to. We are going to work together and solve this so both you and Hunter's dad are safe and don't have to worry about others causing you problems."

"You mean like the two that broke into my apartment?"

"Yes, that is exactly what I mean."

"Ok, but I have to know what's going on to be effective."

"Ok" Allisa said.

They drank their coffee and waited until their flights departure.

Blair knew that Allisa had given her some of this information before but this time she filled in a lot of the blanks. Now she knew the FBI was working on a case that included Hunter's dad's house and hers. She also knew that these documents must be extremely important. I wonder what is in them she thought. Hunter, you must have uncovered something big.

"We should walk to gate 17."

It was at the end of the United concourse.

"Where in New York did you meet Steven?"

"He went to the same college that I did" she answered. "We were in a couple of classes together and we went out a few times."

"He seems to have a thing for you."

"Blair I admire you. You and Hunter seemed to have the real thing going. I've never had that luck. I researched both of you before we met and I found out that you were very loyal to him. I know he was gone a lot and that must have been hard. I also know that you had an offer to do a show on Australian T.V. but turned it down because he was coming home from Afghanistan. You're a special person."

Blair was embarrassed and uncomfortable that Allisa knew so much about her and Hunter.

"I kind of wish you didn't know all that stuff but guess that it was just part of your job."

"That's exactly right; until I got to know you it was just a job. Now I that I know you I think we could be real friends."

Blair liked Allisa and kind of identified with her. She felt that once this was over they could be friends.

The flight to Philadelphia from LAX was going to be a long one.

"I'm going to stop and get a magazine, Allisa do you want something?"

"No thanks, I brought some material that I have to go over before we get there." "Can I help with it?" Blair asked.

"I plan to give you some information to read so that you will be up to speed on the investigation. Nothing that I give you is classified but it is background information that should help. I hope you don't get mad but I had to black out some of the stuff because I would get in even more trouble if you saw it."

"I understand," Blair said.

They sat down at the departure gate and Allisa said, "I want to wait until we're in the air to give this to you. Can't be too safe" she said.

Blair grabbed her magazine and started to look through it. Allisa peeked at a page that Blair seemed to be looking at for a while and laughed.

"I should have guessed shoes!"

"Yes, aren't they great looking? I could wear them with so many different outfits." They looked at each other and both laughed at the same time.

"I told you I just love shoes," Blair added.

"I guess so" and they continued to smile. Other passengers seemed to wonder what was so funny. Both women just winked at each other.

The flight started to load and Steven came out to talk to Allisa and Blair.

"I have a couple of seats in the back for you. I figured that you needed some space away from the other passengers. I'm so glad that we got to see each other again."

"Steven you know that I often think about the times we had in college. It was a lot of fun."

Steven walked back to the check in desk and talked to the two women checking everyone in. They looked toward the two agents and nodded.

"I'll wait until you both are on the flight," he told them.

They grabbed their bags and headed for the check in desk. Allisa again gave Steven a kiss on the cheek.

"I'll call you when I get back," she said.

The plane was about sixty percent full and almost no one was in the back. The two women settled in and left an empty seat in between.

"It's a five hour flight so we can catch a few Z's," Allisa said.

"I've been on this too many times in last few weeks" Blair said.

"Yeah, guess I didn't think about that. Are you ok?"

"Yes, I'm looking forward to solving this and can't wait to see the other information you have."

"Once we're airborne I'll give you the information that should help you."

The voice came on overhead and reminded everyone to put their bags either in the overhead compartments or under a seat. They would be taking off soon. Blair looked at Allisa and said, "Thanks for including me."

"I probably could not do it without your help."

The two were quickly becoming friends.

The Stewardess came down the aisle and started to demonstrate the use of the oxygen mask and continued with the explanation of the safety features of the 747. Blair told Allisa that she had thought about becoming a stewardess for a while after moving to California.

"Why didn't you do it?"

"Hunter wanted me to be home where he could get a hold of me if necessary. I think he didn't like the fact that I would always be in different cities."

"It would be interesting for a while I guess," Allisa said.

"Yes but then I got a role in a play that lasted for six months and I never thought about it again."

The plane took off with a quick lift to its flying altitude of 25,000 feet. Blair looked out of her window and the shore line seemed to disappear in seconds. The only thing you could make out was a string of lights that lined the coast. Blair took a deep breath and seemed to have a tear in her eye. She had just been on the flight from Philadelphia a few days earlier and now she was headed back. So much had happened that it was hard to figure out what was the right thing to do.

"Are you sure that your ok?" Allisa asked.

"Yes, I'm ok, just thinking about all that has happened in such a short time." "You've gone through a lot Blair and it's understandable that you should be upset. It is also evident that you're a strong person. I don't know many 23 year old women that would have handled themselves so well."

"Thanks Allisa. I'll be ok, now let me have some of the information that you have." Allisa knew that she made a good choice asking Blair to come along.

She also knew that she would need Blair to get Hunter's dad to feel comfortable to help with the search in Bridgewater. If she had any chance to solve this mystery she needed Blair's help. Allisa didn't know Thomas Adams but having his daughter-in-law along would be a key to getting his cooperation.

Both women settled in to read the details of the on going case. Allisa knew that when they landed that Dino Tuchy would be there to pick them up. He would not send one of his men. He could not afford to have any of them finding out that he was involved with Allisa and helping her with a case that was so high profiled and important to the FBI. Allisa looked forward to seeing him. Dino was special. She also knew that he would flip out when he saw Blair. Allisa could handle Dino. She was sure of that.

SEVENTEEN

The crime lab technicians arrived at the Adams home in Bridgewater. Dino said, "Kevin, you stay with them as they go through the home of Thomas Adams looking for clues to the men that killed Frank Walker."

Dino liked Kevin. He was new to their group but had performed very well on other cases. Kevin was methodical. He would make sure any information would be recorded and get it to Dino. Kevin was a good investigator. It wasn't clear if either fugitive had actually entered the home but they must be sure. It was also an opportunity to clean the home of any finger prints of the two FBI agents. Once he had his men in place Dino would follow-up with a call to Captain Douglas to meet with him and see what the local police had uncovered. The FBI would not share critical information with the local or State Police but giving them some details might help Dino get key information. Dino called Captain Douglas to set the meeting up. Captain Douglas answered and said he would have to call right back. Dino looked at his phone with a puzzled expression.

"What's wrong boss?" Kevin asked.

"He hung up on me," Dino said!

Both men looked at each other and raised their eyes.

"I'll give him a few minutes and call back" Dino said.

Captain Douglas was driving toward the State Police check point on Highway 13 north of the city. He wanted to tell the State Police Captain in person about the red Harley and one rider headed north past Croydon. He knew that the APB would get through to all the State Police but the Captain of the State police was a personal friend and

Captain Douglas felt he owed him a personal update. He arrived at the road block and saw Captain Campbell talking to his men.

"Hi Ron," Captain Douglas said.

"Hi Bob, I'm surprised to see you here."

"I have an update for you. We found out a few minutes ago that one of the suspects is riding a red Harley headed north and may have just passed Croydon."

Both men walked off to the side of the road to talk about their next move.

"I saw that in the APB," Captain Campbell said.

"I did that and we have sent the information to all the local authorities."

"I should get it out to the State Police in New Jersey" Captain Campbell suggested. "With so many opportunities to cross state lines we need all the help possible to find him."

Both men had a great deal of respect for each other.

Captain Douglas told Ron that he and his men were searching the wooded area of Bridgewater for the missing dark Chevrolet and the other man involved in the break-in and shooting.

"Do you need our help Bob?"

"That would be great Ron. We have three groups combing the woods starting from the Adams house and fanning out north and east. If your men could cover the area south and west we will be sure that everything is searched in as short a time as possible."

"We're on it Bob."

Captain Campbell got on his radio to his men. He told them to move into Bridgewater to start a search on foot south of the Adams home through the wooded area for a black Chevrolet and possibly one of the fugitives. Any search should come under the direction of Captain Douglas of the Bridgewater Police. They would coordinate the search team and cover as much ground as possible. The weather forecast was for a possible rain storm and they needed to get some answers before it started to rain.

Captain Douglas heard his phone and thought about not answering but he picked it up.

"This is Dino Tuchy is everything ok?"

"We have had more information just in and I was trying to coordinate it with the State Police" he said.

"What new information do you have?" Dino asked.

"We found out that the two fugitives may have separated and one of them may be on a motorcycle headed north out of town."

Captain Douglas knew that he had to give the FBI something but was not going to give them all the details, not at least until he found out what the FBI was doing in his town in the first place. Dino suggested a meeting as soon as possible. Captain Douglas said that he was in the field and helping his team search for the other missing fugitive.

"I'll meet you and we can help" he said.

Although he did not want their involvement Captain Douglas had no choice.

"You can meet me at the corner of Apple Lane and Pine" Captain Douglas said.

"It is just a few blocks from where you are now. Do you need directions?"

"No, we have a local map."

He went to get Steve Watkins and reminded Kevin to stay with the crime lab until he called.

Dino and Steve got into Dino's car and headed toward Apple Lane. The town was small but due to so many dead-end streets a few block seemed to take a long time. Dino looked at the street map that Steve had and saw that they were just a few blocks over from Apple. The street was heavily wooded as they came around the corner. They saw a light at the end of the block and headed in that direction. There was a small store on the corner of Apple and Pine and they saw two police cars parked in front of the store. It appeared that the store was closed but Captain Douglas was standing with two young men in front of the store.

Dino pulled his Suburban up to the corner and started walking toward the men. Captain Douglas walked over to Dino and asked him not to tell anyone that they were with the FBI.

"We don't need a panic in our little town" he explained. Dino agreed,

"We will stand off to the side and wait until you have completed talking to them."

When Captain Douglas walked back to the two men in front of the store Dino turned to Steve and said "this actually works best for us. The last thing we need is the Director finding out that we are working with the local or State Police."

Steve understood. He and Dino knew that John Martin was not a forgiving person and getting involvement from local or State Police was always a no in the FBI's book.

Captain Douglas walked over to Dino and Steve.

"We got a report from one of our citizens that a red Harley had been taken from in front of his house. They were having a party and just found it missing. It appears that the Harley may have been used as a get-away vehicle from Bridgewater. We have an APB out for the Harley and the rider. We know that there were at least two fugitives and feel that one of them may still be hiding out in Bridgewater. Perry Wight, who I was just talking to said he saw a red Harley pass by with only one rider. I have all my men searching the wooded areas around town. The State Police are also combing the area."

"Well this does add to the mystery" Dino said.

"Our crime lab is processing the scene at the Adams home and should have some information soon. I will get on the phone to our Newark office so they can alert their men that would cover the area north and east of here."

"That is a good idea," Captain Douglas said.

Dino walked over to his car and seemed to be making a call.

Steve Watkins was surprised that Dino was going to call another FBI office to inform them of the situation. Dino held and phone and smiled at Steve, "I'm not going to be calling anyone" he said, "I just want the dumb shits here to think I'm calling someone." Dino had no use for local or State Police and just working with them pissed him off. He also wasn't going to get anyone else involved in his mission. John Martin gave Dino the mission in Bridgewater and he wasn't going to seek help from another office. Dino wanted to solve this and he knew his team was competent and they didn't need help. Dino and Steve walked back toward the front of the party store and waited for Captain Douglas to come over to them.

"I called our Newark office and they will start searching on their side of the river."

"I would like to know what the FBI has to do with this."

Dino started by saying, "We have had a rash of anti-war activists that are causing a disturbance at the homes of soldiers that have come back from Iraq and now at some of the homes that have had soldiers killed in Iraq. We think they are pretty much just causing concerns for the families of these soldiers but this is the first sign of physical break-in or shooting. The Director wants to make sure we help local authorities keep peace in their communities."

Captain Douglas seemed surprised that Dino gave him that information and understood the concern. He was also smart enough to know that this wasn't the whole story. He told Dino that his men would cooperate in any way necessary.

Dino said, "Let us help you with your search."

"Ok", Captain Douglas said "we'll start right here on Apple Lane. I have two groups of men that have moved west down toward Pine and the State Police have two groups that are moving south through the woods."

Dino said, "Let's head north from here."

The search through the wooded area of Bridgewater could take hours. Dino looked at his watch. He told Steve, "I have an early meeting at the Philadelphia Airport and will stay around here until about midnight. Steve I want you to head the group in Bridgewater."

"Sure," Steve said, "no problem boss."

They walked into the wooded area behind the party store and followed Captain Douglas and his men.

"I don't think they will find anything," Dino said, "let's humor them."

Captain Douglas told his men that if they made a discovery to wait and call for re-enforcements.

"There may be a fugitive hiding and we don't need anyone else hurt."

The men understood and everyone respected the Captain. He had been the head of the Bridgewater police force for over twenty years. Once a highly decorated war hero from Viet Nam he came back home to Bridgewater. He rose through the ranks of the police department and was soon named the Captain at a very young age. Although Bridgewater did not have much in the way of crime his men often would be called upon to help the State Police. He had been offered a high post with the Philadelphia Police Department but turned it down. He loved his town and protecting the people he knew. Captain Douglas married his high school sweetheart and they had three lovely children. His best friend from high school was Ron Campbell. Ron was also in Viet Nam and when he came back he joined the State Police. The two men would often find time to get together with their families. They never seemed to bring home the job which their wives appreciated. It was unusual for the local and State Police to cooperate so well but these were friends and they always worked well together. Both men respected each other and their responsibilities. Neither man wanted to show the other one up. They made a good team whenever they worked on the same case.

Dino suggested that he and Steve should fan out a little further down Apple Lane so that they could cover the area quicker. Captain Douglas agreed but asked them to follow the same rule he told his men.

"This is my town and I'm responsible" he said.

"Sure" Dino said "I'll fall back if we find something."

"Thanks" Bob said.

The local police seemed to be combing the area pretty quickly. With the State Police in on the search it would be a shorter task. Dino and Steve walked slowly through the woods.

"Steve, we need to make sure that if we come up with something that we get a good look around before we phone it in. I don't need these locals guys finding our man and screwing it up."

"Maybe if we do find something we shouldn't tell them."

"That would be great if I thought we would get away with it."

The wooded area off of Apple Lane behind the small party store was very thick. Dino knew that there was no way to hide a car back there. That is why he suggested fanning out further down the street. With all the large pine trees and their branches so close to the ground it was hard enough to walk through the woods. The wooded area down the street had more hardwood trees and it appeared that there was a trail through there. Looked like either kids or snowmobiles had made a path deep into the woods. Dino and Steve came to the path and followed it for over two hundred yards. There was no sign of anything. He called to Captain Douglas to see if their search had come up with anything concrete.

"Nothing so far," Bob answered, "How about you."

"Nothing here either. I think Steve and I are going to double back a little further down the street."

Steve sat on a large rock.

"Are you ok?" Dino asked.

"You know when all the shooting started I thought that Frank was in the middle of the yard shooting toward the woods. I know that I saw a couple of figures escaping and then the individual in the yard started shooting at me."

"I know that Steve, you already told us that."

"Yes, but I now remember that one of the two figures moving toward the woods looked like he was being dragged."

"You think he was shot?"

"Yes and maybe that is why only one person was seen on that Harley."

"Glad you remembered more Steve, that may help us."

Dino knew that Steve was still hurting about the loss of his partner Frank Walker. He wanted Steve to know that he was important and any information that he remembered could be vital.

"Should we tell Captain Douglas?"

"No I don't want to give him any more information than I have to. We will be able to go on the premise that only one fugitive is on the loose and the other is probably hiding here in Bridgewater or dead. They already feel that the information they got about the missing Harley with only one rider is why we are searching these woods."

Both men moved slowly through the woods off the trail and looked carefully into the brush and along the tree line. Then it appeared. It was a car lodged into a clump of small shrubs and covered by tree branches. The branches were on the back of the car and hid it from the street. It was easier to see it coming out of the wooded area than it would be entering the woods.

Dino grabbed Steve and signaled for him to stop. They both crouched down and moved slowly toward the car. It was a dark Chevrolet that was about 10 feet ahead. Dino motioned to be quiet and that they should circle the vehicle. Both men moved around the car to make sure no one else was around. They stooped down about five feet away and Dino drew a plan into the dirt. Steve watched as Dino drew a diagram of the car and angles that they should approach. Dino wanted to keep the news to themselves until they were sure what they had found. Steve knew that Dino was happy that they found the car. They moved closer following the plan that Dino had drawn in the dirt. No one seemed to be in the car. They did not want to use their flashlights in case someone was lying in the back seat. With the information that Steve had just remembered, that there may be an injured fugitive in the car they approached slowly. When Steve got closer he used his flashlight to shine the under carriage of the car. No one was underneath. Dino was on the left side of the car as Steve approached from the right side. Dino knew that this was the missing car due to the damaged driver's side. Anyone in the car would be watching only one direction after the flashlight was used, Dino thought. He could get a lot closer and have Steve hold his ground. Dino was next to the driver's front door and he signaled to Steve with his flashlight. He let it shine under the car back toward Steve so that the direction of the light did not give his position away. Both men held their position for about five minutes. Dino pressed the driver's door handle and felt it release the locking pin. The door was ajar and he could swing it open. Dino stayed low as he opened the left front door. No movement came from inside the car. He signaled for Steve to move in. Steve moved the last five feet slowly and crept toward the right rear door. He also reached for the door handle on the right side and pressed it open. Both men had their guns drawn as they pulled the doors open and waited to be met by the missing fugitive. The car was empty! Dino looked at Steve and they quickly searched the interior with their light. There was nothing inside the car. Dino looked for the trunk release and found it under the left side of the dash. Dino motioned to Steve to move toward the back of the vehicle so he could be in position when the trunk popped open. Steve slid toward the rear of the car. The trunk popped open and Steve pointed his gun into the trunk. A light came on in the trunk and it was empty. Both men moved back to recheck the cars interior. The rear seat was soaked in blood. It looked like the person or persons in the back seat had bled on the seat and the floor. They now knew why only one person was seen riding the Harley.

"We must have gotten one of them," Steve said.

With this much blood one of them had to be dead. Steve felt better that at least they got one of the fugitives. But now where was he?

"We should close the doors and trunk" Dino said.

"We can tell Captain Douglas that we just found the car but haven't moved in to examine it."

"Good plan" Steve said. "They will know that we want to help and are following their plan."

"Before we call it in let's search around for a possible body."

Dino had left Steve to close the car and wipe the doors off while he moved toward the passenger side to see if there was a trail of blood that would help his search. No trail was found on the ground. They could use bloodhounds Dino thought. He would call the find in to Captain Douglas and even offer his crime lab technicians to check the cars interior when they finished at the Adams home.

Captain Douglas heard his cell phone ring. "Damn Feds!"

He could not get away from their interference.

"Captain Douglas this is Dino Tuchy, we have found the get-away car hidden in the woods further east off Apple Lane. Steve and I are about fifteen feet away from it and there doesn't look like any movement in the car."

Don't touch anything we're on the way was the answer.

"We will let them have their fun" Dino said.

"Dumb shits really think we're going to wait for them."

Dino and Steve continued to look through the wooded area for a body. They were sure that the individual in the back seat could not have survived losing this much blood. They figured that it would take at least 10 minutes before Captain Douglas and some of his men would make it to their position. Dino's cell phone rang. He saw it was Captain Douglas. The request was for specific directions. Dino said they would move away from the car further and shine their flashlights so that it would be easier to find them. This was also a great cover for the search for a possible body.

Bob Douglas headed toward the flashlights in the woods.

"We're over here" Dino called out.

"Glad that you called us so we could search the car together."

Dino almost felt guilty but knew that his mission was much more important than helping the local police get too involved. Captain Douglas suggested that Dino and Steve approach from the driver's side while he and his men took the passenger side. "You're sure this is the car?"

"Yes, the driver's door is badly damaged and it fit's the description."

Dino no longer felt guilty with that question. Damn local shits. Like there would be more than one abandoned car fitting that description in the woods.

The two teams moved in and all five men held their guns in position in case there was a fugitive aboard. Captain Douglas called out to the car.

"This is the police, toss out your weapons and we won't shoot."

Dino looked at Steve and almost laughed.

"I told you, dumb shits," Dino whispered.

There was no answer. Captain Douglas signaled that they should all move in. The five men were less than five feet from the car and were doing a search with their flashlights as they approached. No movement in or around the car. Bob Douglas was the first to pull open the right front door. There was nothing inside. They all moved in and had the doors opened. Captain Douglas pointed out the pool of blood on the back seat and floor. Andy must have gotten one of them. Let's open the trunk and check it out. They opened the trunk but found it empty. Steve and Dino just looked at each other knowing that they had already been through this search.

"Must be someone badly wounded" Captain Douglas announced. "Let's fan out and search the area."

Ron Campbell and his State Police team were called by Captain Douglas to let them know that the car had been found. Ron said his team would head in that direction and help search for the wounded man. Dino said that his crime lab could process the car once they finished at the Adams home.

"Thanks" Captain Douglas said.

Dino was pleased that he had the local police thinking that he was working with them. He also hoped that he and Steve would find the missing fugitive. He knew that the search could take a long time. He looked up in the sky as rain started to fall. The sky opened up and a hard rain started to fall. The men tried to take cover under some of the larger trees. This was not going to make the search any easier. Any trail would soon be washed away. The rain was very hard and it started to lightning and thunder.

"We need to get out of the woods" Captain Douglas said.

"This storm is going to be short but could be dangerous."

They all agreed and headed toward the store on the corner.

Bob Douglas marked the spot the car was found so that they could set up the next step of the search. He placed an orange cone on the street so that it would be easy for them to find the spot that they came out of. The rain was now falling at a very heavy rate and the ground that was already soft could not absorb the water. We can go back in when this slows down they said. Captain Douglas called to his other teams that they should get shovels and boots for everyone.

"This is going to be a long night" he said.

Dino looked at his watch. It was close to eleven and he knew that he had to be at the Philadelphia airport early the next day.

"Steve I want you to get with Kevin and see how the search at the Adams home has gone. You both should stay with the local police and see if you can search some of the area on your own. Call me if you find anything."

Steve was glad that Dino was still confident enough to leave him in charge. He was afraid that Dino would be mad at him for the mess at the Adams home earlier.

"You can count on me boss" Steve said.

"I need to get back to Philadelphia and the office before my morning meeting."

Dino knew that Allisa was on the red eye from Los Angeles and even with the time change that her plane would arrive around 8:00 a.m. Eastern Standard Time. Dino had not seen Allisa for a couple of years but the thought of her being back in Philadelphia started to stir old memories.

EIGHTEEN

The night was dark and the sky had grown heavy with clouds. The ride up Highway 13 along the Delaware River was smooth and without incident except the earlier road block that Yawer had evaded. He had passed one police car before Croydon but had not seen anything since. West Bristol was ahead a few miles and he planned to cross the Burlington Bristol Toll Bridge. Once across the Delaware River he could head back toward Mansfield Square and El Jaafi. The search of the Adams home had not accomplished anything he thought. Not only did they not get into the house but now the local police had shot and killed Omar and would be on his trail soon. He knew that the Harley would be reported stolen and that an APB would be out for it. He hoped to get across into New Jersey and on Highway 130 headed toward Mansfield Square before having to look for another get-away vehicle. Yawer was a very accomplished motor cycle rider and was able to handle the Harley well. He thought that it was the fastest bike he had been on. It seemed to glide along the highway and he and the Harley felt as one. The bike was very quiet for a Harley. He saw the sign for the Burlington Bristol toll bridge ahead. The sky had seemed to darken and he felt rain drops on his helmet and could see that the road was starting to shine from the rain. It had started to thunder and the heavier rain would be coming soon he thought. He turned right onto the bridge and pulled in the automated lane. He quickly paid the toll and proceeded across. The town of Springside was on the other side of the bridge and he would head north on Highway 130. The Toll Bridge had two lanes and Yawer had passed through the unattended lane. He tossed a variety of coins in the catch basin and after the gate opened he proceeded across the bridge. The other lane was operated by a young bridge employee that occupied his time watching a Philly's ballgame. Not much happened at this time of night and with high hopes of the new baseball season everyone in the area thought this was the year. The Philly's had added some big name players and felt that they would rule the division that the Atlanta Braves had owned for the past thirteen years. The rain started to come down harder as Yawer turned north on Highway 130. He hoped that he could make it up the highway before having to try to change rides. The Harley was so impressive of a ride and he felt that he could go anywhere with it. It would allow him in the case of a chase to out maneuver a car. Maybe no one noticed it missing, he hoped.

A State Trooper vehicle pulled up to the toll booth on the Burlington Bristol Bridge. Connor slid open his booth door while still watching the ballgame and held his hand out for the toll.

"Have you seen a red Harley cross came a voice from the car?"

Connor looked up and asked "What did you say?"

"Have you seen a red Harley come through here?"

The rain had been coming down harder and Connor had kept his window in the booth closed. He would open it if a car was coming but he had not seen any cars for over an hour.

Connor was surprised to see that it was a State Trooper.

"No sir," he said.

"How many people have crossed in the past hour?" was the next question.

"There haven't been any cars through here in over an hour."

"Are you sure that none of the people crossing were on a motorcycle?"

"I haven't noticed one," Connor answered.

The trooper proceeded across the bridge and called back to his Commander. He reported that there was nothing at the Burlington Bristol Bridge. He would go back across and head up the highway further north. Maybe he's headed for Levittown and the crossing at Highway 276 was the response.

The APB had been sent by Ron Campbell of the Pennsylvania State Police to the New Jersey State Police. The local Captain headquartered in Trenton dispatched four cars to head to all the bridge crossings along the Delaware River. There were three crossings north of Croydon Pennsylvania into New Jersey. They would stake each one out and send a car along I-295 south. The red Harley would be easy to spot this time of night. Not much traffic would be on the roads, at least not until after the Philly's game. The Captain of the New Jersey Police knew that with the Braves in town that a lot of people may be coming back across from Philadelphia after the game. Southern Jersey was Philly's country and many of the locals had moved across the Delaware River but kept their hopes of a Philly World Series alive.

The rain started to fall harder and the sky became alive with lightening and thunder. Yawer slowed down and looked for a spot to get under cover. Mansfield Square was only about 30 minutes north of Springside. He kept an eye out for any police vehicles in the area. He hoped that he could somehow ditch the Harley for another ride. If only he had a way of getting another ride and keeping the Harley. The thought of it being the perfect get-away ride stayed in his mind. Yawer found a gas station near Springside that was closed. The overhang was perfect cover from the rain storm. He got his cell phone out and called back to El Jaafi in Mansfield Square. It was close to midnight when the cell phone rang. El Jaafi picked it up and looked to see who the caller was. They had purchased one time use cell phones in New York so that no one could trace any calls or who was using the phones. El Jaafi had used a stolen credit card to make the purchase. No trace would be found.

The caller was Yawer and El Jaafi had expected to hear from him earlier.

"I am on my way back," Yawer told El Jaafi.

"How did the search go?"

"Not good, we had some problems. The local police had the place staked out and we were sure that we could handle the Officer we saw. In fact Omar shot him and we thought that we could get into the house but two or three more police were in the house and ambushed us. We did get one of them but Omar was wounded as we tried to escape into the woods. He was wounded badly and did not make it. Our brother is dead!"

"He did not die in vain, Praise Allah," Jaafi said.

"Where are you now?"

"I just crossed into New Jersey and headed toward Mansfield Square. I have another ride and had to ditch the car. I took care of everything. I hid the car and I buried Omar's body in a ditch. They will not find it for quite a while. I took the license plate off the car and all our belongings out of it. I have Omar's identification with me."

"How did you get out of Bridgewater?"

"I have a Harley that I am riding but will look for another ride before I get to Mansfield Square."

"We should go back to New York and regroup," Jaafi said.

"I will get our stuff together here and you should just head to the safe house in the Bronx. We cannot fail in our mission. We can travel to California if necessary and let everything calm down here."

El Jaafi planned on checking them out of both rooms and making sure nothing was left behind. They would clean off all the possible fingerprints as they left the motel.

Yawer was hoping to join El Jaafi but knew that this was a better plan. Why endanger the whole group as he tried to escape. Right now they were just looking for one other person. At least El Jaafi and Abdulla could continue with the mission if necessary. The rain seemed to slow down and he could get back on the highway. It was no longer necessary to try to get to Mansfield Square. Yawer looked at his map before getting on the road. The best route to New York would be highway 95 toward Newark. He had many options to cross over into New York from highway 95. He still needed to change rides and the night time offered many options. It would make sense to stay off the main roads until he had a new ride. He moved the motorcycle onto the local road that would lead back to highway 130. As he rode through town he looked for his next ride. He passed a farm house that seems to have a lot of pick-up trucks out in front. Everything was dark and he stopped to look around to make sure no one was around. It appeared that it was a working farm and the vehicles were parked until the next work day. He searched through them and found most of them had keys either in the ignition cylinder or on the seats. He wanted to take one of the trucks but also did not want to ditch the Harley right there. The Harley was very heavy and Yawer struggled to hoist it into the back of the pick-up. He found one of the trucks near a mound and was able to get the Harley in the bed from that angle. Once the motorcycle was aboard he closed the tailgate and started the truck. He headed to highway 130 and would take some back roads to the interstate.

El Jaafi and Abdulla gathered their stuff and cleaned out the rooms. They loaded everything into the second vehicle that they had rented under a false name and proceeded to make sure everything was out of the second room. They would call back to the house in the Bronx to inform them that they were on their way back. The Days Inn lobby seemed to have a lot of action at night. The Air Force staff staying there from McGuire Air Force Base was watching a late ballgame in the bar just off the lobby. El Jaafi decided not to go into the lobby and he and Abdulla slowly pulled out of the lot and headed toward the interstate. They would get back to the safe house in about three hours. Traffic would not be an issue this time of night.

Yawer was pleased that he was able to get the Harley into the pick-up truck. He thought that he would keep it because there would not be any check points until he crossed the toll bridges into New York. The Harley would allow him a second escape vehicle if necessary. Most of the toll booths had automated lanes and he could pass through them without being noticed. He planned to cross at the Verrazano Narrows Bridge and take highway 278 all the way back to the safe house. It was still raining but the rain had slowed down and he would be at the safe house in about three or four hours. He knew that El Jaafi would call ahead to inform the rest of the group what had happened. The night was very quiet as Yawer pulled the pick-up through town. The ride would be safe as long as he did not bring attention to himself. He looked at the gas needle and it read about a quarter of a tank. Damn, he knew that was not enough to get to New York. He would have to stop and get fuel. The best place would be along the Interstate where there were plenty of non descript rest stops with fuel and food. He would not even have to get off the highway. The ride to the Interstate from Springside was short. He had to enter on highway 295 north because there was not an entrance at Springside. He could jump on the New Jersey Turnpike before Mansfield Square. The pick-up was a late model Chevrolet 1500 series Silverado. Yawer was headed north toward Highway 95 when he saw a State Trooper headed south on the other side of the highway. He made sure that he was doing the speed limit and kept one eye on the fuel gauge. The Trooper passed Yawer's

vehicle and kept heading south. He felt some relief as he saw the sign
for Highway 95. Yawer wanted to call El Jaafi once he got the truck
fueled to let them know where he was and that he was able to get a new
ride. When he entered Highway 95 north he looked in his rear view
mirror and saw another State Trooper behind him. The hair on the
back of Yawers' neck seemed to rise. He again checked his speed and
kept an eye on the fuel gauge. He came to the first of the toll booths
and saw that the only lane opened was an attended lane. He would
have to get a ticket for the toll charges on the Turnpike. He kept his
head down and took the ticket from the attendant. Yawer entered the
Turnpike and headed north.

The State Trooper was two vehicles behind the pick-up. When the
Officer got to the toll booth he asked the attendant if there had been a
red Harley that had passed through the booth that evening.

"The only one I saw was in the back of a pick-up truck."

"When?" the Officer asked.

The attendant pointed to the Chevrolet Silverado that was just
disappearing onto the highway.

"Thanks," said the Officer.

The call came into the State police headquarters at 12:31a.m. It was
from Trooper Greg Jones.

"I have a late model Chevrolet Silverado dark blue headed north on
the New Jersey turnpike with a red Harley in the trucks bed."

The response was hurried but clear.

"Follow the vehicle but do not give your position away. We will
send back-up before you should try to apprehend him."

The trooper was a long time member of the New Jersey State Police
force. He followed the pick-up leaving about three or four vehicles
between them. There was an exit at Crosswicks about 8 miles ahead.

The Captain of the Trenton State Police Headquarters called to Ron
Campbell to inform him that they may have found the fugitive headed
north on the New Jersey Turnpike in a late model Chevrolet Silverado.
He had a red Harley in the back of the pick-up. They were not sure if
it was their man but it was the only lead they had. Captain Campbell
thanked them and asked to be kept in the loop. Ron quickly called
Captain Douglas.

"Bob the New Jersey State Police have a trail on a man driving a pick-up on the Turnpike. He has a red Harley in the bed of the pick-up."

"Thanks Ron, I hope it's our guy."

"I'll keep you informed Bob. How is the search for the missing fugitive going?"

"We had to fall back because the rain was almost blinding but it has slowed down and we are going back in the woods soon."

"If you need my men a little longer just let me know."

"I think we can handle it from here but I will keep you up to date on our search. Thanks Ron for all your help."

"That's what friends are for Bob."

The Chevrolet Silverado kept going north on the Interstate and Officer Jones stayed a good distance behind. His goal was to keep tabs on the vehicle but not to cause the driver any special concern. He knew that there would be back-up coming soon and his job was just surveillance. He kept in radio contact with the main post and they informed him that there would be back-up at Crosswicks. If the Silverado stays on the Interstate we will continue to follow him with both of you he was told. The Crosswicks exit was one mile ahead and the Silverado made no move to the right exit lane. The driver of the Silverado was doing the speed limit and did not seem to be aware of being followed. A sign ahead said that there was a rest area with a gas station and food in two miles. The officer saw that the second patrol car entered at Crosswicks and fell in behind him. He radioed back to the post to inform them that both cars were now following the possible suspect. The main post said that they were putting stakeouts at the next three exits and the upcoming rest area. This could be a long night they all thought. The Silverado driver put his right turn signal on and moved into the right lane. It appeared that he was getting off at the rest area. Officer Jones got on his radio.

"I have our suspect exiting the Interstate and entering the rest area three miles north of Crosswicks."

The answer came back to follow the car but keep your distance.

"We have a car stationed in the rest area at the gas station."

They thought that with a squad car already parked it would not seem out of place.

Yawer looked down at the fuel gauge and was happy to see the gas station. He figured that he could fill the truck up and grab something to eat. He pulled into the left fuel island and got out of the truck. Yawer noticed that a squad car was parked in front of the station but it appeared to be empty. He ran the credit card through the pump and began to fill the truck. While he was filling the truck he looked around to see if anything appeared unusual. The only thing he saw was the one squad car with no one inside. Using the automated pump to pay for the gas would allow him a quick get-away if necessary. He was putting the pump handle back in the pump when he saw a second squad car along the side of the restaurant. That car had one occupant behind the wheel. Yawer decided to get back into the truck. Yawer did not want to make any sudden moves but slowly pulled out of the gas station and watched the squad car along the restaurant. He drove slowly like he was going to re-enter the Interstate when he saw the squad car pull out and head in the same direction. He also saw an officer come out of the gas station and head toward the parked squad car. Yawer circled the lot and pulled the Silverado next to an 18 wheel Semi-truck. He walked around the back of the pick-up and pulled the tailgate open. Yawer started to pull the Harley out of the truck. The driver of the semi saw what he was doing and asked if he could help.

"Yes, thank you."

They got the bike out and Yawer tossed a backpack on it and took off toward the wooded area behind the restaurant. The semi truck driver just stood there wondering what had happened. Both State Police Squad cars took off and headed in the direction of the Harley that was now closing in on the wooded area. Yawer jumped the curb and was now on the walking path heading into the dense woods. The squad cars could not follow him. Officer Jones called to the post to inform them what had happened.

"Shit," came back the answer.

"He made us and now we will have a hell of a chase on our hands."

NINETEEN

The flight was long but Blair was able to sleep for a couple of hours. She woke up and saw that Allisa was reading some documents.

"Are you ever going to tell me what the FBI is searching for?"

"I told you that Hunter had found some key information and we can't find it. We thought that somehow he may have sent it to either you or his father."

"I understand that but what's in this key information?"

"Blair I don't know. Just that we feel it is critical to our operation in Iraq. The orders for the search came from the Director in Washington."

Blair settled back in and asked what time it was.

"We should be landing in about an hour," Allisa answered.

"Guess I should go freshen up. I must look like a wreck."

She headed to the bathroom that was just two rows behind their seats. When she got inside, she looked into the mirror.

"Hunter, I need you to help me. Make sure I'm doing the right thing."

Blair washed her face and thought she needed some make-up. She knew that they would be picked up by someone that Allisa had arranged to meet them at the Philadelphia Airport. I need to look professional she thought. Allisa had make-up on and I guess thats ok.

The pilot's voice came on the speaker above requesting everyone to return to their seats. They would be landing at the Philadelphia Airport in 25 minutes. Blair went back to her seat and Allisa said, "You always look nice Blair."

"Thanks, with my fair skin it is hard sometimes."

The Southern California sun had given Blair a nice glow. Although she had naturally fair skin she also had an even tan that helped make her always look radiant.

"Allisa, who is going to pick us up?"

"I have a friend in the Philadelphia Bureau, his name is Dino Tuchy. He will pick us up and take us to a hotel. We can get settled in and get caught up on the investigation there."

Allisa also knew that she had not told Dino about bringing Blair with her. She hoped that he did not flip out. This was the best way in her mind to gain the confidence of Hunter's dad and move the investigation along as quickly as possible. With the failures in Santa Monica, Allisa had to get something positive or she was going to be relegated to a desk job.

The plane made its final approach into the Philadelphia Airport and Blair thought that she had just left there a few days ago. So much had happened in such a short time. Blair was hoping that coming with Allisa was the right thing to do. She knew that she had to get answers to all her questions. They were soon on the ground and both women searched the overhead compartment for their baggage. They both had carry-on luggage so that getting out of the airport to meet their ride would not take too much time. Allisa reminded Blair not to talk about the operation to anyone.

"Blair, it is important that we stay out of the limelight as much as possible. Once we get to our hotel I have planned to get two rooms so that I won't put you in any danger."

"Guess that makes sense. What do I say to the person who is picking us up?"

"I'll do all the talking; he doesn't know that I brought you yet."

"Is that going to be a problem?"

"He may freak out at first but I know it is the only way to solve this and having you with me I can protect you."

"You really think someone will try to hurt me don't you."

"I'm really not sure but I just don't want to take a chance".

They exited the plane and headed toward the main terminal. Blair was pulling her duffle bag and Allisa said that it looked pretty easy to manage.

"I got it at the flea market in Santa Monica. I thought that it was just super because it has wheels on one end and can be carried or pulled."

The walk was very quiet because their flight must have been the first one to arrive at the terminal that they came in on. It was a little after 8:00 a.m. and most everyone in the airport was departing for their trip not arriving.

Allisa moved toward the curb when they got outside. She seemed to be sure what type of car she was looking for.

"Dino, were over here," she waved to a black Chevrolet Suburban.

The Suburban pulled up a few feet past the women and a nice looking man about 45 got out.

"You always look beautiful kid," he said.

Dino Tuchy grabbed Allisa and hugged her.

"Don't kid around," she said.

Dino was taken back by her statement.

"You know that I will always have a special place for you Dino. I want to introduce you to a friend I brought along. Dino Tuchy this is Mrs. Blair Adams."

Dino looked puzzled and didn't know what to say.

"Jesus Christ, are you crazy?"

Blair didn't know exactly what to say or do. A police officer came over and told them that the vehicle had to be moved now. Allisa opened the back of the Suburban and tossed their bags in.

"Let's get going. We can talk on the way to our hotel."

They all got into the truck. Allisa jumped in the front with Dino and Blair got in the back seat. The Suburban had so many gadgets on the dash that Blair didn't know what most of them were for.

"Wow, I have never seen so many different types of radios and gadgets in a car before."

"This is a government vehicle Mrs. Adams and we have to make sure that we have various types of communication equipment to do our job."

He looked at Allisa and hoped that she had a good reason for bringing the main person they were investigating in California with her.

"I'm sorry for your loss Mrs. Adams," Dino said.

"Thanks it has been very difficult especially with all that has happened since".

"Dino, I told Mrs. Adams, I mean Blair that you have reserved two rooms for us at the hotel so that she would not be in any extra danger. I know that we can put her room in a false name to protect her."

"I need to call to confirm that to the desk."

Dino got his phone and made a call to confirm the room reservations. It appeared that there was a little mix-up but he seemed to make sure the person understood that they needed two rooms and neither room would be listed under Blair or Allisa's name.

The drive from the Philadelphia Airport to the hotel was about 25 minutes. Allisa brought Dino up to speed on all the details of the California investigation. She seemed to leave out a few details but Blair felt it was because she was in the vehicle. Dino said he would go over the information that he had once they were in the hotel. Blair sensed some tension between Dino and Allisa and figured that it was because Allisa did not tell Dino that she was bringing Blair along. They pulled up to a Marriott hotel on Cottman Avenue. Blair noticed a large mall across from the hotel.

"Looks like a very nice area", she said.

"I thought it would be better to put you out here because there are stores and places to eat nearby. I'm not sure how long you will both be here and I know that you don't have a car so the location seemed to be a good one."

This was the new trendy area in Philadelphia. A group of businessmen had opened a few chic bars and shops that seemed to catch on with the locals. They had a New York sort of flair.

They parked in front and Allisa said, "Let me go in with Dino and get our keys Blair."

"Whatever you say."

Dino and Allisa got out of the Suburban and walked into the lobby of the Marriott.

"Now are you going to tell me what in the hell you were thinking by bringing her here."

"We had a lot of trouble in California and I had to give her some information about the investigation. Now with her here she can't tell it to anyone else and she seems to be willing to help us with Hunter's dad."

"I guess that make sense. How much does she know?"

"I had to tell her that Hunter was in the FBI and that he had some critical documents that we haven't found. We were thinking that maybe he sent them to either her or his dad. I didn't tell her much of anything else."

"Hell she knows as much as we do."

Allisa touched Dino's hand and looked at him.

"I hoped by getting separate rooms we could spend some time together."

"Allisa, you know that I've never forgotten the time we spent together. I missed you a lot."

The two Agents came out of the hotel and said that everything was arranged.

"I thought I would leave you two here to unpack and get some rest before I come back for you later. I will be back here for you both about 3:00 p.m. I have some unfinished things that I was working on."

Allisa said that they were going to rest first and they would meet Dino in the lobby at 3. They grabbed their bags and headed for the lobby. Dino got in the Suburban and drove away.

"Allisa, I hope that he isn't too mad to let us help in the investigation here."

"Blair he's like all guys, if it wasn't his idea it isn't a good idea. I convinced him that having you here was the only way we would be able to get the information we need as quick as possible."

"I'm glad that I came."

"Bet your tired, Blair."

"Maybe a little, I need to call Olly in a little to let her know that I'm ok. I promised to call her everyday."

"You're lucky to have so many special friends."

They got on the elevator and Allisa pressed both the 7th and the 9th floor.

"You're on 7 Blair, room 716 and I'm in room 925. I have to make sure that you are not in any danger ever and keeping us apart will help protect you. Other FBI agents may find out that I am here but they

will not know that I brought you along. Dino won't tell anyone and he
knows that I promised to protect you."

"I appreciate that Allisa."

Blair got off on the 7th floor and asked, "Should I call your room
later?"

Allisa said she was tired and she would call Blair's room around
2p.m.

"Get some rest Blair, we will be very busy later on."

Allisa opened the door to her room and looked around. Nice room
she thought. It had a king size bed and two very comfortable looking
chairs with a small table in front of the window. There was a desk with
a desk chair in the far corner. She put her bag on the end of the bed and
sat down. Her feet were tired and she slipped her shoes off.

The phone on the night stand next to the bed rang.

"Hello."

"Hi, how is the room?"

"Real nice!"

"Did you get Mrs. Adams off to her room?"

"Yes, I told her that I would give her a ring about 2 p.m. I'm sure
she is tired and needs some time alone."

"Do you need time alone, or can I come up?"

"I'd love to see you, come on up."

There was a knock on her door. She looked out the peep hole to
see who it was.

"That was quick, where did you park?"

"I parked in back of the hotel. You don't know how happy I am to
see you again. It has been a long time since we have been together".

"Yes, a couple of years. I'm happy to see you too. You know how
much I appreciate your help. Unless I can recover and find some critical
information here my career is over."

Dino put his hand on Allisa shoulder. He looked into her eyes and
moved closer to her.

"I would do anything to help you. You mean a lot to me. I'll never
forget the times we had together."

Allisa put her hand on the side of Dino's face and touched him so
softly.

"When I left here for California and my new assignment I was excited to get the promotion but leaving you was very hard".

Dino moved closer and kissed her on the cheek, then the lips. They embraced and held onto each other as Dino slipped his hand around her back and pulled her tight toward him. They fell back on the bed and Dino moved his hand on her thigh. Allisa had leaned back and her head rested on the bed as Dino moved his hands to her waist. Allisa had a strong and lean body. Dino moved his hands back to her face.

"Allisa I will do whatever necessary to help you with this investigation. We have had some problems here that I need to fill you in on."

"Not now Dino, I just want to be with you."

Dino unbuttoned her blouse and moved his hands on her breast. Allisa opened her mouth but nothing came out. She pulled Dino down to kiss him. They undressed each other as they kissed on the bed. The luggage tumbled to the floor. Allisa rolled on top of Dino and sat on him as he stroked her breast. She kissed him all over and they found comfort in each other as if they had never been apart. It had been a long time since Allisa had made love to anyone. She was a career FBI Agent and that always seemed to come first.

When she was assigned to Dino's team some of the other Agents thought that she was having an affair. Most of the men felt she was getting some of the easier assignments. When she was put as an undercover Agent and helped Dino solve a major case her career took off. The two laid on the bed for over an hour. Dino wanted to tell Allisa how much he missed her and wished she would come back to him but he knew that was not what she wanted. He knew that she wanted to help solve this investigation. He wanted to help her save her career. Maybe someday they would be together. Right now this moment was to be savored.

"Allisa I need to make a call and get you up to speed on everything here."

"Yes, that's a good idea."

Allisa was happy to be back in Dino's arms and working with him. She hoped that their lovemaking would not get in the way of this case. She watched as Dino sat on the edge of her bed and called to one of his men.

"Boss this thing has really gone to hell on us!" Steve said.

"We thought the New Jersey State Police had him on the interstate headed north when he entered a gas station. He ditched the truck that they tailed him in and got back on the Harley."

"How in the hell did he have time to do all that?"

"He had the Harley in the back of the truck and pulled it out with help from a trucker who just happened to see him and helped. He took off into the woods behind the buildings and we have a manhunt on for him now."

"Did you question the trucker who helped him?"

"Yes, it seems that he was getting out of his semi when he saw a man struggling with the Harley. He said he asked if the guy needed help and they pulled the bike out of the bed of the truck. Then the guy just took off."

"Shit, how did that all happen so quickly?"

"He really didn't give us much of a description."

"I need to update the Director. He's going to go nuts."

Allisa sat up and asked what had happened. Dino brought her up to speed on the action at the Adams home in Bridgewater and now the chase for the fugitives. They knew that they had to get moving now.

"I have to get back up there", Dino said.

"Let me call to Blair's room and tell her that you called and we need to get moving in fifteen minutes."

"You really want to bring her along?"

"We can leave her at the Adams home with Hunter's dad if necessary but I think she is the key to the documents."

"Ok give me a few minutes to get dressed and downstairs. I'll wait for you in the lobby."

Dino left Allisa's room and headed for his Suburban. He had to call John Martin and update him on the situation. This was a call he didn't want to make unless he had positive news.

"Hi, is the Director in?"

John Martins' secretary would put the call through to the Director's phone regardless of where he was. She knew what line he would be on and where to forward the calls. He had told her as soon as Dino Tuchy calls put him through.

"This is John Martin."

"Sir, I have an update for you. After the incident at the Adams house last night that I told you about we found the fugitives car in the woods. It appears that one of them stole a Harley and headed north on the Interstate through New Jersey."

"Son of a Bitch! This damn thing is growing like a cancer. Who else is involved now?"

"The New Jersey State Police were trailing the fugitive."

"So they know that we are chasing this man?"

"Yes sir, but no one knows why. I gave the local police a cover story and they bought it. The State Police had a tail on our guy but lost him at the rest area north of Crosswicks. They don't know what is going on just that he was one of the men that was involved in the incident at the Adams home."

"Shit this is really getting to be a mess Dino. Not only do we have fugitives on the loose but you lost one of our men in the process."

"I'm sorry sir, but I have contacted all of our Agents in the area to be on the lookout for them."

"Dino, I will talk to the President and the Homeland Security Chief about putting out a code Red terror alert. We can say that an informant gave us information regarding a possible terror cell on the East Coast."

"I will keep you informed boss."

"Don't screw this up or your ass will be in South Dakota protecting the monuments."

"Yes sir, you can count on me."

"That's what I'm doing but don't prove me wrong. The Director of Homeland Security is up to pace on this. I need to report some kind of a success."

"I guess the President is concerned?"

"The dumb shit only cares about his personal interest. Unless it involves Texas or his oil connections he doesn't have a clue."

"Yes, sir we're on it."

Dino knew that many of the high ranking officials in Washington did not feel that the President was very smart but this was the first time he heard John Martin say it out loud.

John Martin said, "I just got some weird news from California that Dean Curry doesn't know where Mrs. Adams is. He has tried to contact her at home and at her work but no one seems to know where she is. He has men stationed at her apartment and her place of work."

Dino knew that he had problems. Allisa was counting on him to help her. Mrs. Adams was now here and he didn't want too many people knowing that. Now John Martin was putting him on notice that he will be held responsible for this fugitives capture. Why me he thought! This should have been a simple search and report back to the Director. Now it was a chase through a couple of States for fugitives that may or may not be involved in the original case. He wondered if the two men that were shot in Mrs. Adams apartment by Agent Baxter had any relationship to the men they were now chasing. He also remembered that Allisa said that one of the men had been identified as an Iraqi National. This thing may be bigger than any of us knew.

Dino pulled the Suburban to the entrance of the hotel. He waited outside for Allisa and Mrs. Adams. It was close to noon and he had to get back to Bridgewater. Dino also needed to call the Trenton FBI office to get them involved. As he sat in his Suburban he was wondering how cold it was in South Dakota this time of the year.

TWENTY

Thomas Adams thanked his brother Bill and Martha for the evening and the nights stay.

"I need to get back," he told Bill. "It is almost noon and I think the stay was good for me. I have to call Bob Douglas and see what he wanted from me. Guess they may have a lead in the break-in at my house."

Thomas got in his car and headed toward Bridgewater. The night before had seen a heavy rain storm and there were spots along highway 13 that had water standing over the road. He drove slowly along the highway and watched as a road crew did some repairs along the way. Must have had a couple inches of rain he thought. He passed a State Police car that seemed to be driving slowly toward Croydon. Maybe there had been a report of an accident. The sun was bright as he headed home. The rain the night before brought our more leaves that sprung from the tree branches. Rain seemed to bring life to many of the trees and flowers. The ride from Croydon to Bridgewater was always enjoyable. The road followed the river and you would often see boaters and fishers along the river banks. He dialed Captain Douglas as he got closer to Bridgewater.

"Bob, this is Thomas Adams. I am headed home and you said to call before I got there."

"Glad you called Thomas. I will meet you at your house in a few minutes."

Thomas wondered what had happened that Bob needed to talk to him in person. Maybe it was the new neighborhood kids that did the break-in and they wanted to apologize. It was probably nothing serious

he thought. At least everything was put back and no real damage
occurred. Thomas pulled down his street and saw the Captain's car
in his driveway. There was also another car in the street. He didn't
recognize it as he pulled along side Bob's squad car.

"Hi Thomas," Captain Douglas called out.

"Hi Bob, what's up?"

"Thomas, this is Steve Watkins from the Federal Bureau of
Investigation. He and I want to go over a few things with you."

"What's going on, why is the FBI involved?"

"We'll explain everything Thomas. Can we go inside?"

"Sure, has something else happened?"

Bob Douglas covered the second break-in for Thomas and the
shootout in his yard. Thomas was so stunned that he just sat there
listening. He never asked any questions. Steve Watkins told him the
story about a group that was causing trouble for families of soldiers
that had been in Iraq. He was explaining that the FBI had heard about
the break-in and just wanted to make sure that Thomas's family had
not been harassed by this group. With the shootout now it was more
serious.

"We will be involved from here out," Steve Watkins told Thomas.

"My chief will be here in a little and he can go over more details for
you. His name is Dino Tuchy."

Thomas didn't quite know what to think. He asked if anything had
happened in his house.

"We had our crime lab people go through your house to see if
anything had been disturbed or if any fingerprints were found. We
didn't find anything," Steve Watkins told him.

"How about the men that got shot?" he asked.

Captain Douglas said that Andy Emery was in the local hospital.
Thomas said he remembered Andy. He is a nice young man and I
hope that he will recover. Captain Douglas told Thomas that Andy's
girlfriend had called and said the surgery went well and that Andy
would be in the hospital for only a couple of days. Unfortunately the
FBI agent that had been shot had died at the scene.

"I'm sorry to hear that," he said.

"Thomas I will be with you and my men will be here 24/7 to make
sure your ok. I'm not going to let anything happen to one of our

citizens and a good friend of mine." "Thanks Bob that does make me feel better."

Steve Watkins asked to be excused for a minute.

"I have to check in with our Agent that is at the rest area north of Crosswicks." Kevin Reese was working with the State Police team that had mobilized their local force to search the wooded area that was behind the rest area. They knew that Groveville was due north of the area and that the fugitive could make his way to State Route 524. They had stationed a squad car at each end of that road in case he came out of the woods and headed that way. The fugitive had a head start before the State Police could get their men into position. The search started in the dark and they felt that he could not travel too far even on the Harley in the dark.

"You would have to be one hell of a bike rider to pull that off," the State police Captain said.

Kevin answered his phone.

"Kevin, this is Steve, how is it going?"

"They have the area covered and brought in some motorcycles that have headed into the woods. It is so muddy that I don't see how anyone could get very far."

"Did you search the abandoned truck?"

"Yes, and we found some papers that Dino is going to want to see."

"I hope it helps, he didn't seem too happy when I talked to him a few minutes ago." "They may be a little confusing but it looks like it may lead to a group headquarters in New York. It appears they have a headquarters somewhere in the Bronx."

"Wow, that is great news. I'm going to call the boss and tell him. I bet he will get the Director to mobilize the New York unit."

Steve looked at his watch and saw that it was about 1:00 p.m. I should call Dino now and not wait he thought. Dino heard his phone and saw it was Steve calling.

"I'm on my way Steve, what have you got?"

"Kevin has found some papers with a map. They were in the abandoned truck. We think it may lead to a cell at a house in New York."

"Good work!"

"He found the information searching through papers the fugitive left in the truck before he escaped into the woods."

Dino thought, finally something positive.

"I want to report this to the Director but I would like to see the documents first. Have Kevin fax them to you."

Steve went back into the house.

"Captain Douglas do you have a fax machine in your office?"

"Yes we do."

"I need to get some information faxed to me right away."

"I don't mean to butt in but I have a fax machine here," Thomas said.

Steve called Kevin and gave him the fax number to Thomas Adams' house.

"Dino is going to want to see as much of that information as you can fax to us."

Steve stood by the fax machine as the pieces of paper started to come through. He looked at each one and saw what Kevin was talking about. There was a map that had a circle drawn around the exit off interstate 87 and 3rd Avenue in New York. It was just a few blocks from Yankee Stadium. Steve wasn't sure if it was the location of a possible safe house or signifying Yankee Stadium as a target. Steve put the documents in the order that Kevin had faxed them. There were 7 pages in total.

Dino called Steve to see if he had gotten the documents yet.

"I have them all right here sir. Mr. Adams let us use his fax machine."

"We will be there in a few minutes, Steve. You need to tell Mr. Adams that I have his daughter-in-law with me. Don't get him too excited but explain that we wanted to make sure both of them are safe and having them together was the best way to accomplish that. You also have to tell him for her safety no one should know that she is with us."

"Holy shit boss, you pulled that one off without any of us knowing."

"Yes, guess I just thought it was the best move for now."

Dino thought that since he would get blamed for Mrs. Adams being along he might as well take credit for the idea. He also didn't want Thomas to have a heart attack when Blair walked in. He told Allisa and

Blair that they would arrive at the Adams home in a few minutes and they would enter from the rear of the house. He didn't want anyone to know that Allisa and Blair were with him. He would handle Steve and knew that he could count on his keeping it quiet. Blair was happy that she would see Hunter's dad and hoped that they could have some time together. She also wondered what roll she would play in this adventure. The black Suburban pulled into the Adams driveway. Dino had to park behind Thomas Adams Chevrolet. The three passengers got out of the vehicle and walked around the back of the house.

Blair stopped at the back of the garage and asked, "What happened here? Is Thomas ok; is there something you're not telling me?"

"Calm down Blair," Dino said. "Thomas is fine and in the house. We had an incident here last night and I lost one of my men."

"Sorry," Blair said.

She walked into the garage with Dino and Allisa. Thomas came into the kitchen and when he saw Blair they hugged. They both had tears in their eyes.

"I'm so glad that you're ok they both said at the same time."

Blair was glad to see Thomas. He was such a nice man and she knew that he would be so lonely after losing Hunter. Thomas thought that Blair was the best thing that had happened to his son. She brought him closer to his family. Girls have a way of bringing sons back home. Dino asked them to all go into the living room.

"Blair, we need you and Thomas to think back to the last things you may have gotten from your husband. It is critical that we know if he sent you anything that may help our cause in Iraq."

Thomas said that he had talked to Hunter several times but he did not send anything to him. Blair sat on the couch next to Thomas and did not answer. Dino looked at her and again asked if she had received anything from Hunter in the past few weeks.

"I haven't opened anything from him in close to a month," she said.

Blair turned to Thomas and apologized for the surprise visit.

"Don't be sorry, I'm just happy to see you."

Captain Douglas seemed puzzled but just listened to the questions that Dino had asked.

"Are these so called papers the reason Mr. Adams home has been broken into?" he asked Dino.

"We think that may be the case. We also think there is a group causing problems for our soldiers that have returned from Iraq."

Dino had to toss that in to cover his earlier statements.

"Captain, I want to leave both Mr. Adams and Blair here. Can I ask your people to help keep an eye on them? I want to make sure they are safe."

"I have already ordered a 24/7 watch and will be involved myself to help protect Mr. Adams and his daughter-in-law."

Steve and Dino went out onto the porch and Dino wanted to look at the faxes that Kevin had sent.

"Steve, I don't want you to say anything about Blair or agent Jones being here. It is for our benefit that they have come along."

"I don't know anything boss."

Allisa came outside to see what they had found from the search of the abandoned truck.

"I want to be involved," she said.

"Don't worry, we will need everyone on the case that we can get."

Dino showed her the fax and the map that showed the area circled near Yankee Stadium. He said that they were not sure if it detailed where there was a safe house or if Yankee Stadium was a target.

Allisa said, "I know the area. I went to NYU and lived in a loft near Yankee Stadium. It makes sense if I was to go there with you."

Dino knew that she would be great value to the investigation. He also knew that the Director would have his ass if he found out.

"Let's think about the best way to proceed."

He wanted to report something positive to the Director as soon as possible.

"I am going to report the map that we found to the Director and let him suggest the next step. We can make our plans once we know the direction he will want to take."

Dino walked off the front porch and called the Director. His mind went back to the director's last statement about guarding the monuments in South Dakota.

It was just past 1:00 p.m. when the phone call came through.

"Director, this is Dino Tuchy, I have an update and some good news."

"About fucking time you got something for me."

"We found some documents that the fugitive left behind that may lead us to something real big."

"How much bigger do you want this thing to get Dino?

Dino just knew that he had to get the Director off his case.

"Sir, we may have a terrorist on the loose and we have a map that shows the location of their possible location and their next target."

"How did you get this map? Where does the map show this location?"

"The map has a circle around the area that Yankee Stadium is in."

"Holy shit! The Red Sox are in New York tonight and after last year, this series has been sold out for months. There will be 60,000 plus people at the game. I will need to mobilize our units to put special precautions in place around the stadium."

"How do you want my team to proceed?" Dino asked.

"You need to continue to try to find the fugitive that got away. Also we need to know what this has got to do with the Adams situation."

"Sir, I would like to be involved in the New York search."

"Dino, you get your men on the fugitive search and I will call you later to possibly get you involved with the Yankee Stadium thing."

"Thank you sir."

Dino had hoped that Mount Rushmore could find someone else to guard it.

Dino walked back toward Allisa and Steve. He told them that they need to get the fugitive captured and maybe he could head to New York.

"The Yankee Stadium thing could be my ticket," Dino said.

"Steve, I don't want anyone to know that Allisa is here. I want you to take her with you to the search site at Crosswicks and introduce her as special Agent Mary Kathleen. You both should take control of the situation and report to me as soon as possible."

Allisa was happy that she would be involved. Maybe if they could get the fugitive they would get the information to help solve her case.

Blair asked Captain Douglas if it was ok for her and Thomas to go into the kitchen. He said, "no problem," and she asked if he was hungry.

He said, "no thanks, but bet you are." Thomas walked with Blair to the kitchen and she opened the fridge.

"You need to listen to me and pretend that we are making lunch," she said.

Thomas looked confused but went along with her.

"None of this makes any sense," she said. "I'm not sure why the FBI is involved but I may have what they are looking for."

"How do you know?" Thomas said.

"I got a package from Iraq a couple of days ago. I didn't open it because that was the day I was going to meet the FBI Agent, Allisa Jones."

"Why didn't you open it?"

"I had picked it up at the post office and went to The Pub to meet Ms. Jones. I left it downstairs at The Pub and that's when I found out that there was a second break-in at my apartment. I was so shook up that I forgot about the package until just now. When Mr. Tuchy started asking his questions it triggered the memory of that package."

"We should tell the FBI," Thomas said.

"No," said Blair. "I want to know what's going on first. What if this is bad for Hunter?"

Thomas understood and agreed with her.

"I have to get back to Santa Monica and get that package."

"You could call and have someone open it for you."

"No, there have been too many people hurt already and I don't want any of my friends hurt. I have to do this myself."

Thomas remembered that Hunter told him once, when Blair made up her mind there was no stopping her.

"With all the police protection how do you get back to Santa Monica without them knowing?"

"That's what we have to figure out."

Captain Douglas walked into the kitchen and asked what they were going to make. "Guess I could have something," he said.

Blair looked surprised to see him but started pulling out some packages that Thomas had in the meat keeper.

"Looks like we have some lunchmeat and I'll make us some sandwiches," she said. "Sounds good to me", Thomas said.

"Me too," Bob answered.

Blair made them all lunch and thought that she had to figure out a way to get back home. She could not call Olly and put her at risk, besides, what could be in the package that has caused all this. If she was to get back home she would need Olly's help. Allisa came in with Steve and said that they were going to head up to Crosswicks but should be back around dinner time. Dino had left for Crosswicks and wanted to have a meeting with the State police and his people. This investigation needed to be resolved because there was another case that needed his attention they said. Blair didn't want to hurt Allisa but it was important that she be the first one to open the package. Maybe it wasn't anything but she had to know. She told Thomas and Captain Douglas that lunch was ready.

They sat at Thomas' table and the Captain expressed how sorry he was that all of this had happened.

"I know that you both have had a great deal of grief with the loss of Hunter and this on top of it is almost too much for anyone to handle."

They sat and ate without much being said.

Once she had picked up the dishes she told Captain Douglas that she was tired and was going to lie down for a while. Thomas walked her to one of the spare bedrooms and Blair told him that she would try to make some plans and would let him know what she was going to do.

It was close to 10:00 a.m. in Santa Monica when Olly's phone rang. "Hi Olly."

"Blair I'm so glad to hear from you. Is everything ok?"

"I said I would call once we got here and would let you know what was going on. It appears the FBI is on the lookout for some terrorist that may be involved in the break-in at my place and his dads place."

"That doesn't make sense."

"I know, but that's what they are telling us. Thomas and I agree that I need to be back in Santa Monica."

"Why do you need to come back here?"

"I'll explain once I figure out how to get out of here."

"Blair, there has been a couple of FBI Agents asking about you. We all have said that we don't know where you are. They seem to be worried that you have been kidnapped or in hiding. We know that they have a man stationed outside of your apartment building and at The Pub."

"Olly, somehow I will get back there as soon as possible. I will need your help and continue to tell everyone that you don't know where I am."

"Ok but you need to be careful."

"I will."

Blair sat on the bed and planned her escape back to Santa Monica. She knew that she would have trouble shaking the FBI but maybe they will be moving on to the other case Allisa mentioned. Knowing that they have men stationed at her apartment and The Pub would make this even more difficult. She might have to get Blake involved because they are probably watching Olly too. She also knew that the local police were watching Thomas's house so just getting out of there will be a task.

Blair had to think up a plan and get back to Santa Monica and see what was in that package.

TWENTY ONE

Kevin came back to the State Police mini post that had been set up at the rest area. He told the State Police Chief that his Bureau Chief and a couple of Agents were on their way to Crosswicks. He also wanted to gather any details that Dino may want to know. Kevin had just been promoted to the Philadelphia Bureau, and wanted to make sure that he could fill Dino in without getting him angry. He had heard from the other agents that Dino had a temper. He did not want to look bad in front of his new boss. Kevin learned that the State Police had covered most of the areas that the fugitive could escape from. That included the wooded area around Groveville and State Route 524. He also knew that the Trenton FBI office had their men mobilized and were covering the Interstate's that led north to New York. Brad Ferguson was the New Jersey State Police Chief headquartered in Trenton. He gave Kevin a local area map that had the main routes marked so that Kevin knew where the State Police had positioned their men. Kevin was good at working with the local and state guys and Brad had been assigned to an FBI task force so they got along well.

Brad was new to his position. He enjoyed working with the FBI on the task force but did not like the way they treated local cops. Kevin seemed different. He asked questions and listened for answers. Kevin took advice from Brad on the search and was appreciative for the documents that Brad turned over to him. Kevin had a feeling that Brad would not like Dino.

Dino arrived at the Crosswicks rest area and Kevin brought him up to date on the search. Dino wanted to review the papers that Kevin found at the scene in the abandoned pick-up truck. He told Kevin that

Steve Watkins and Mary Kathleen, another Agent that was bought in, would be arriving soon. He wanted to cement the identification of Allisa as Mary Kathleen. Dino could not take a chance on someone slipping up and calling her by her real name. Dino wanted to gather all the information possible before talking to the State Police chief. Dino did not want to deal with any local authorities unless they understood that he was in charge. Dino and Kevin walked to the abandoned pick-up and Dino asked who had searched through the truck.

"The two local State Police officers that were trailing the fugitive were the only ones in the truck," Kevin said.

"I want our crime lab guys to go through this and report back to me. Get those two local State cops to give us their fingerprints so that the crime lab can rule those out." "The two State Officers are still here and the crime lab is on their way up here Boss."

Dino was pleased with Kevin's progress on the case. Dino and Kevin walked toward the wooded area and saw the motorcycle tracks. He knew that the local State Police had also sent in three other motorcycle riders to see if they could locate where the fugitive was headed. How far could you get in all this mud he thought? He saw that Steve and Allisa were arriving at the rest area. He wanted to make sure that Allisa was introduced as Mary Kathleen, special Agent from Washington. He waved to Steve as Kevin came walking over to meet Mary Kathleen. The four Agents were talking when the state police chief came over to cover his team's strategy.

"Hi, I'm Brad Ferguson of the New Jersey State Police. Our team has made some progress through the wooded area but it is so muddy that it has been difficult."

Dino put his hand out and greeted Brad.

"Dino Tuchy, Federal Bureau of Investigation, and these are my Agents, Kevin Reese, Steve Watkins and Mary Kathleen."

"We have been working with Mr. Reese, and I have an update that just came in. The fugitive's motorcycle tracks were followed through the wooded area that leads toward state route 524. Mr. Reese has that marked on his map. We lost the tracks near a small stream that ran through the woods. We have gone up and down the stream but the tracks do not re-appear."

"How far into the woods are these tracks?"

"They stopped about three and a half miles into the wooded area."

"Where are your men now?"

"They have split up and one is headed south along the stream and the other two have headed north along the stream. Our other teams are stationed along the state route so that if he comes out of the wooded area they would be in position to track him."

Dino thought for a minute and put his hand on Brad's shoulder.

"Your people are doing a good job. I want to be kept informed on their progress. I have our Agents from Trenton also in position along the major routes in case he was to make it past your men."

Dino knew that this posture signaled that he was in charge. That was the initial impression he wanted to make on the State Police Chief.

Brad knew what Dino was doing, and he didn't like it. He had some questions that needed to be answered.

"Who is this guy we're all chasing anyway?"

"I can't divulge that just yet!"

"It would help if we had more details."

"Once I have clearance from the Director I'll pass the information along."

Brad Ferguson walked away from the meeting shaking his head. Most local and State Police thought the FBI people were crap. Brad felt that Kevin was different but his Bureau Chief was not. The FBI never shared what they knew, and always wanted you to give them all the information you had. If the case ever was solved they always took the credit. He had told Dino that he would keep them informed but he felt that his men were more than capable to track this guy. Brad felt that he gave Dino everything that he knew but Dino never answered any of Brad's questions.

Captain Douglas told Thomas that his men were making constant passes around his house.

"Thomas we will be here to protect you and your daughter-in-law. I have to leave but I will be back in an hour so. If you need me just call my cell phone number."

"Bob, I appreciate everything that you are doing for us. I know you have other things to attend to so just take your time. We will be ok."

Thomas was hoping that when Captain Douglas left that he and
Blair could plan her attempt to get out of the house and back to Santa
Monica.

Captain Douglas and Thomas walked outside to the Captain's
car.

"Thomas, I will be back. Do you need anything?"

"Before you get back Bob maybe I could get one of your people to
go with me to the store."

"Sure that won't be a problem."

Thomas was looking for as many different opportunities that they
could use to accomplish Blair's plans. He wasn't too sure what she had
in mind but knew that it would not be easy getting out of his house,
let alone making her way to the airport. Thomas walked down the hall
and stood outside the bedroom door.

He quietly asked, "Blair are you awake?"

"Yes, you can come in."

He opened the door and saw Blair had changed.

"You look so different."

She had put on some jeans and an old sweatshirt of Hunter's. She
had tied her hair back and had on boots.

"I need to make myself look as different as possible without causing
too much attention."

Thomas told Blair that Captain Douglas had left for a while but
would be back.

He also told her that there would be local police cars passing by to
keep a watch on the house. It was about 3:00 p.m. and they knew it
would not get dark until about 9:00. They needed a plan.

Blair thought for a little, "What if you said you had to go out?"

"I did tell Bob that I had to do some shopping for groceries."

"Ok, lets think about a good plan," she said.

Dino wanted to make sure that everything possible had been covered
at the rest area. He also had to update John Martin but needed more
positive news. He called to the Bureau Chief in Trenton to give them
the latest information. He told them that John Martin wanted all the
information to be filtered back through him and he would contact
John Martin with the data. Dino was an authority freak. Everyone
that worked with him knew that. They also knew he was one of the

best people to handle this type of situation. Dino told Steve that he and Kevin needed to stay at the rest area and call him as soon as they had any news. He would take Mary Kathleen with him to head toward Trenton and coordinate the search from the other side of the wooded area.

"We might get a couple of motorcycles and have some of our men enter the woods and follow that stream from the northern end."

Dino did not want to leave Allisa at the rest area for fear of someone recognizing her. He knew if John Martin had any idea that Allisa was with Dino that he would be on the next flight for South Dakota.

Thomas called Bob Douglas and said that he would like to go to the store.

"I'll have one of my men come by and get you," Bob said. "Is Blair going with you?"

"No, she is really tired and will stay here."

"We will continue to cover your house while you are at the store. Tell her that she doesn't have to worry."

"Thank you again Bob for everything you are doing."

Thomas felt guilty that he was miss leading his friend but knew that Blair was right. They had to know what was in the papers that the FBI was determined to find.

He told Blair that he was going.

"I'll still be here when you return, but if I am gone I will leave a note in the top dresser drawer for you. Once you read it make sure that you tear it up."

"Blair, I'm worried that you're taking on too much."

"I don't have a choice. I have to see if there is anything in that package back home and if so I have to protect Hunter."

Thomas knew she was right. He wished he could be that strong. Blair was a determined person.

"Blair, what if I called my brother Bill to help us?"

"Sure what do you have in mind?"

"Bill could drive down and meet you on the street behind my house. You could sneak through the yard into the woods and come out on the next street. He could take you to the airport."

Blair thought for a minute. "Are you sure he would do it?"

"Bill would do anything I ask. He has been a great help with the funeral and everything. I can explain it to him and I'm sure he will help."

"That's a great idea. Let's call him," Blair said.

Thomas called Bill and went over the situation. Bill said that he would do anything to help them. He could not believe that so much had happened since Hunter's funeral and now more problems for his brother and Blair.

The rendezvous was set up on Bloom Bird Street. Thomas said it helps because they would be doing this at night time. He felt that if the police thought that Blair had gone to bed for the evening she would have eight to ten hours before anyone suspected that she was gone. This might give her the time to get to Santa Monica before they started to look for her. Blair agreed that this was a good plan. She called the airlines to check on flights to Los Angeles. There were two flights that left Philadelphia that evening. One was at 10:46 p.m. and the other was at 11:23 p.m. With the time difference she would be in Los Angeles before midnight, Pacific Time. That would be good. She could have Olly or Blake meet her. They would have make up a plan to get the package out of The Pub. It would be open until 2:00 a.m. and with the FBI watching The Pub she would need help. The plan was set. Thomas decided to go to the store and Blair said she was going to change clothes.

"I'll hang on to the disguise for later."

Dino and Allisa headed to his Suburban.

"You need to be in the background as much as possible" he told her.

"I will make sure that you are involved and anything that helps you will be yours."

Allisa knew that Dino would keep his promise. She also knew that he was taking a great chance having her along with him.

"Dino I can never tell you how much this means to me."

"Maybe we will get lucky Allisa and catch this guy. But if the shit hit's the fan, I will have to get you out of here."

"I understand," she said.

Yawer pushed the Harley out of the stream onto a path that seemed to be hard enough to ride on. He was soaked but still on the move.

Finding the stream in the woods helped to cover his tracks and would buy him time to escape. The Harley was heavy but he was able to maneuver it through the wooded area. When he came to an area of the stream that had some dead tree limbs in the water he pushed the Harley out of the stream on a tree limb. He covered the tracks by pulling the limb out of the water. He wasn't sure what direction he was going in. He still had some maps in the saddle bags on the bike and now that the rain had stopped he could check them out. He wanted to get out of the woods and into an area that he could change his form of transportation. He was sure that people would be tracking him. When he looked at the map he could see that Trenton was due north and that he should be close to Yardville. If he could make it out of the woods he could get to Highway 130 north and maybe steal a new ride. It would be light soon and he had to make his way out of the woods and get as far from here as possible. Yawer knew that he had a head start on anyone that was tracking him through the woods. He also knew the police cars that chased him at the rest area would mobilize men on the roads that surrounded the woods. The wooded area was very dense and because it was night time he was able to ride the Harley deep into the wooded area. Once out of the deep woods he saw a clearing ahead and rode the Harley to the edge of what appeared to be a gravel road. He turned right and headed north on the gravel road. It was still dark but he could see a few farm houses as he rode past them. He slowed down when he saw a large barn with the doors opened. He rode the Harley into the barn and thought that it would serve as a place to clean up. Once Yawer got into the barn he found some work clothes hanging up. He quickly changed and buried his dirty clothes in a hay pile. He walked around the inside of the barn and looked out the back and saw some late model trucks parked there. Yawer knew that he had to keep moving. He got the stuff out of the Harley's side bags and pushed the Harley into a hay pile. He was able to cover it with a few bales of hay and hoped it would not be found for a few hours. Yawer hot wired a truck and pulled out around the back of the barn onto the gravel road. The gravel road led to a blacktop road about ½ mile past the farm house. Yawer turned right and was glad to see that he had over ¾ of a tank of gas in the truck. He stayed on the blacktop road until he came to a sign that said Groveville one mile. Yawer headed toward Groveville and figured Highway 130 was straight ahead.

The State Police were still far behind. Brad Ferguson had mobilized his men and cars as soon as possible but Yawer had a big head start. He also found it difficult to get help from the local police in Groveville. They had only two cars and because it was night time only one man was on duty. The FBI had said that they would cover any escape routes that lead to the interstate. There were not enough men and too much territory to cover.

Yawer found his way to Highway 130 and headed north. He would hope to get up the road before he would have to change vehicles again. He figured that he would have at least a two hour head start with the pickup truck before it was reported as missing.

Thomas called his brother Bill and explained the situation. Bill was stunned to find out about the FBI involvement and that Blair had some break-ins. He said he would be willing to help in any way that Thomas or Blair needed. Thomas told Bill their plan. Bill said that he could leave his house in Croydon and be on Blue Bird Street to meet Blair whatever time she wanted. Thomas said that Blair wanted to get to the Philadelphia Airport by 9:00 p.m. so that she could catch one of the two departures for Los Angeles. Bill offered to fly to L.A. with Blair if she wanted him to. Both Thomas and Blair were very appreciative but said that it would be best if Blair traveled alone. The plan was set. Blair would make an excuse to go to bed early and sneak out to meet Bill for the ride to the airport. It was about a 45 minute ride from Thomas's house to the airport. Blair asked Thomas to make sure that he made excuses for her as late into the next day as possible. She said she might try to return to Philadelphia before anyone knew she was gone. Thomas doubted that the plan would work.

He said, "You have two flights of 4 to 5 hours plus having to get the package from The Pub."

"Yes I know but I have the time difference on my side. Traveling at night gives me an additional advantage. If I get to L.A. by midnight and can get the package in a couple of hours I can do it. The flight back would put me here about noon tomorrow."

"Blair, you have to get everything to go perfect for that to work out."

"So far nothing has worked out for us, maybe this time it will."

Blair and Thomas went back into the living room. Thomas was getting ready to go to the store.

"Blair, don't do anything silly while I'm gone."

"I won't, I'll be right here waiting for you."

Thomas noticed a squad car pulling in his drive.

"I need to go now. I will be back in about 30 minutes. I really don't have much in the fridge. Is there anything you need or want?"

"Pick up something for dinner. I made a small list of stuff. I can make dinner for anyone that is here. It would be a good diversion."

"Sure, sounds good."

"Could you also pick up some English breakfast tea?"

"Sure, is that all?"

"Once we get our hands on that package, then I be ready for some food."

"I understand," Thomas said.

Dino told Allisa that they should head back to Thomas's house.

"You could get some rest and I will pick you up later. I would also like you to question Blair and Thomas to see if something might trigger a memory that would help us."

"I still want to be involved Dino. I'm not going to stay out of sight at the Adams' house."

"I promise that I will come back for you later. I'm thinking maybe about 8:00 p.m. I can come for you. There will be more progress here by then and we still have a fugitive or fugitive's body in Bridgewater to find."

The two drove back to the Adams home. Allisa knocked at the front door when they arrived. Blair came to the door and looked out the small glass window to see who it was.

"Hi Allisa, I didn't know when you were coming back."

"I need to rest some and Dino thought it would be better if we continued our search later this evening."

Blair stepped outside and waved to Dino. She wanted to make sure she was seen as often as possible.

"Where is Thomas?"

"He went to the grocery store with one of the local Bridgewater police officers. They have a car down the street watching the house while he is gone."

"Dino pointed it out when we drove up."

The two women sat in the living room.

"Do you want anything?" Blair asked.

"No, I'm just happy to sit for a while and rest. While we were gone did you or Thomas remember anything that might help us?"

"We just have been talking about Hunter and really don't have any ideas that would help. Guess that this is all so confusing that we are just trying to catch up ourselves."

"That's understandable. If you do have anything no matter how small you might think it is just let me know. Blair you know I will do everything to help you and solve this puzzle."

"I know that Allisa. I promise to tell you anything that might help."

Blair felt a little guilty not telling Allisa what she remembered but until she knew what the package held there was no sense in telling anyone. It might be nothing but Blair had to know.

Allisa said she was going to catch a little nap.

"Blair, if I fall to sleep please wake me in two hours."

"Not a problem," Blair answered.

Allisa walked toward the bedrooms and Blair said just use mine, it is the first one on the right."

"Thanks, I guess I am more tired than I thought."

The front door opened and Thomas walked in.

"Can I help you with those bags?"

Just then one of the Bridgewater officers came in carrying two more bags.

"Did you buy the whole store?"

"I just followed your list. You have to remember I haven't shopped for a group in a long time."

"Is there anything else I can do for you Mr. Adams?" the officer asked.

"No thanks Jeff, you've been a big help."

"Allisa is here, and I said she could sleep in my room."

"When did she come back?"

"Just a few minutes after you left for the store."

Thomas carried the bags into the kitchen. Blair started to put the groceries away with him.

"Thanks for the breakfast tea. I enjoy tea more than coffee except for an occasional latte'."

They talked quietly as they put the remainder of the groceries away.

"Do you think I should tell Allisa about my plan?" Blair asked.

"I really don't trust them Blair. They have an agenda that is different from ours. We just want to make sure nothing bad is said about Hunter, they want something and we don't know what it is."

"Your right, I needed your prospective. I wonder what they think he found." "It must be big Blair or the FBI would not be involved."

Blair knew that Thomas was right. She again wondered why the FBI had been involved. If Hunter was one of their agents they must think he did something wrong. She wanted to trust Allisa but didn't trust the other agents. What to do next was her dilemma.

TWENTY TWO

Bill pulled down Blue Bird Street and turned off his headlights. He had some reservations about Thomas and Blair's plan but he would do anything to help them. He had met Blair two years ago when she and Hunter had come to Thomas' house for Christmas. His first impression was that she was a very beautiful girl but probably just another California type. He judged her looks not her. He was surprised when he talked to her about current issues regarding the war in Iraq. She was very informed and had some valid reasons for her position. Blair was against the war although she supported Hunter's position. She had her own opinion on our involvement. Bill was also surprised to find out that Blair had a normal childhood growing up and like all kids she had to work in various fast food type jobs to earn money for extras. Blair's dad worked for a major corporation and they moved quite a few times. She had lived in Cincinnati, Louisville, St. Louis and Atlanta before moving to Birmingham, Alabama. Because they moved so many times it gave Blair a well rounded outlook on life. She made friends easily and remained friends with so many of them by mail, phone or visiting. Her parents often would take trips back to one of the cities they had lived in so she could spend time with an old friend. When she moved to Santa Monica many of her friends came to visit. Blair and Hunter always made room for them. Bill realized that Blair was a strong person and that she had a great influence on both Hunter and Thomas. He understood that because she had him sitting on Blue Bird Street waiting to help her escape back to Los Angeles for some reason he was not privileged to yet. Bill had many questions and he hoped that Blair could fill him in on the trip to the Philadelphia airport. It was a little before eight o'clock and he was in position earlier than he should have been but he wanted to be there in case the plans changed and he was needed sooner. He dialed Thomas on his cell to let him know that he was there and to re-confirm the plans.

When the phone rang Thomas almost jumped out of his skin. He was getting more nervous as the time got closer to nine. Allisa was still sleeping in the extra bedroom and Blair was making dinner. Thomas picked the phone up and was happy to hear Bill's voice.

"Hi Bill."

"I just wanted to call and let you know that I'm where you said I should be."

"Plans are still the same. We may have a little variance in the time because we have company here."

"Thomas, is everything ok?"

"Blair will fill you in when she sees you."

Thomas told Bill that he would try to ring his cell phone once when Blair leaves the house so that Bill will know that she is on the way. The woods behind The Adams house were very dense and at night they could be hard to make your way through. These woods have seen a lot of action. With the night of the shoot out in the yard and the chase with Captain Douglas and the FBI in pursuit of the fugitives the woods were becoming heavily traveled.

Allisa came out of the bedroom and said, "I really needed that rest. What time is it?"

Thomas looked at his watch and said that it was ten minutes until eight.

"Wow, I can't believe that I slept so long. Where is Blair?"

"She's making dinner."

Allisa walked into the kitchen and saw that Blair was busy setting the table. It appeared that she had made a roast with all the fixings.

"This is a great looking dinner! I wish you asked me to help."

"You needed the rest. I got to sleep when we got here. I hope you're hungry."

"I can't remember the last time I ate."

"I made a large meal because I didn't know if Dino or some of the other men would be here. Do you know what their plans are?"

Blair was fishing for information. She had her plans but would be somewhat flexible depending on who was at Thomas' house.

"Dino had said that he would pick me up about 8:00 p.m.," Allisa said.

"Blair, I need to tell you something. I cannot let you be in the dark about anything. Washington thinks that Hunter found some information that may lead to a discovery involving a lot of money. They also think now that Hunter was going to sell this information."

Blair stopped setting the table.

"When did you find this out?"

"Dino told me before he dropped me off. He said that John Martin, the FBI Director, told him that yesterday. They think that is why you or Hunter's dad may have had the information sent to you."

Blair was shocked. She sat down and was very quiet.

"Blair, I am telling you this because you have taken a chance on coming here with me. I also think that you have been very honest with me. I am betting that Hunter just didn't have time to get the information to his superiors before he was killed."

It was very quiet in the kitchen for it seemed like an eternity.

"Blair, please talk to me." Blair took a deep breath.

"I don't know what to say."

"This is the first time we have been alone since I found this out and I had to tell you. I hope you can understand that I trust you and hope you trust me?"

Blair wanted to think before she said anything.

"Allisa, I do trust you but I don't trust the other FBI people."

"I understand and don't blame you. You've been through so much and now this added to it."

"Allisa, I'm going need to have some time alone to figure some of this out. Could you help me get that time alone?"

"I don't know what you mean."

"After dinner I would like to go and check out a few things. I might be able to give you some help once I have the time to check them out."

"What kind of time do you need?"

"I will say that I'm going to bed and if you could cover for me until tomorrow." "What time tomorrow?"

"Maybe close to noon."

"That's a lot of time. Where are you going? You promise that you won't leave me holding the bag here?"

"I would not do that. I'd rather not say where I am going to yet."

"If I did this I could cover for you by saying that your sick in the morning to Dino." "That would work."

"They are going to want to see you tomorrow."

"I am thinking that I would have some answers by late afternoon tomorrow. Allisa I cannot do this without you're help."

"I'm not sure we can pull this off but I'm willing to give it a try."

"Just where are you going to?"

"I have to get out of the house for a while."

"How are you going to get out of the house?"

"I have a plan."

"Blair you and I have a lot in common. You're my kind of agent." Blair laughed. "Yeah, a real FBI agent."

"Remember Blair you have all the credentials, use them if needed."

Blair forgot that Allisa gave her a full set of FBI credentials. That could be her key to getting on the flights she needed without a reservation. Blair and Allisa hugged in the kitchen. Thomas came into the kitchen and saw the two girls hugging. "Sorry, Blair and I just had to have a girl moment."

"Dinners ready," Blair said.

"Wow, everything looks great. You made so much."

"I didn't know how many people would be here, plus left over roast makes for great sandwiches."

Blair was a good cook. Although her schedule at The Pub did not leave her much time for cooking. When Hunter got home from a mission she always made all his favorite things. Blair's mom was a great cook. She made Blair a copy of all her recipe's so that Blair would have her own book of them.

The door bell rang. Thomas went to the door and it was Dino, Steve and Kevin. "Come on in," he said.

"You must have smelled dinner."

"We don't want to interrupt we just came to get Allisa," Dino said.

"Blair made enough for a small army. You should all come in and eat with us." Dino looked at the others and said that sounds good. He wanted to make sure that Thomas and Blair were comfortable with them. Maybe by eating dinner with them he might find out something to help in the case. Dino also thought that Kevin and Steve could use a break.

Allisa and Blair came out of the kitchen.

"Dinners on the table," Blair said.

This would work out great for her plan. Everyone would see her late in the evening and no one would wonder where she was. With Allisa helping to cover for her the next morning, she could follow her planned escape and get back to Thomas' house with the package.

"Wow, great looking dinner," Dino said.

Being single he often ate fast food or frozen dinners. This looked like a feast. They all sat down at the kitchen table. Blair and Allisa put the roast and potatoes on the table. There was corn, salad and bread. Blair said, that she had pumpkin pie cooling in the fridge for dessert.

"You really went all out for this," Dino said.

"The pie is my Grandmothers recipe, and my mother taught me how to make it. I love to cook; I just don't have the time at home to do it."

Steve and Kevin were happy to have a good meal after the last few days of fast food and sitting in their cars searching for the fugitives. Everyone started to pass the food and Blair was happy that they seemed to be enjoying everything. The dinner conversation was about the escaped fugitive and the search for him. Blair seemed to ask a lot of questions and Steve and Kevin were free with information. Allisa knew what she was doing. Feed them and ask questions. Seemed innocent enough and now Allisa was realizing that Blair was cunning and very good at finding out information that she was after. Dino cautioned Blair and Thomas that the investigation was still in progress and nothing should be repeated outside of the room. Steve started to tell them about the connection with a possible terror cell in New York when Dino stopped him.

"Steve, we don't need to bore them with all our stuff, let's just eat and enjoy the meal that Blair has made."

Everyone was eating and the talking continued to focus on the investigation.

Blair looked at her watch and saw that it was eight forty five. She hoped to get to Bill's car and off to the Airport by nine.

She gave Allisa a look and said, "Boy am I full. I could almost use a nap after a meal like that."

"Blair, why don't you let us clean up for you. After all, you did all the work preparing this great meal."

Thomas knew that time was getting close for Blair to have to leave.

"Yeah Blair, let Allisa and me clean up, you go and rest," Thomas added.

"Guess I'm just a little tired from the trip and all. I hope everyone had enough. Don't forget about the pie in the fridge."

Dino and Steve got up and thanked Blair for the dinner. Kevin said he would help Allisa pick-up.

"I was the youngest of six and was always stuck in the kitchen with my mom," Kevin said. Kevin was down to earth and very polite. "I can help Allisa and then we can get going."

Blair said goodnight to everyone and hugged Thomas. She went off to her room and Allisa and Kevin helped Thomas pick-up the dinner dishes. Dino said, "we need to get going." He hoped that the State Police in either New Jersey or New York would have some updated information for him.

Blair pulled the disguise out that she had hid under the bed in her room. She heard the front door close and looked out the bedroom window to see that Kevin, and Steve were getting into the back seat of Dino's Suburban. Dino and Allisa were getting into the front seat and Blair headed down the hall toward the back door.

It was a few minutes past nine.

"Be careful," Thomas said.

"I will. Should I call you when I get to Santa Monica?"

"It might look too suspicious because of the time of night when you would get there. Instead, just call me once you found what you are looking for."

Blair hugged Thomas and headed out the back door. Thomas dialed Bill and let it ring one time. He went to the front porch and stood outside watching to see if the local police patrol car was out front. He did not see anything. Blair ran from the back of the house into the wooded area. She found the brush thick and some low lying branches almost knocked her to the ground. She made her way through the woods to Blue Bird Street. She waited at the edge of the woods to make sure that Bill's car was in sight before she ran out toward him. Bill was glad to see her and pushed the passenger front door open so that she could jump in. Blair ducked down and winked at Bill.

"We make a good Bonnie and Clyde," she said.

"This is a bit more excitement than I normally have," he said. "I'm at your service."

"I want to go to the Philadelphia Airport."

"That's what Thomas said you wanted to do. I'll get there as quick as possible."

Blair sat on the floor until Bill got on the interstate. They headed toward the airport and Blair started to put her disguise on. She pulled her blond hair back and put on the boots and sweat clothes.

"I need to make sure that I don't look like the image that the FBI would be looking for in case they find out that I'm gone."

She also knew that they were looking for her in Los Angeles and she had to be careful. She called the airport and asked for the United flight information. They confirmed that there was a flight leaving for LAX at 10:46 p.m. and that there were seats still available for that flight.

Bill said that they would make it to the Airport in about 45 minutes. She would have to hurry but she could make that flight. If necessary she would use the FBI documents that Allisa made for her. Bill pulled up in front of the Philadelphia Airport and looked for the United sign. Blair said that she really appreciated his help and Thomas would call to let him know if she would need to be picked up.

"Be careful," he said. "I'm not quite sure what you are doing but if you need my help just call me."

"Thank you for everything. I'll explain everything to you once I get back."

Blair jumped out of the car and jogged down the terminal toward the United desk.

"I need to get on your flight to LAX," she told the lady at the desk.

"We have one that leaves at 10:46 but your going to have to hurry."

Blair gave the lady her credit card and the FBI identification fell out on the counter. "Sorry, I didn't know that you were with the FBI. I will issue you a gate pass and call the gate to let them know that you are on the way."

"Thank you," Blair said.

She turned and headed through the terminal toward the departure gate. The United gates were the closest to the main terminal and she was able to make it there in about ten minutes. The longest part was getting through security. She walked up to the gate and handed her boarding pass to the gate Agent.

"Headed to L.A. in a hurry tonight?"

"My fault, I should have been on an earlier flight but the meetings lasted longer than expected."

"You can grab a seat in the back. The flight's not full and most everyone wants to sit closer to the front."

Blair thanked the gate Agent and boarded the plane. She could relax for the four hour flight and figure out a plan on how to get the package. Once she was aboard she called Olly and let her know what flight she was on and when she would arrive.

"I'll pick you up," Olly said.

"That's probably not a good idea. If they are watching the Pub they may be watching you too. I'll grab the local hotel shuttle to the Holiday Inn on Colorado and Second Street. We can meet there and make our plans to get what I'm looking for."

"Just be careful."

"I'm on the plane and ok. I'll see you in a few hours."

Blair leaned back and took a deep breath. I need a plan to get back after I get the package she thought. What if the FBI was right? What if Hunter did send her some information that she should not have? Only time would tell.

The pilot's voice came on overhead and said that they would be departing in a few minutes. He then said that he wanted to recognize a special person on the plane and asked everyone to acknowledge Captain Dennis Montgomery. Captain Montgomery had just flown in from Iraq and was headed to Los Angeles. The people on the plane applauded and Blair watched as a soldier sitting about four rows ahead of her waved. The pilot said that Captain Montgomery was part of the special forces that was stationed in Baghdad. Blair became very nervous. Hunter was stationed in that same group. This was a strange coincidence, or was it. Blair was on her way to discover what the package held. Now she wondered who was this soldier and why was he going to Los Angeles. Blair could not remember the name of Hunter's commander, although he had mentioned him a few times. Brian had also mentioned their commander but what was his name. Blair slouched in her seat and was glad that she was in back of the plane. She had hoped to catch some sleep on the flight. She asked the stewardess for a pillow and blanket. She leaned toward the window and covered her shoulder and part of her face with the blanket.

Captain Montgomery seemed to be reading something. What was it she thought? Blair drifted off as the 747 banked toward the west and climbed to a cruising altitude of 28,000 feet. Captain Montgomery had been looking at some papers that he had on his lap. He read them and was looking at some pictures. They were of Hunter Adams and his wife. Little did the Captain know that Blair Adams was just four rows behind him on the same flight?

TWENTY THREE

John Martin had just finished his phone call to Dino Tuchy. He gave him an update on the situation in New York.

"I have brought our task force up to date on your information regarding the situation in New York. Of course no one is sure what we have yet but we're sure that this could be significant. Dino, once we catch this guy on the motorcycle I will want you to head to New York to help with rounding up this possible terror cell. I feel that they are somehow related."

Dino was happy that the Director was placing this responsibility in him.

"Dino, I'm going to call Don Goth in Manhattan to let him know what we have so far. He will wait to hear from us when we have more details."

Dino was hoping that he could get the situation handled in Bridgewater too.

Don Goth was one of the top FBI Bureau Chiefs. He had been instrumental in the aftermath of the September 11th Twin Tower disaster. Don was also a good friend of John Martin. He once worked as John's Chief Inspector early in their careers. John Martin knew that he could trust Don to handle the situation and work with Dino on it. Not all the Bureau Chiefs worked well together, but Don was the exception.

It was after midnight and Dino pulled into Thomas Adams driveway and got out of the Suburban. Allisa said that she would stay at the Adams home with Thomas and Blair. Dino thought that was a good idea. He figured that she could keep an eye on them. It was close to midnight and she said that Thomas had given her a key.

"I'll call you tomorrow about 9:00 a.m. and we can touch base with Blair and Thomas one more time."

"Can we make it a little later? I was thinking that if I could eat breakfast with them alone maybe I would have more luck getting some questions answered."

"That will work. What if I show up about noon?"

"I like that plan," Allisa said.

Allisa opened the door and said goodnight to Dino. He walked back to the Suburban and told Kevin that he should stay behind and kept an eye on the Adams home.

"You can use Steve's car that is still in the driveway. Just keep an eye on the house and make sure no one comes in or goes anywhere."

Steve offered to do it but Dino said, "We should stay together. I want to make one more pass at the rest area and the abandoned truck."

Allisa knew that she had bought Blair a lot of time. Blair said that she needed until the afternoon and at least this would get her close to noon. Allisa hoped that her trust in letting Blair leave the Adams house would not backfire. She had no idea where Blair was going to but it must be big. When Dino and Steve drove off Dino's cell phone rang.

"Dino, John Martin here. I just got confirmation that our man is on his way from Iraq to Santa Monica. It will take some time to get him from Iraq but I will keep you appraised of his progress. I got confirmation that he is on the last leg of the journey. He should be on a flight to Santa Monica as we speak. We think that he might be able to get some information from Blair, or be able to snoop around because of his relationship with Hunter."

"Thanks for keeping me in the loop sir."

"You're my main man on this one, don't let me down."

Dino knew that everyone still thought that Blair was in Santa Monica.

Dino turned to Steve, "We have to close this thing up here so I can get up to the Big Apple. This is my career opportunity. If it all works out Steve, you know that I will take you with me."

Steve was happy that Dino still trusted him and wanted to keep him as a partner. After Frank was killed and the search of the Adams home had not gone well Steve was concerned that Dino would not trust him with any important assignments. "Thanks Dino, I will do anything to help."

Steve was pleased and sat a little taller in his seat as they drove north toward the rest area at Crosswicks.

The night was cool and Yawer was driving north on Highway 130. He decided to stay on that road because it ran parallel to I-95 and was less traveled than the Interstate. He had looked at his map and saw that the he would meet Highway 1 at North Brunswick. He could stay on that all the way until Elizabeth and than cross over into New York on highway 278 and the Narrows. Yawer wanted to get to a larger city before he changed rides again. It would be less suspicious if a stolen vehicle gets reported in a big city verses in a small town. He would contact El Jaafi when he was a little closer to the Bronx. Yawer remembered back to when his parents were killed in fighting along the Iranian border. The war between Iran and Iraq was deadly for all the civilians. Yawer was taken in by a group of men that gave him food and shelter. El Jaafi was the head man in the tribe of rebels that took him in. Being alone and on the run in the woods, and now trying to get back to the safe house sent his mind spinning back to that time. El Jaafi was like his older brother. Jaafi taught Yawer the art of fighting and how to flee to safety when needed. He was smart and had learned much from El Jaafi. When Jaafi was in trouble and captured by Iranian guerrillas it was Yawer to his rescue. He wanted to prove his value to his mentor. He knew that he would have to tell El Jaafi that he had left some documents in the abandoned truck, but he wanted to tell him in person. He didn't know exactly what he had left, but he felt that he had gathered most of the important documents. He was cunning and was making his way to New York.

The New Jersey State Police were still looking for a single rider on a red Harley. They had cars patrolling the Interstate and sent some cars to check out various sections of Highway 130. Brad Ferguson had contacted Captain Campbell of the Pennsylvania State Police to advise him of their progress. Captain Campbell kept his best friend Bob Douglas in Bridgewater aware in case the fugitive doubled back.

The night and a new ride were the best allies that Yawer could have. He wished that he did not have to escape from the state troopers at the rest area because he was sure that he had left some documents in the pick up truck, but what?

El Jaafi and Abdulla had told the group in the safe house about the situation in Bridgewater. They did not detail their mission but wanted to make sure they had an escape route if necessary. El Jaafi remembered the September 11th incident and that he had to flee the area and stay hidden for weeks until he was able to return home. El Jaafi knew that Yawer would make it back to the house in the Bronx. He had trained Yawer from the time they found him laying on the bodies of his parents. Jaafi treated Yawer as if they were brothers. The war between Iran and Iraq took its toll on many families that lived in small villages along the border. Yawer's family was one of them. The house was a refuge for the group of men that had been planning to disrupt American lives. They had initially planned to plant bombs during the annual Times Square New Years Eve event that always drew a million people and was seen around the world, but security was so heavy that the plan did not come off. They were now hoping to accomplish a disaster that would be carried world wide. A splinted group that was headquartered in London had just successfully created havoc by placing bombs in the London subway system. El Jaafi and Abdulla would have liked to help in this endeavor but they had a mission to complete.

Kevin circled the Adams home and saw the local police cruiser pass him by. The cruiser slowed down and Kevin was sure that it was the same car that had just passed him on Blue Bird Street. Guess he is wondering who I am especially at this time of night Kevin thought. He kept driving and turned on Apple Lane and figured that he should drive out of the area for a little. He saw a donut shop with its lights on at the corner of Apple and Green Street. Kevin thought a cup of coffee and a donut would help him stay awake. He was sure the donut would not be a match for the pumpkin pie that Blair had made, but he needed something, and he pulled into the parking lot.

Kevin was placing his order when the voice behind him said, "put your hands up." Kevin started to turn around and the voice said, "don't move or I'll shoot."

He believed the voice because it sounded a little shaky. Never mess with a shaky person holding a gun, he thought. He could see in the reflection of the counter glass that it was a local police officer.

"I'm with the FBI." Kevin said.

The donut shop clerk fell to the floor behind the counter. This was a small town and a Bridgetown officer holding a gun on an FBI Agent would be big news.

"Put your hands on the counter and spread your legs," the officer said.

Kevin did as instructed but again identified himself.

"I know that your people are in our town but I must make sure you're who you claim to be."

The officer patted Kevin down and felt his gun in the shoulder holster. The officer took the gun out of the holster as Kevin kept his hands on the counter. He then told Kevin to turn around.

"Let's see some identification."

Kevin felt embarrassed that he was not paying attention to anyone following him. Now he had to show his identification to a local cop. Kevin took his right hand and reached into his breast pocket.

"Stop right there. I'll get that for you."

The officer patted Kevin's pocket and reached in and pulled out a FBI badge. The officer looked at it and lowered his gun.

"I'm sorry but I've seen you passing the Adams home a couple of times and I wasn't sure what you were up to."

"Just doing my job," Kevin said.

The officer handed the badge back to Kevin and apologized. Both men laughed a little. Maybe they were just both a little nervous and now were feeling relaxed.

"Can I buy you a coffee and donut," Kevin asked.

They both realized that the young clerk was still on the floor behind the counter. "You can get up, everything is ok."

The clerk looked up from the floor and said, it was just his second day and he was sure it was a holdup. He didn't seem to have heard the conversation between the two lawmen because he was scared to death. They both noticed that he had a large wet ring in the center of his pants when he got off the floor. Neither man mentioned the wet spot but smiled at each other.

"How about two cups of coffee young man," Kevin said.

The clerk was Tom Cappy, a student at Holy Family College, located about 10 miles south of Bridgewater. Tom had just finished his first year at the college and had come home to get a part time job. It was just his just second night at the all night diner and coffee shop. Kevin asked Tom if he was ok.

"What was all that about?"

"We are just looking for someone and mistook each other for him," Kevin answered.

"Is it dangerous for me to be here late at night?"

"We never have any trouble in this town," Jerry McCarthy the local officer answered.

Jerry was on the Bridgewater police force for over ten years, and was the second in command to Captain Douglas. He had noticed Kevin circling the area around the Adams home and had been keeping an eye on him. When he passed Kevin's car he turned and followed him to see where he was going. Jerry wanted to make sure he was protecting Thomas Adams and making sure that it wasn't the fugitive they were looking for in Bridgewater. Tom got the men two cups of coffee and a couple of donuts. The men took their coffee and sat at a small table near the large window in the center of the shop.

"Since we are both doing the same thing lets work out a pattern so were not chasing each other instead of watching the home."

Kevin knew this was a good idea although Dino would not want him to work with local authorities.

"How about if I just positioned my car down the street and you could do the surveillance of the neighborhood," Kevin suggested.

"I have been running past the home about once every fifteen minutes on my route. I also have been circling the back side where the fugitives had hid their car."

"Here is my cell number if you see anything and need assistance just call me," Kevin said.

"Thanks, that's a good idea," Jerry answered.

Both men headed out of the coffee shop and back to their cars. Kevin had been working with the State Police at the Crosswicks rest area, and was good at working with other local authorities. He was originally a local police officer in Philadelphia before joining the FBI. He had been placed on a joint task force working with the Feds and impressed them. The offer to work for the Bureau was a dream opportunity. Kevin's wife Cindy, didn't like the hours. She had to do most everything for their two girls when he was on assignment. He would often be gone on assignment for days without being able to contact her. This was a normal situation for both federal and local officers. A stable home life was hard to have.

Allisa decided to use Blair's bedroom. She knew that Blair would not be back for hours and wanted it to look normal in case someone was watching. She sat on the edge of the bed and hoped that Blair was telling her the truth. She had put a lot of trust in Blair but knew that Blair had put a lot of trust in her. She wondered where Blair had gone to. Allisa set the alarm for 7:00 a.m. and figured that she would ask Thomas in the morning if he knew what Blair was up to. She wondered if Thomas was even aware that Blair had left. Maybe I'll just play it by ear, she thought. Sleep was something that she didn't have much of lately. She lay back on the bed and fell into a deep sleep in minutes.

Dino and Steve headed toward the rest area in Crosswicks. The State Police had a car stationed at the pick up truck and had closed that area of the parking lot off. They finished a fingerprint analysis of the truck and would have the results by early morning. Dino wanted to go through the truck one more time himself. He had left Kevin at the scene when it all happened and felt that Kevin did a great job faxing Steve copies of documents that were found. What about this thing in New York with the area in the Bronx circled? Could this be linked to their original assignment? Dino had questions and he wasn't ready to stop until he had answers. Steve Watkins knew Dino would want to head to New York and there would be no stopping him. Dino was head strong and determined to do it his way. That is what broke up Dino's first marriage. He was engrossed in his work. Dino's wife, Tina, would often tell the kids that their dad was on a special project and would be home soon, but in her mind she never knew when he would be home. The life of being married to a police officer or special Agent was lonely. Many officers and Bureau members had been divorced because of the job. They got out of the Suburban and approached the State Police Officer.

"We would like to take one more look around," Dino said as he displayed his badge. The Officer obliged and handed Dino the keys to the truck.

Dino said, "He didn't take the keys?"

"No, Steve said when they approached the truck he got the bike out of the back with help of the man parked next to him and took off. When they searched the truck they found the keys still in the ignition."

"Do we know anything about the man that helped him get the bike out?"

"He was just a truck driver thinking that he was helping out. The state guys questioned him and got all his information in case they wanted to talk to him again."

They searched the truck and the truck bed for any information that would help their case. Dino knew the crime lab guys would pick up every small item in case it helped to detail who the fugitive was. Dino had to see it for himself.

"Do you know when the report will come in from the crime lab?"

Steve looked at Dino and shrugged his shoulders.

"They said we should have something in the morning."

"If we could find out who this guy is we might be able to get a jump on him. His identity might lead us to where he is going."

Steve knew that Dino was grasping for straws. He hoped the crime lab would give his boss some answers. They came back to their Suburban and the officer said that his Chief Brad Ferguson wanted to know if any identification had been found?

"We hope to have something by morning," Steve answered.

Nothing was learned from this secondary search but Steve was going to follow any lead that Dino felt was important. They would head back to Bridgewater without any more information. The ride back was quiet. Both men were exhausted.

TWENTY FOUR

The flight to Los Angeles was a red eye flight. Most of the passengers would fall to sleep for the whole time and the stewardess service would be minimal. Blair had closed her eyes and kept the small blanket over the corner of her face in case the soldier was to walk by her on the way to the rest room. She did not know who he was but the significance of him being in the same group of Hunter's bothered her. So much has happened that she didn't trust anything to just coincidence. Flying east to west always took a little longer because of head winds. The pilot did not make any announcements because most of the passengers were sleeping. The three stewardesses would take turns walking down the aisle to check on passengers and see if anyone needed something. As one of the stewardess approached, Blair signaled to her.

"I've got a question. Do you know anything about the soldier that the captain introduced when we were taking off?"

"I didn't talk to him but one of the girls said that he got on early in Philadelphia and said he was from Georgia."

"He looks young to be a captain," Blair said.

"Yes," Tammie said, "He told her that he had just left Baghdad yesterday morning."

"I wonder why he is going to Los Angeles if he is from Georgia."

"I'm not sure but maybe his family has moved out there."

Blair was even more concerned about the soldier. What is he on the plane for, and how did it work out that he was on her flight. Did Allisa know where she was going and was he watching her? No that didn't make any sense, he just came in from Baghdad. Blair wished she knew more but figured that she needed to catch a few hours of sleep before landing in Los Angeles.

"Don't say that I asked about him," she told the stewardess.

"I won't," she said. "He is cute!"

Blair left it at that, figuring the stewardess was thinking that she was interested because he was a young cute soldier. She leaned toward the window and closed her eyes. Tomorrow would be a long day and she needed to get back to Philadelphia as soon as she got that package. If things bogged down, she had Allisa's cell phone number to let her know what was going on.

Olly looked at her watch and figured that Blair would arrive in about three hours. The time difference would put her in L.A. about 11:50 p.m. Pacific time. She looked out the front of The Pub and saw the man that had been sitting at a table in front of Hooters for the last couple of hours. Olly knew that he was watching The Pub. He wasn't the normal tourist that would eat and check out the girls for a while then leave. He was drinking something other than alcohol, maybe coke or tea and had not ordered any food. She figured that he was on a one man stake out. I'll keep an eye on him and hope that he's the only one watching us, she said to herself.

Olly had told Blake and Ashley that Blair was concerned that the FBI was watching both her apartment and Hunter's dads place. Blair was trying to find out what was going on. Both of them said that they wanted to help.

"Blair knows that you want to do something to help. She might call one of us later tonight."

"Do you have any idea what is going on?" Blake asked.

"I'm not really sure but she had to go to Bridgewater to check on Hunter's dad." "Is he ok?"

"Yes, but the FBI is also involved in searching Hunters fathers place, and Blair wants to get to the bottom of this."

"I don't blame her," Blake answered.

Blake said, "when I came out of my apartment I noticed a man sitting on a park bench and figured he was watching the apartment. He wasn't a tourist, not the way he was dressed.

Olly said, "I do know that the FBI has been watching her place and The Pub, probably looking for her."

"If we could pretend that she is around that might help." Ashley said, "I still have her apartment key, why don't I go there and they might think I'm Blair."

"That might work Ashley but your hair color would give you away."

"I'll wear one of those crazy hats that Blair loves. It can't hurt."

Olly thought for a minute.

"Let's do that, but wait until near midnight. If you go in the apartment stay there for about an hour. It might cause them to be thrown off the trail here at The Pub."

"How about if I spend the night in her apartment?"

"I don't think you will want to do that Ashley."

"Why Blake?"

"I don't think anyone has cleaned up after that shoot out yet."

"I forgot about that."

Olly said, "The main thing is, we want to just throw them off the trail. Let's set a plan to have Ashley go to the apartment about midnight. Blake you go there to pick her up around 1:00 a.m. like you are going somewhere together. Head off toward Venice, you know around The Whaler, on the corner of Washington down by the beach."

"How about the Halo bar upstairs?"

"Yes, it's always jumping about that time. I know Blair would go there after we closed some times."

"You think they are watching us too?"

"No, I think they are watching to see where Blair is!"

"At least we will feel like we are helping her."

The plan was set. Blake and Ashley would try to throw off the FBI by pretending that Ashley was Blair. This might help Blair get to The Pub and get the package. Olly didn't tell Blake and Ashley that Blair was coming back from Philly that night. She just hoped that the two friends could help buy Blair some time. They would understand and Olly was not sure herself what was happening. She was sure that Blair was in too deep and not experienced enough for this type of espionage.

Blair got out of her seat and went into the bathroom at the rear of the plane. It was about 10:15 p.m. pacific time. She would be in Los Angeles in less than an hour. She wanted to make sure that her disguise was ok and didn't bring too much attention. She had her hair pushed up under the hat she found in Hunter's room and the boots added a flair that was almost stylish. She came out of the bathroom and looked down the aisle to peek at the soldier four rows ahead of her. He seemed to be sleeping. Should she take the chance to walk on past him? She wanted to get a look at him in case they would run into each other. Blair walked down the aisle looking forward only to peek at the soldier as she made her way up the aisle. She noticed that he was sleeping but there was some papers on his lap. Blair continued past the row he was in and stopped about ten rows past him. She looked back and saw that very few people were awake. Those that were seemed to be reading or looking out the windows hoping to catch a glimpse of the Grand Canyon or the lights of a big city they were over. Blair saw the soldier hadn't moved. She headed back toward her seat and slowed as she passed him. The papers were in a folder on his lap but she stopped dead in her tracks when she saw a picture of her and Hunter on his lap. She wanted to grab it off his lap. Why did he have a picture of her and Hunter? Who was this soldier? Blair continued to walk down the aisle toward her seat in row 32. She stood in the aisle for a few minutes when a stewardess asked if she was ok. Blair almost jumped when she heard the voice behind her.

"Yes, just a little stiff from sitting so long."

"One of the girls said you asked about Captain Montgomery."

"Oh, I was just curious."

"Hi, I'm Tammie and I talked to him when he came aboard. He said that he had been flying from Iraq to London and then to Philly before boarding our flight." "Without stopping?"

"That's what he said."

"I wonder why he would do that."

"I asked him, and he said that he was going to the Los Angeles area to see a friend. Must be a chick. Why else would you go to LA when you're from Georgia?"

"I was just interested because I have friends in the military."

"Can I get you anything?"

"No, I'm fine. Just looking forward to getting home."

Blair sat down in her seat. She wanted to find out what the soldier had to do with all of this. She couldn't think. How much more could she take. She decided to sit back down. Her main objective was to get that package. Maybe she would follow the soldier a little when they got off the plane. No better not, I forgot about that picture he has. The pilot told everyone that they were about to make their final approach into the Los Angeles area. Blair had one small carry on and it was in the luggage bin above her seat. It was a duffle bag that she found in Hunter's room. She wanted to bring a few things to change into as a cover. She stood up and got it out. She grabbed a make-up bag out and put the carry on under her seat. She knew that she had just been in the bathroom but she needed to make sure she looked different from the picture that Captain Montgomery had.

"Do you think I could use the bathroom before we land?"

The stewardess looked up.

"Sure we are probably about 30 minutes from landing."

She opened the bathroom door. The term bathroom on a plane was almost an oxymoron. It was more like a closet than a bathroom. She opened her make-up bag and got out her hair brush and some mouse.

"Maybe if I get all this hair under the hat and put a little make-up on I will look different from that picture."

Blair tucked all her hair under the hat and looked in the mirror. She thought about that picture that Captain Montgomery had on his lap. It was from a trip that Hunter had taken her on. They had just finished changing after skydiving and the pilot had taken their picture. The skydiving trip was a real rush. He didn't want her to try it but she insisted. The instructor had taken a video of her and she planned on sending it to her Mom and Dad. She knew that they would be ok because it was over. Couldn't tell them about it before she did it. Her dad would give her a thousand reasons why she should not try it. Guess he was just being a normal dad. She finished with the make-up and looked in the mirror once again. No one knew where she was except for Olly. She didn't tell Allisa that she would be flying somewhere just that she had to go out for a while. Hunter's dad would not tell anyone and she just had to know more about Captain Montgomery. She was going to follow him when they landed. Blair was determined to find out what he was doing and why. The pilot's voice came back across the loudspeaker. We would like everyone to please place your seats in the upright position and return your tray tables to the back of the seats in front of you. We should be on the ground in a few minutes. So much for thirty minutes she thought. I could not have been in here that long. Blair opened the door only to jump back. Captain Montgomery was standing in front of the bathroom door.

"I'm sorry miss, I didn't mean to startle you," he said.

"That's ok."

Blair bent her head down and turned away from the soldier. She headed back to her seat and made sure that she was watching for him to come out of the bathroom. Did she seem too obvious when she walked away? Did it appear that she was hiding something? Holy cow that was close. Captain Montgomery came out of the bathroom and walked back to his seat. Blair noticed that he just looked straight ahead and she felt relieved.

The plane glided to the right and made a large sudden turn. The movement seemed to be a harsh maneuver. The pilot came back on the intercom and asked everyone to please be seated and put their safety belts on. Passengers had worried looks on their face. Was something wrong? The pilot came back on the intercom.

"Folks we were waved off our approach and I'm sorry that I had to make such a sudden turn. Please be assured that everything is ok. It appears that another flight had been on the same approach and we were too close to their airspace."

All the passengers seemed relieved. There was a little laughter and conversation after the announcement. Blair also felt relieved. You never think about crashing but when something like this happens it is your first thought. She leaned out of the aisle to check on the soldier. He was talking to the couple that was sitting across the aisle from him. They seemed to be having a conversation and he was demonstrating something with his hands. The pilot came back on and said we have been cleared to land on the western runway.

"We are the only plane on this approach."

Everyone laughed.

He added a, "I think!"

That made everyone laugh even more. It was a good idea to make a joke of it and it did relieve the passengers. The landing was smooth and everyone applauded as they glided to a stop. The pilot came on and thanked everyone.

"Guess this wasn't too bad, especially because it is my first flight."

The laughter was contagious. Blair chuckled as she stood up at the gate to get her bag from under her seat.

The stewardess said, "The pilot, Dan is a 20 year veteran and he always makes jokes, guess it helps to keep people calm."

"I'm sure he has seen many strange things and laughter always makes people feel less stressed."

"Tammie said that you're with the FBI."

"Yes."

"I bet that's real interesting."

"Not really, I spend most of my time on background research. Not that interesting." "Are you on an assignment?"

"No, just headed home."

Blair had almost forgot that she had to show her FBI identification to board the plane. Guess they don't get too many FBI people on their flights she thought. She tried to keep a watch on Captain Montgomery as she waited to get off the plane.

She kept watching the soldier and if he turned toward the rear of the plane she would look down or toward the back. She was in the last row and although the plane was just a little over half full it was still about ten minutes for all the passengers to collect their bags and unload the plane. She walked about ten feet behind the soldier as they all made their way to the baggage area. She didn't have any luggage just the carry on but she was determined to follow the soldier.

Blair dialed her cell phone.

"Hi Olly, I just landed and will catch the limo to the Holiday Inn as planned."

Olly told her about the plan she worked out with Blake and Ashley.

"Sounds good, anything to throw someone off the trail would help."

"Blair they have a man watching The Pub and we are sure one is watching your apartment. Officer Tuttle came by earlier and asked about you."

"What did you say?"

"I told him that you needed some time and said that you were maybe going to take a ride up to Santa Barbara."

"I really could use a trip like that."

"I'm sure once this is over you could use a long trip alone."

Olly said she was using Sonia's car in case they were watching her. The Suburban would still be parked in her spot behind The Pub.

Blair didn't tell Olly about the soldier. She just wanted to follow him and see if she could get any information that would help her.

"I'll call when I'm close to the Holiday Inn."

"Ok, just be careful."

They approached the luggage area and the soldier seemed to be looking for someone. Blair watched from a distance and saw him approach a tall man in a suit.

Wonder who that is, she thought. Blair took her camera phone out and pretended to be dialing and pointed it toward the two men. She took three pictures and put the phone away. She headed out of the terminal toward the limo pick-up area. She jogged across to the pick-up zone. The limo ride was always the quickest way back to Santa Monica. She would often tell her friends, don't pick me up I'll just take the limo. LAX was always a nightmare to get into and out of especially with the tightened security. The limo headed toward the pick up area and she saw that there was only one other person waiting there. When the limo stopped Blair turned back to make sure no one was watching her. She put her bag on her lap as she slid into the back seat.

"Where is everyone going to?"

The limo driver was making his drop off plan. Many of the passengers were regulars and knew the route.

"Going to the Shutters on Pacific," was the first passenger's response.

"The Holiday Inn on Second," Blair said.

The limo driver headed down Lincoln toward Santa Monica. The ride through Marina del Rey and Venice was always nice. He turned on Ocean Park in Venice and then turned right on Neilson. That would lead into Ocean Avenue and the first drop off at Shutters. This was an exclusive hotel on the beach side of Ocean Avenue that many Hollywood types would stay at. The first passenger thanked the driver and got his bags out of the trunk. The driver got back in and said your next honey. Blair said thanks. The limo pulled off of Ocean onto Colorado and stopped in front of the Holiday Inn. Blair got out and grabbed her bag. She tipped him five dollars and headed into the hotel.

She walked into the lobby and got her cell phone out.

"Hi Olly, I'm here."

"I'll be there in ten minutes to get you. I'm driving Sonia's car."

TWENTY FIVE

Captain Douglas was excited. The call had just come into the station and he was rounding up his men to head out to the field along Apple Lane. He headed to his squad car and thought about calling Dino Tuchy of the FBI but figured that it was late and he would wait to see what his men had found for sure. Captain Douglas had gotten the call about 12:30 a.m. and usually would be home but with all that had happened he decided to stay in the office that night. He was monitoring the car that had been covering the Adams house and had talked to Jerry McCarthy after Jerry had the altercation with Kevin Reese at the all night diner & coffee shop.

Captain Douglas turned onto Apple Lane and slowed down when he saw the two squad cars parked along the north side of the street. He grabbed his flashlight and headed toward the wooded area.

"Hi Captain, hope it wasn't too late to call but I knew that you would want to be here."

"Your right, we needed a break of some sort in this case."

The Bridgewater officer and the State Police Officers were pleased that they were the ones to find the body. As they headed off into the woods two more squad cars pulled up. This was the first break in the disappearance of the second fugitive from the Adams shooting. The team of Bridgewater and State Police Officers had combed through the wooded area for over a day and a half with no results. The heavy rains had flooded the woods and made it almost impossible to search too close to the abandoned car. After the rains had quit the spring winds and a good sunny day helped dry the ground around the abandoned car so they could resume the search for the missing fugitive. The Officers led

Captain Douglas to a spot about thirty feet from the abandoned car to a ravine. You could see a partially exposed body lying in it. It appeared that the legs had been exposed under some tree limbs that may have covered the rest of the body.

"Let's get down there and see what we have."

"We didn't know if we should disturb it before you got here, sir."

"You did the right thing."

It was a drop of about four feet to the body and it looked like a large tree limb was on top of the chest area. The two officers that found the body moved down the ravine to remove the tree limb and see if they could pull the body up. Captain Douglas told them to take care, something may fall out of the clothing. It might give them clues as to who this was.

While they were bringing the body up Kevin Reese called out to the Captain. Captain Douglas was startled to hear him.

"We're over here Kevin."

"I was on my scanner and heard your call. I figured that you probably already called Mr. Tuchy but thought I should be here too."

"I didn't know for sure what we found so I haven't called him yet."

"Guess that make sense. Do you want me to call him for you?"

"Lets get the body up here first and make sure it is who we think it is. It might not even be related to our case."

The local police had a good feeling about Kevin. Maybe because he was once a local cop in Philly and he understood them. He didn't seem to talk down to them like the other FBI personnel.

The body was laid flat on the edge of the ravine and Captain Douglas and Kevin bent over to look at the face. They realized that this was their man because he could not have been dead very long.

"Kevin, you go through his stuff and I will call your boss."

"Thanks Bob, that will sit well with Dino."

The phone rang and Dino jumped. Who would call at this hour? He had just gotten back in the Suburban after looking around the abandoned truck at the Crosswicks rest stop. He didn't recognize the number on the phone's screen.

"Hello, Dino Tuchy here."

"Mr. Tuchy this is Captain Douglas."

"Oh yes Captain, what can I do for you?"

"Hope it isn't too late to call but we believe we have found the body of the missing fugitive."

"That's great news. I appreciate you calling us."

"Your man Reese is here with us and he is going through the personal effects of the man as we speak."

Dino was surprised that Kevin was on the scene. He knew that Kevin was good with local authorities and that was one of the reasons that he left him in Bridgewater. "Can I talk to him?"

"Sure, but before I give him the phone, I want to take the body to the local hospital for examination."

"That's probably a good idea. I can get our crime scene people over there to help with the identification."

Bob Douglas knew that the FBI would want to be in charge. He also knew that it was his men and the state police that had gotten the results and was proud of his people. He would tell them that when they all got together to cover the details of this on going case. Bob handed the phone to Kevin.

"Mr. Tuchy wants to talk to you."

"Hi boss."

"Good job Kevin. I'm very proud of you. Glad you were on the spot with those local guys to make sure everything went ok."

"They found the body sir and were good enough to call me so that we would be involved."

Kevin wanted the local authorities to know that he appreciated what they did and hoped to be able to have them keep him in the loop. He was a good politician.

"Don't let them screw this up Kevin. We are just leaving Crosswicks and should be in Bridgewater in 30 minutes."

"Boss, this is the guy. He was down in a small ravine and covered with branches. Looks like his partner tried to hide him."

"Ok, I'll call the crime lab people and get a CSI team out to the field. Get it all staked out and I want you to stay with the body the whole time."

"No problem sir, but now no one here is covering the Adams house."

"Allisa is in there so I'm not too concerned. She's a good Agent and will watch out for any funny stuff. Maybe you could ask Captain Douglas to keep sending a car past the house."

"I'm sure that's not going to be a problem."

Dino turned to Steve and said that they needed to get back to Bridgewater.

"What's going on?"

"Looks like they found the second fugitive's body in the woods. Either you or Frank must have shot him like you thought."

"Maybe we will have that break you're looking for boss."

Dino wanted out of Bridgewater and onto the bigger action in New York. His early career was solid with a few high spots. The last big bust he was involved in was when Allisa worked with him and they made the major bust of a group selling documents to the Russians. That was a few years ago and he needed one more big case to get the next step on the ladder. A possible terror cell in New York and something to do with Yankee Stadium would be the ticket. Dino was in his mid-forties and time was running out. This was the break he was waiting for.

Steve was happy that they may have gotten one of the fugitives. He was still hurting over the loss of his partner Frank Walker but maybe now they will get some answers. He headed back to the interstate and was glad that there was no traffic this time of night. The traffic would be heavy on a normal morning rush hour. Many commuters used I-95 to get into Philadelphia for work each day. Southern Jersey was a bedroom community for those that worked in the Philadelphia area.

Kevin was pleased that Captain Douglas was willing to have him ride along with the body. He made sure that he gathered any loose items found at the scene in case they belonged to either fugitive. Kevin was a good Agent. He looked at his watch and figured that Dino and Steve would be in Bridgewater in about a half hour. He was hoping that he could get some key information to help the case along.

Yawer was getting close to New Brunswick and where highway 130 and highway One would meet. He was planning on staying on highway One the next ten miles until he could get on Interstate 287. That would lead to the crossing at the Narrows on 278. He planned on calling El Jaafi from Staten Island. Yawer looked down and the truck still had over a quarter tank of gas and he hadn't seen any sign of the police.

Everything was quiet in the safe house. It was tucked into a residential neighborhood that had a mixed population of mostly Hispanic and Arabic people. El Jaafi and Abdullah knew that they were hoping to be there for a few days. The group that was there had their mission and El Jaafi was not part of that plan. They knew that things had gone wrong in Bridgewater. Yawer would make his way back to them and they would make their next move. El Jaafi wanted to head to California. He felt that Blair Adams was the next step in their search.

The group in the Bronx kept a constant lookout because they were always suspicious of everyone. They had noticed that police cars had traveled down the street a little more than normal that night. They never stopped or seemed to be going slow like they were searching for something but seeing police cars coming down the street made everyone nervous.

Yawer had made his way to Perth Ambot and crossed into Staten Island on 440. He wanted to avoid interstate 95 and hoped to find a spot to ditch his latest ride. He continued on highway 440 and looked for an exit that appeared residential. Yawer got off at Arden Avenue and pulled onto a quiet street. He dialed El Jaafi.

"I am close and will be there in about an hour."

"We must make our next move. I will start our plans to travel to Los Angeles." Yawer wanted to tell El Jaafi about the papers that he left in the truck but wasn't certain which ones he had left. Maybe once he was in the safe house he could look through the documents that he had and then he would know what he left behind?

"I must get a new ride," he said to Jaafi.

"You could ditch that one and take the subway here?"

"That's a good idea. I have been afraid that the truck would lead someone to the safe house."

"Get into an area that the subway runs to, and leave the truck."

"I'll call when I'm closer."

"You need to follow the subway to Yankee Stadium. We can come get you if you need."

Yawer felt that was a good plan. Jaafi was rested and Yawer was exhausted. Jaafi helped him keep focused. He got back on Highway 440 and headed up to Interstate 278 and the crossing at the Narrows. The ride had been without incident since he headed off into the woods.

He knew that he must have covered his tracks pretty good at the barn where he found the truck and some fresh clothes. Yawer continued along Highway 278 after crossing at the Verrazano Narrows Bridge. He was in Brooklyn and would get off the highway to look for a subway entrance. This was a highly residential neighborhood along Prospect Park and the Zoo. Yawer parked the truck along Coney Island Avenue and started to walk toward the subway entrance. He would travel by subway through Manhattan to the Bronx. The idea that El Jaafi had was a good one. He made sure that he cleaned the interior of the truck and wiped it off so that no fingerprints remained behind. He left the keys in the ignition and hoped that some kids would take the truck and when they were caught it would throw the authorities off his track. He had his documents in a saddle bag and tossed it over his shoulder like a backpack. It was about 3:00 a.m. and not many people were around. The subway line was about a half a mile away and he could see the entrance ahead. Yawer checked to see that he had change to go through the turnstile. He walked down the steps and entered the tunnel to head toward the Manhattan line. Yawer was very tired. It had been a long time since he had any rest.

Kevin arrived at the Bridgewater hospital and walked with the two ambulance attendees to the morgue. They entered an elevator and went down two flights to the basement. It was a dark and dreary hall that led to a large room with steel tables and sinks around the perimeter. Kevin felt creepy as he watched them move the body from the gurney to the steel table in the center of the room. It was cold in the room and the attendees left him alone once they had completed their job. Kevin looked around and noticed the instruments that were on a roll around steel table near the large sink. He figured that these were the tools that would be used to carve the body of the fugitive open. He hoped that Dino and Steve would arrive soon. Being in the morgue by himself was not something he enjoyed. While on the Philadelphia police force he had been involved in a double homicide investigation. It appeared that a man had shot his wife and then killed himself. The wife had been shot numerous times and they had to get the bullets for evidence. Kevin was assigned the task of overseeing the autopsy and making sure he gathered any evidence from the body. He never forgot the sight of the Medical Examiner sawing the breast bone of the woman open and removing vital organs. There were three bullets lodged in her body. One in the skull and the other two in her torso. The bullets matched the gun found near the husband's body. They also matched the bullet found in the husband's skull. Kevin hoped that he would never have to view that scene again.

Steve crossed the Delaware River at West Bristol and headed toward Bridgewater. He and Dino had been talking about the possibility of both of them heading to New York to continue the investigation. They felt that there was a definite connection with the fugitives and the map that had the area of Yankee Stadium circled. What did this have to do with the Adams investigation? Why did the fugitive that got away have a map to the New York area? Steve and Dino had discussed many possible connections but neither of them came up with an idea that made any sense.

The ride to Bridgewater was short from West Bristol and Dino dialed Kevin. "Where are you now?"

"I'm in the morgue with the body of the fugitive."

"Are the local guys there?"

"No, I came on the ambulance with the body and have been here alone."

"We'll be there in a few minutes. I called the crime scene people and they have dispatched a team back to Bridgewater to meet you at the hospital."

"See you soon boss."

Kevin knew that Dino was happy that he was with the body. Dino never trusted the local police. He would often say that they could not find their dick with both hands in the dark. Kevin wanted to make sure that he covered his ass with Dino but also wanted to keep open the lines of communication with Captain Douglas and the State police. They might have some useful information and they would be more willing to pass it along if he showed respect to their investigation. Captain Douglas came into the room with two other men.

"Kevin, this is Sandy Banks and Paul Marker. They are the Bridgewater Medical Examiners. It will be their responsibility to do the autopsy on our fugitive." "That's great Captain. I just heard from Mr. Tuchy and he will be here in about 5 minutes. I hope it would be ok if we waited for him to be present."

"Shouldn't be a problem. It's not like our guy is going anywhere."

"You've got that one right sir."

Captain Douglas had done some research on the FBI guys that were on this case. He found out that Kevin had been a local cop in Philadelphia and was highly regarded by his peers. He liked Kevin and was willing to make sure that Kevin looked good to his boss. He did not like Dino Tuchy. Dino came off as an arrogant bastard. Captain Douglas told his men that Dino Tuchy was a SOB and only acted like he respected their jurisdiction. It was his town that had the shootings and the FBI was his guest.

It was close to three a.m. and everyone was tired. Finding the body gave them all an adrenalin rush but that was now starting to wear off. Captain Douglas had sent his men home. He knew that tomorrow would be another day of searching for more clues. Kevin sat on a small round metal chair that spun around. It was on wheels and he was moving around the room nervously as he waited for Dino and Steve to arrive. He was concerned that Dino would raise holy hell when he saw the local medical examiners there. Dino had already put a request for the FBI crime scene team and they should be there soon.

Dino and Steve parked in front of the Bridgewater hospital and walked inside. They stopped at the front desk and asked for directions to the morgue. The attendee said that he would take them there. They got in the elevator and Dino looked at Steve."

Guess there is more than one floor to this place."

"The attendee looked back and said we have four floors plus two lower levels."

He knew that Dino was being a smart ass and didn't mind answering him back. He walked them down the hall and they entered the morgue. Dino looked at Kevin who had been wheeling himself around the room on a small metal chair.

"What's going on here?"

Before Kevin could answer Captain Douglas spoke up.

"I asked our team of Medical Examiners to be here to help perform the autopsy on our man. Your guy, Mr. Reese, insisted that we wait until you arrived."

"I know that this is important Captain but I want our CSI team involved. The Director feels that this is a multiple state investigation and that the FBI should take the lead."

"When do you think they will be here?"

"I talked to them a few minutes ago and they are only ten minutes away."

"Mr. Tuchy we need to get an understanding. I am responsible for anything that happens in Bridgewater. You and your people are my guest. We will be every bit a part of this investigation." Dino was taken back by Captain Douglas and his statement. He wanted to push the FBI issue down their throats but knew that the Director John Martin was interested in results and that arguing would only slow those down.

"Of course your team will be an integral part of this investigation. I just want to make sure all the resources of the FBI and our forensic team could help solve this case."

Kevin and Steve were surprised to hear what Dino said. It was not like him to be so cordial.

"Ok Mr. Tuchy, we will wait for the FBI team to arrive. I'm glad that you see that we would be more successful together than just one of us handling this case."

Dino turned to Kevin and said, "Why don't you come with me so you can fill me in on what you found in the woods."

Kevin didn't like that idea. He was sure that Dino would eat his ass out for something.

"Sure boss."

Kevin and Dino walked into the hall leading to the morgue.

"Kevin I'm glad that you were here to hold those assholes off. I wish I could shoot the son of a bitch instead of having him think it is his case."

Kevin knew that Dino was mad, but at least he wasn't mad at him.

"I'm going to have Steve head upstairs to wait for our guys. You stay with the body and don't let them touch anything until I get back."

"Yes sir."

"Send Steve out here."

Kevin walked back into the morgue and told Steve that Dino needed him in the hall. He waited for Steve to leave and than thanked Captain Douglas for covering for him.

"Kid I've seen these FBI types before. You seem like a nice guy and no sense both of us going down in flames."

Kevin smiled at Captain Douglas. "Thanks."

TWENTY SIX

The traffic along 4th was very congested as Olly pulled out of her parking spot to head for the Holiday Inn. This was the first time she had driven Sonia's car. She was going to drive toward Arizona then down Ocean so that she could pull up in front of the hotel. It was a warm night and there were a lot of people still walking through the Promenade. The Pier was crowded with people as she made the left turn onto Colorado Blvd. Olly pulled up in front of the Holiday Inn and Blair came out to meet her.

"I'm so glad to see you," Olly said.

Blair jumped in and Olly looked at her.

"What's with the boots and hat?"

"I wanted to get out of the house and to the airport without being seen. When I was on the plane a strange thing happened."

"How many more strange things can happen to you?"

"There was a soldier on the plane and he was just returning from Iraq. The strange part is when they announced where he was from it was the same group that Hunter was in.

"Your kidding, did he know Hunter?"

"I didn't want to take a chance on talking to him but when I walked by his seat he was holding a picture of Hunter and me on his lap."

"What!"

"Olly I almost froze. I looked down and could not believe that he had our picture. I kept away from him on the flight but followed him to the baggage area."

"Why would you do that?"

"I just had to know what was he doing and why did he have our picture. I got a good picture of him with my camera phone. Maybe Allisa knows who the man was that he met at the airport."

They continued along Colorado to 4th Street. Olly pulled into a parking garage and found a spot on the first level.

"Ok, what is the plan?" she said.

"I left a package at The Pub on the day I was suppose to meet with Allisa. I just picked it up at the post office before I got to The Pub and left it behind the bar. I think that package is what everyone is after."

"What's in the package?"

"I never opened it. It was from Hunter's address in Iraq and I couldn't bring myself to opening it up. I need to get that package and see what's in it."

"I could have opened it for you. It would have saved you this trip."

"I have to open it myself."

Olly understood. Everything that has happened could be related to the package and Blair needed to see its contents.

The CSI team from Philadelphia arrived at the Bridgewater hospital. Steve met them and escorted them to the morgue on the lower level. He explained the situation and that the two local medical examiners were also waiting to perform an autopsy. They were accustomed to friction between local authorities and the FBI. It seemed that anytime there was possibility of a case being solved that everyone wanted to take credit.

Sandy Banks was the Chief Medical Officer and had never worked on an autopsy with these type of implications. He actually was relieved that the FBI was sending an experienced CSI team to help with the process. His assistant Paul was new to the office and had very little experience. Sandy would often be called in on an accident or questionable deaths but never in his ten years in Bridgewater for a murder. Sandy was a nice looking man about forty five years old. He was originally from Scotland and had moved to Bridgewater after his family came to the United States. He had been the Chief Medical Officer for over twenty years and was well respected. His wife Vicki had been a nurse at the Bridgewater hospital when they met. Bridgewater was the normal small town. Sandy appreciated the assistance from the FBI team. They had more experience and could help move the identification along faster to solve this case. Bridgewater had its share of problems but all of them were minor compared to those that the FBI handled.

Steve walked into the morgue and Kevin was sitting on the steel roll around chair. Steve looked at him like you would look at your children.

"What is it with the damn chair?"

"I don't know. Just a place to sit I guess."

Steve smiled. "If it's just a place to sit why are you wheeling around the room?" "Just nervous I guess."

Captain Douglas had left the morgue and Dino was still outside. The two agents thought that Dino would want them to be present during the autopsy. Kevin introduced himself to the CSI team leader. The two medical examiners and the FBI team seemed to be just fine together and started to perform the process of getting ready to start their investigation. The body was in the center of the room on the steel table and Kevin and Steve moved to the back of the room. This was a task that neither of the agents relished.

Dino looked at his watch and figured that they should have some results in the next couple of hours. He wanted to go to the scene in the woods where the body was found. It was a little past three am and he was dead tired. He remembered that he told Allisa that he would be at the Adams house around noon. That was before this development and he would call her in a little while to change that plan.

Yawer had transferred from the Manhattan subway line to the one that would take him to the Bronx. He would get off at the Yankee Stadium stop and walk the last three blocks to the safe house. He looked at his watch and figured that he would call El Jaafi when he got off the subway. There were always people riding the train regardless of the time. He sat in the corner of car and closed his eyes. It had been a long night. Yawer had not been to sleep for close to 48 hours. He still had to go through his back pack to see what documents he may have left in the truck at Crosswicks. He needed to let El Jaafi know in case it would compromise the safe house location. Yawer fell asleep in the corner of the subway car as it rocked on its way to his final destination.

Olly and Blair had set their plan. The Pub would be very busy that night. It was always busy on Karaoke nights. Big John the bouncer always had his hands full with someone drinking too much and thinking they were Elvis. Tommy would be behind the bar and not many people would be paying attention to Manual. Meaghan was the new bartender that was working the same shift with Tommy. She was a tall blond that had been doing some magazine print ads in New York before moving to California. The fun always started slow but as the patrons had a few more drinks it seemed that you could not get them off the small stage in the front corner.

Olly called back to The Pub to tell Manual that there was a package in her office with Blair's name on it. Just take it out the back door and put it in the dumpster. He was confused but would follow here request. Olly thought if she had him do this it would be more normal because every night he would take items out to the dumpster from The Pub. She also didn't want to get anyone else involved because they would ask a lot of questions. Manual was a good employee. He had been at The Pub for over three years and was a hard worker. His English wasn't too good, but he managed to get by. Manual went into the office and found the small package that had a lot of foreign stamps and Blair's name across the front. He took the package from the office and put it on top of some trash that he had collected from behind the bar. He walked to the back door and headed for the dumpster. The dumpster was a small metal trash bin that the city of Santa Monica had stationed behind restaurants along the Promenade. It was about six feet long and four feet tall. It would be perfect for them to retrieve the package from.

Blair had checked with the United Agent before she left the airport for the schedule to return to Philadelphia. There were two direct flights. One left at 6:24 a.m. and the second one left at 8:15 a.m. The goal was to get on the 6:24 a.m. flight. With the time change and help from a western tail wind she would be in Philadelphia before 2 pm. She would have to call Allisa and see if they could buy her some extra time.

Captain Montgomery had settled in his hotel room. He had been flying for over 36 hours from Baghdad to London then Philadelphia and finally to Los Angeles. Dean Curry the Los Angeles FBI Bureau Chief had taken him to his hotel. He was going to catch some sleep before Dean would pick him up in the morning. He had studied the documents that were sent to him and he had planned on using them to help find Blair Adams and use his relationship with Hunter to get information about the missing documents. Captain Montgomery had been an undercover FBI agent for many years. He had been recruited while at West Point. As a young military officer he was highly regarded by his commanding officers. The opportunity to join the FBI was a tough decision to make. He loved the military but thought that he could serve two masters and help protect his country. Being from rural Georgia he had a deep love for his country. He felt that southern young men had a deeper feeling of patriotism than people from other parts of the country. Captain Montgomery was a conservative and religious individual. He also was a fierce fighter. He would find Ms. Adams and use the pretence that Hunter asked him to visit his wife if anything happened to him. He would get the information and those documents if she had them. Dean Curry had informed him that Ms. Adams had not been seen for close to 36 hours. They heard that she had gone to Santa Barbara but one of his men spotted her coming out of her apartment a few hours ago with her friend Blake. They went down to Venice beach and a bar called the Whaler. His men were watching the place to see where she would go to next.

Dino took the elevator back down to the morgue. The CSI team should be in the process of the autopsy. He would get Steve to go with him to the wooded area where the body of the second fugitive was found. Maybe they would find a clue that would move this case along. Dino wanted results and to be able to get to New York.

He knew the FBI Chief in New York pretty well. They had been in Washington early in their careers together. Dino knew that he would be able to work with Don on this case. Don was in a secure position. He had been promoted to the New York post after September 11th and had been instrumental in helping gather critical information in the aftermath of the Twin Towers being hit by the two airplanes. Don was in his 50's and would retire from the New York post. He was well respected by the other agents and John Martin trusted his judgment.

Dino told Kevin to stay with the CSI team and to call him with any updates. He told Steve to come with him to the wooded area where the body was found. Dino hoped that the CSI team would come up with an identification of the body. He knew that the two men found in Ms. Adams apartment that agent Baxter had shot had been identified as Iraqi Nationals. One of them had been identified as Ahmad Aswar an Iraqi National with close ties to Saddam. Ahmad had been held at Abu Ghraib prison by the U.S. Army but let free just a few weeks earlier. The other body was that of El Hassen, also an Iraqi National. The identification of the two men in the Santa Monica shoot out had caused a red alert by the Homeland Security Department. Dean Curry and his agents had been on twenty four hour duty making sure these were the only two men involved in the incident at Blair Adams apartment. There was still no motive but the desire to find the missing documents grew with the identification of these men. Could there be a link with the body found in Bridgewater? Dino had to know and wanted that information as soon as possible. The CSI team had a direct link to both Washington files and those of Interpol.

The trip out to the scene in the wooded area off of Apple Lane was short. It was still very dark but Dino and Steve had brought search equipment. Captain Douglas had one of his men stationed at the scene. Dino called out to him as they approached. The Officer was Jerry McCarthy. He had been on the scene to make sure that it was not disturbed. Jerry had not met the two FBI men but Captain Douglas had told him that they would probably want to conduct their own search. Steve showed Jerry his badge. Dino just said we're here to take over.

"Captain Douglas said you would be here. I will help in any way necessary if you want."

"No we can handle this, "Dino answered.

"That's ok, but I will have to stay until the Captain tells me something different." Dino just gave a look of distain and walked by Jerry and Steve followed him. They walked past the car that had been found the night before. The ravine was about 30 feet beyond the car. It was still muddy around the area but you could see where the body had been hidden. It was about four feet down to the place where the tree limbs still lay on the ground.

"I'm glad that Kevin was here," Dino said.

"The bag of items he retrieved may help us in this investigation. It might be better to send the CSI team out here in daylight to see what they can come up with." "That's probably a good idea Boss."

Both men searched around for a few minutes but found nothing new. The mud had caked over their shoes and Dino struggled to pound it off. They walked past Jerry to their Suburban. Neither man said anything as they got into their vehicle.

Jerry smiled to himself. Dumb shits, only thing they found was mud. He laughed and went back to his squad car to keep a lookout at the scene.

Dino wished that they had found something that would move the investigation along. He was tired and Steve knew that they should rest because it would be a few hours before the CSI team had anything.

"Boss we should go back to the hospital and wait for results. I could use a nap." Steve thought if he suggested it then Dino can blame him for the needed rest. "That's a good idea. I'll give the CSI team the location of the wooded area so they could head there to continue the quest at daylight."

The team at the morgue was busy at work. They had fingerprints faxed to the FBI central bureau in Virginia and to Interpol in London. Photo's were taken and sent along with the fingerprints. The medical examiner from the hospital had waited until the FBI team had the information they needed. Sandy Banks was excited to be involved with such a high profile case. The team also was going through the items that Kevin had retrieved from the scene. There was a gun that had been tucked in the back of the fugitive's belt along with a few items from his pockets. Dino came in and talked to the team leader. He gave them a map with the location of the wooded area off of Apple Lane. They would go over to the scene that had been roped off by the Bridgewater police. Dino told them to call him as soon as any update came in. He covered the plans with Kevin who was still on the metal chair. He was in a corner of the room near the entrance. Everyone was tired but there was still work to be done. Dino said that he and Steve were going to catch some rest, and that they would relieve Kevin in a few hours. Kevin said, "thanks I'll be ok." Steve found a spot in the hospital waiting area that they could catch a nap in. It was empty and they both needed some rest. Once they had some positive information the next step in their plan would be set.

Olly walked down the alley way between The Pub and Brookstone's. It was still busy on the street ahead. She ducked behind The Pub and looked in the dumpster. There it was. The package had a lot of foreign stamps across the top of it and had Blair's name in the center. It was about ten inch's long and maybe weighed three pounds. What was in it she thought? She could hear the music from The Pub. Karaoke had been going good when she left and it was really cooking now.

Santa Monica was full of Hollywood hopefuls and many of them found their way to The Pub on Karaoke nights. Never know when that big break would come. She retrieved the package and headed back down the alley way to the parking garage. Soon they would have the answer to the package contents. Olly walked back to the parking garage on 4th Street. She held the answers that Blair had been looking for.

What could it be that Hunter sent her that would have caused such a high level search from the FBI? The parking garage was almost empty at this time of night. Many of the tourists would have headed back to their hotel rooms and those still in the Promenade would be locals who could walk home or take public transportation. The Pub was the busiest place at this time of night because of Karaoke. It had been very popular and getting in was always tough.

She got into the car and handed Blair the package. Blair held it on her lap and just studied the outside. The package was fairly heavy and had her address on the front. It was not Hunter's writing. He always made a little heart over the I, in her name. The address in the right hand corner was that of the APO Battalion location that Hunter was in. She looked over at Olly.

"I'm not sure what's in here, but it's not from Hunter."

Olly looked surprised. "How do you know?"

"He always had this cute way of writing my name, and this isn't his handwriting. I'm not sure who sent this but it wasn't him."

Blair turned the package over and studied the bottom. It had been taped up with the 2 inch type of package tape that you could buy at a Fed Ex store. She turned it back over and again looked at the front of the package. It was from Iraq. The foreign postage in the left corner was very prominent.

"You're killing me," Olly said. "You have to open it so we can see what the fuss is about."

"I know but I'm afraid to."

"Do you want me to open it for you?"

"No I have to do it."

Olly opened her purse and took out a small pocket knife.

"Here, you can use this to open the package. In case it has something important you don't want to damage the front. The FBI would want it as proof that Hunter did not send it to you."

"That's a good idea."

Blair took the pocket knife and slit open the side of the package so that she could remove the contents without damaging the outside. There was a cardboard carton inside the brown wrapping. She removed the carton and put the outside wrapping on the dash of the car. Olly watched with great anticipation. She wanted to help Blair or at least hurry her up. The carton was folded at the top and easy to open. Blair pulled open the flaps and removed two rubber banded packs of letters. They were all in envelopes and the one on the top was addressed to Hunter from her. She looked over at Olly and said, "These are letters that I sent to Hunter. This doesn't make any sense."

There was a note on top of them. She held it and read it out loud.

Blair,

I know that you must be hurting with the loss of Hunter. Although I had just met you for the first time at his funeral, I felt like I've known you for a long time. Hunter and I were close, and I wanted to send these to you. I found these letters in his foot locker and felt you should have them. I hope that when I get back to the States we can get together. I would like to share some stories of Hunter with you. He was a great friend when we were growing up and a brave soldier. If you need anything please let me know.

Your friend,
Brian

"Olly, these are my letters to Hunter that his friend Brian has sent to me. There isn't anything in here but my letters."

"Who is Brian?"

"Remember I told you about Hunter's friend Brian who was with him on the roof top. He brought his body from Iraq and they had gone to high school together. I introduced you to him at the funeral."

"That was such a difficult time Blair, I just don't remember."

As she looked at the front of each letter she noticed the dates were almost in order. She wasn't sure if Hunter or Brian had done that. They were in two bundles and banded together. Blair was looking at the front of each envelope in the first bundle and Olly watched her. Neither of them spoke. Olly could see tears in Blair's eyes as she fingered the envelopes. Love letters that she had sent to her now dead husband. Blair's words that she shared with Hunter were now back in her hands. Olly had tears in her eyes and didn't know what to say. Blair reached for the second bundle when a small brown manila packet fell on the floor. She leaned over to pick it up. It was sticky on the front and seemed to be stuck to the last of the letters. There was nothing on the outside of the manila packet.

"What is that?" Olly asked as Blair held it in her hands.

"I'm not sure, it was stuck to the last letter."

The manila packet was about 5 X 7 and a seemed to be stuck in the middle of the two packets of letters that Brian had sent to Blair. Blair held the packet and looked over at Olly.

"This isn't anything that I sent to Hunter."

"Open it up."

Blair held the packet and studied it again. She flipped it over and saw that it was closed with two metal tabs. She pulled them up and opened the packet. There were papers folded in the packet and she slid them out. The top paper was written in a foreign language. She looked over at Olly and had a puzzled look on her face.

"I'm not sure what this is, it's in a foreign language."

"Let me see it."

Blair handed the contents to Olly and she looked at the top piece of paper.

"This is Arabic, Blair."

"How do you know?"

"Remember Mr. Thomas who comes in every Friday morning for breakfast. His brother lives in Saudi Arabia and often sends him letters. Mr. Thomas was showing me some pictures from his brother in a letter sent to him and the writing was the same as this."

They started to look through the rest of the contents of the packet. Blair took out what looked like a map and there was a small metal key taped on the corner. All the documents were in Arabic.

"Olly this is probably what the FBI is looking for. Why would Brian send it to me?" Neither woman had any answers and continued to look through the documents in the packet. Blair put all of them back into the small manila envelope and looked over at Olly.

"I need to get back and see if I can find the answer to what these mean and why I have them."

"Blair, we know that there are people killing others to get this information. It will be dangerous. Maybe you should just call the FBI and let them handle it from here."

"I can't because I still don't know why I have them. Did Hunter want me to get these or did Brian do this. I have to get more answers before I give the FBI the packet."

"Yeah, I guess your right. You have to be careful."

"Olly, please get me back to the airport."

Olly started the car and headed back out of the parking garage. She turned right on 4th street and left on Colorado to Lincoln Avenue. She would take Lincoln all the way to LAX. Neither of them spoke for quite a while. Blair had put all the letters and the manila packet back into the larger envelope that they came in.

"Olly, I will call you once I get back to Philly. The plane ride will give me some time to think of how to handle this information. I think I can trust Allisa but I will have to see what has happened in Bridgewater before I tell anyone about this stuff." "How are you going to get back to Bridgewater?"

"Thomas' brother Bill will pick me up and get me back. Allisa is covering for me. If I can make the 6:24 flight I will get back close to noon Eastern time."

"Blair you still have a few hours before that flight leaves. Let's stop at the little diner that you like on Lincoln and Rose and get something to eat."

"I'm ok Olly."

"You have to eat. There's a lot going on and you have to keep your strength up." "Ok but I can't miss that flight."

They stopped at the diner and got something to eat. Olly was trying to keep Blair on an even keel. This was a good idea because she could help Blair put her plan into a clear thought process. Olly knew that Blair was in an emotional turmoil and that she needed some time to think.

Olly suggested that before Blair got the FBI involved in the packet she should find out what the material was about.

"I don't know anyone that reads Arabic."

"Maybe Hunter's dad does."

"That's a good idea. I'll see once I get back."

After they finished Olly and Blair headed to the car.

"Breakfast was a good idea, Olly. I guess I was a little hungry after all. I needed some direction and time to think. Thanks."

"Blair, with all the mental and physical stress you are going through you need to stay healthy. I will get you to the airport in about ten minutes."

The two women sat quietly as Olly drove to LAX. Blair held what she thought might be the reasons for all the break-ins and FBI intrusion into her life. She wasn't sure exactly what she had but knew she should not have them. Olly pulled up to the front of LAX and Blair leaned over and hugged her.

"Call me when you get back."

"You know that I will."

"Blair, I'm worried about you. You are taking too much on and this is very dangerous." "I know, but my apartment has been broken into and men have had a shoot out there. Thomas has had a shoot out in his yard. How much more danger could there be?"

"Just be careful darling."

Blair got out of the car and headed toward the United terminal. Maybe she would get some answers with this new information.

TWENTY SEVEN

The subway car rocked back and forth as Yawer leaned into the corner sleeping. It had been close to two days since he had any sleep and being on the run for the past 24 hours had taken its toll. The next subway stop was at 145th Street. Three young men entered the subway car and looked at each other as they watched Yawer sleeping in the corner. It was not unusual to see someone sleeping on the subway but this passenger had a large backpack that had slid to the floor. One of the men sat across from Yawer and another sat on the seat next to him. The third man stood as the car rocked on its trip through Manhattan toward the Bronx. As the subway slowed to its stop the man standing reached down and picked up the backpack off the floor. They kept an eye on the sleeping man in the corner, he didn't move. The doors of the subway opened and the three men ran out of the car and headed up the stairs to the street level. Yawer moved as he heard the noise of the doors closing and looked to his side for the backpack. It was gone. Yawer jumped up and looked around hoping that the bag had just fallen under his seat. There was no sign of the backpack. He saw that the next stop was 155th Street. That was the exit for Yankee Stadium on that line. He ran back and forth in the subway car but there was no sign of the backpack. He remembered that the safe house was a few blocks east of Yankee Stadium. He would have to get off at the next stop, but where was his backpack and who took it?

The three young men ran down 145th street toward Lenox. They looked back and saw that no one was following them. They stopped on the corner of 145th and Lenox. The man holding the backpack opened it and started to look through its contents. The first thing he found was a silver pistol. None of them recognized what type of gun it was. It was the glock that Yawer had carried with him. The rest of the contents were papers in a foreign language. They studied the papers and none of them could make out what they were but they recognized that it was in Arabic. The neighborhood was very ethnic and many Arabs had moved into the area. They pushed the papers back into the backpack and tossed it into a trash can on the corner. The men took off toward St. Nicholas Avenue. They were hoping that they could find their friend that they knew purchased guns. This one looked expensive.

Kevin found Steve and Dino sleeping in the waiting room off the lobby in the hospital. He called to Dino.

"Sir, they have an identification of the body."

Dino moved slightly but Kevin realized that he would have to physically wake him up. Kevin put his hand on Dino's shoulder.

"Sir, I hate to wake you so soon but they have identification."

Dino slid to a sitting position.

"I was just about to get up. What did you say about identification?"

"They have the identification on the body sir. Interpol was able to trace the fingerprints that the crime scene people sent them."

"Holy shit!"

"He is an Afghanistan rebel with a long association to the Taliban. His name is Omar Kabole. His father is Mohammed Kabole, the former Taliban Deputy Interior Minister."

"What the hell! Now we've got a Taliban rebel involved. The men in Santa Monica were Iraqis. The shit will hit the fan in Washington with this information."

Dino jumped up and yelled at Steve.

"Steve, get up we got to get to the office. The Director is going to go nuts when he has the news of this identification. He will want to mobilize as many men as possible."

Steve looked dazed. He got to his feet and almost stumbled over his own feet.

"I'm with you sir." Steve had no idea what had happened but he knew Dino was headed out to the Suburban and he was going to follow him. You stay here Kevin and keep the situation together here. I'll call Allisa in a little while and let her know what is going on."

Kevin stood in the lobby and watched Steve and Dino jump into the Suburban and drive off. What was he suppose to do? What situation? The one last fugitive had gotten away and the identification made this chapter of the case closed. He headed back toward the morgue to see if there was any follow up to the information he gave to Dino.

Blair entered the LAX terminal and headed for the United desk. Blair was able to get on the early United flight to Philadelphia. Not many people on this flight the attendant said. She used her FBI identification when she was at the desk and was getting use to showing it. The desk clerk, a young man smiled at her and tried to strike up a conversation. Blair was tired but now had a purpose and didn't feel like talking. She thanked the young man and took her boarding pass. She started walking down toward her gate when she was startled by someone calling out her name.

"Ms. Adams."

The voice was not familiar and Blair was afraid to turn around. She knew that the FBI had men looking for her. Did they have someone at the airport? Should she run? The voice sounded close and she had no choice but to stop and turn. "Ms. Adams, I'm so surprised to see you again so soon." Blair looked and was relieved to see that it was Allisa's friend Steven that they had talked to when they left LAX a couple of days ago. She was sure that he would question why she was flying again from Los Angeles to Philadelphia just two days since her last trip on the same route.

"Oh hi," Blair said.

"I'm so surprised to see you. Is Allisa with you?"

Blair was glad that the subject of Allisa seemed to be what Steven wanted to talk about. She remembered that Allisa told Steven that she would look him up when she was back in L.A.

"No she stayed on the east coast. I had to come back and get some documents that were necessary for her case. They were too important to put them in the mail."

"Please tell her that I am looking forward to seeing her again."

"No problem Steven. I am hoping to get a seat in the back of my flight to Philly. Need to catch a few Z's."

"I can help you. What flight are you on?"

"I'm on the 6:28 a.m. flight to Philly."

"Would you like me to get you a first class seat?"

"I don't want to be a problem. A seat in the last row would be just fine."

Blair didn't want everyone on the plane walking by her. Never know who you might see. Having run into Steven was proof that you might meet someone that you just don't want to see, or want to see you. The memory of the soldier on her flight out to LA was still in her mind. She had to find out who he was and who was that at the airport that met him.

"I'll walk with you to the gate."

"That's very nice of you."

Blair thought more people would think they were a couple going on a trip and pay less attention to them. She didn't know if the Los Angeles FBI had put out an APB on her where-a-bouts. They walked to the United gate number 26 and Steven went up to the desk and started to punch in some information. He came back with a new boarding pass and handed it to Blair.

"Please don't forget to tell Allisa I said hello."

"I won't, thanks so much for your help."

Blair could tell that Steven was pleased that he had helped her. She also knew that he could be used for this sort of assistance and figured that is why Allisa kept him on a string. She settled in a chair near the next flights gate that was empty. Steven asked if he could do anything else for her.

"I just wish I could get on the plane first so that I could settle in before all the other passengers."

"I'll come back before they start boarding and get you on the plane."

Blair said thanks and gave him a peck on the cheek. Steven smiled and strolled away.

She had close to an hour before her flight would depart. Blair looked up and saw that it was 5:25 a.m. She got her cell phone out and dialed Allisa's number. It was three hours later in Bridgewater and she was sure that Allisa would be awake.

"Hello Blair, I'm glad that you called. A lot has happened here. Did you find what you were looking for?"

"Yes, and you will be happy with my results."

"What is it?"

"I don't want to say over the phone but I'm on my way back. It might be a little later than noon."

"You're going to be ok because they found the body of the missing fugitive in the woods and have discovered his identity. He is a son of a high ranking Taliban Minister. It looks like the investigation here in Bridgewater is close to being over."

"You're going to want to stick around for the documents that I have. Allisa, you and I can break this thing wide open. I also have a picture on my cell phone and I will need your help to identify the individual that was on my flight out to LA. He might have been from Hunter's battalion in Iraq."

Allisa was silent for a moment. She wanted to be involved if the case was headed to New York but she knew that she would have to be in the background because she was still suppose to be in Santa Monica. If Blair had a key to the mystery Allisa could be in the lead role.

"Blair, I have to at least get an idea of what you found?"

"What if I told you that I found a map, Allisa."

"Oh shit, that's got to be the key. Where did you find it?"

"I will give you all the details when I get there. You have to promise not to tell anyone until we are together and I know what these documents have in them. One problem is they are all in Arabic."

"That's not a problem, I have a friend in the bureau that can help us."

"Wait until I get there and we can handle this together."

"That's a deal Blair. Do you need us to come and get you?"

"No I have that arranged."

"Where are you now?"

"I'll give you all that in a few hours. Give me until around 2:00 p.m."

"Ok."

Blair hung up and dialed Bill. She had told him when he dropped her off at the airport in Philadelphia that she would let him know about picking her up. She gave him her flight information and he said he would be there to meet her in Philadelphia. Everything was set for her return. She was sure that she could trust Allisa and knew that she had what was the key piece to the puzzle. Blair figured that if she had what the FBI and everyone else was searching for that it would be important enough for Allisa to keep it quiet and to want to be the one to reveal the finding.

Allisa was excited with the information that Blair had given her. This could be the break she needed. She would tell Dino when he called that it would be best if she stayed out of the picture and kept an eye on Blair in Bridgewater. She knew that he would want to grab some glory and if he didn't have to worry about her being along it would be easier. Allisa was in the kitchen drinking coffee when Blair had called. Thomas was outside getting the newspaper. He always took a stroll around the yard in the mornings. It was so nice to hear the birds singing and he stopped to watch the small field animals that were making their summer nest and homes. The wooded area behind his house was teaming with squirrels, raccoons and an occasional beaver building a dam. There was a small stream that ran along the edge of the woods and he could watch the activity from his kitchen window. Thomas had been so sad the past few weeks that he had not paid much attention to this rite of spring. He had some excitement now with Blair bringing him into a bit of espionage and he forgot about his sorrow and was nervous about her findings. Thomas came into the kitchen and saw Allisa at the table.

"I'm surprised that we have not heard from Blair yet!"

She told him that Blair just called to let them know that she was on her way back and would tell them what she found.

"I hope that she is being careful," Thomas said.

"She's a bright girl and very smart. I'm sure she will be ok."

Dino called to the Adams home to talk to Allisa.

"The Director has given me the assignment to head to New York and to work with Don on the suspected terror cell. Because we have the background on the escaped fugitive we will be in a lead position."

"That's great Dino. I don't want to mess you up by being involved. How about if I stay here and keep an eye on Blair and Mr. Adams for you?"

"Are you sure that will be ok with you?"

"Too much could go wrong if I'm discovered with you in New York. Too many people know me there."

"I promise if we solve this Allisa I'll give you some of the credit."

"Thanks Dino you have been a good friend and I want to wish you good luck in New York. If you get a chance to call me with an update I would be grateful."

Dino was relieved that Allisa had let him off the hook about going to New York. He wanted to be able to handle the assignment without the fear of people finding out that he had Allisa involved.

"You know that I will keep you in the loop if we have something."

Allisa didn't feel guilty by not telling Dino about Blair's documents. She wasn't sure what Blair had, but it could be as big as Dino's search for the terror cell.

Allisa knew that they could all have success if things worked out right. She would start watching the time with excitement waiting for Blair's return.

The flight was about half full and Blair had a seat in the back of the plane. She had taken a bottle of water from the stewardess as they first came down the aisle and settled in to catch a nap. She clutched the bag she was holding. It was lodged against her left side toward the window where no one could even see that she had anything. The row ahead of her was empty and no one was across from her. She needed the nap just like she needed the breakfast that Olly had forced her into having. The flight was a direct one and she should land in Philly around 1:15 p.m. Allisa said that the coast was clear and Dino would be headed to New York. Blair slept the best she had in a long time. There were still questions to be answered but she felt that she had some of the answers with her.

Yawer walked up and down 155th street hoping to find evidence of his missing backpack. He would have to call El Jaafi and tell him what had happened but did not want to make that call until he had time to search for the backpack. He only knew that when the subway door closed he saw some young men running up the stairway. He could get back on the subway and head back in the opposite direction. It was just one stop back that they got off the train. Did they take his backpack? Yawer thought that they had to be involved. He needed to get the documents that were in the backpack back as soon as possible. It was about 5:00 a.m. and not too many people were on the street. Yawer headed back to the subway station and entered on the other side of the street to head back into Manhattan.

Pat was usually up early but never ventured out at this time. She was watching her sister's dog and he was crying to go outside. It was not exactly what she had planned this time of the morning but here she was out of her brownstone and down the street with the puppy leading the way. She turned off of 7th Avenue toward Columbia University. It would be a good spot for the puppy to run around. She crossed the corner on Lenox and saw what looked like a backpack in a trash can. The puppy stopped to perform his morning deed and Pat looked in the trash can. The bag looked fairly new and was full of maps, books and papers. Maybe a student from Columbia had been robbed and needed this back. She pulled the backpack out of the trash can and opened it. There were a lot of documents all in Arabic and maps. She figured that it was important to someone and would drop it off at the local police station on the way to the campus. The puppy was done with his morning deed and Pat put the droppings in the plastic bag she carried and left it in the trash can that she found the backpack in. She continued on her walk with the backpack over her shoulder.

Yawer got off of the subway at 145th Street and started walking toward the west. He came to Lenox and turned south. If only he knew that at the exact same time Pat was walking on St. Nicholas headed in the same direction, one block west of him.

The Columbia campus would be quiet at this time and there was a police station on the corner of St. Nicholas and 135th Street. Pat saw two Officers standing on the steps of the police station.

"Good morning Officers. I found this backpack on the corner of Lenox just off of 7th in a trash can. Looks like it might belong to a student."

"Thanks Ms. we will get it to the lost and found. It might have some identification inside."

"I looked through it but it is all in Arabic."

Pat was happy that she may have done a good deed for the day. She continued toward the Columbia campus on Cathedral and St. Nicholas. She passed a man that looked suspicious headed in the opposite direction. He had farm hand clothes on and looked out of place. He was looking around like he had lost something. Pat continued on her way, puppy in tow.

The Officer at the Columbia University campus police station took the backpack into the station house. He gave it to the desk clerk and said that a lady found it on the street. It probably belongs to a student. Look through it and see if you can find any identification inside. The desk clerk opened the package and saw that all the documents were in Arabic except for the local maps. He put it on the floor and called upstairs to the detective's desk. One of the local Detectives was Arabic and might be able to help. He was told that Wahid would be in around 10:00 a.m. The bag was left on the floor of the station house with a note to be delivered upstairs to Detective Wahid.

TWENTY EIGHT

The flight from LAX to Philadelphia seemed shorter than expected. Maybe it seemed short because she had slept most of the time. Blair held her package tightly as she heard the pilot tell everyone that he was making his initial approach into the Philadelphia area. He said that they should be on the ground in about 30 minutes. Blair was looking forward to getting back to Bridgewater and finding out what the documents she found held. She had told Bill that she would meet him in front of the United terminal. She would call his cell number when the plane landed. It was about 45 minutes to Bridgewater and she was rested and excited.

Allisa looked at her watch and figured that Blair's plane should be landing soon. She called to her friend Baltazar that she went to NYU with. He had moved to Philadelphia and had majored in Mid-Eastern studies. The FBI had used him many times as an interpreter and she knew that she could trust him. He said that he would be glad to help with some documents and for her just to call later when she had them. They could meet wherever necessary. Allisa had been pacing and Thomas said she was making him nervous.

"I can't help it. Blair is due back at any minute and I hope she has found something that can help solve this."

"So do I," Thomas said.

Blair found her way out of the Philadelphia Airport and had called Bill to tell him that she would meet him in front of the United drop off point. She hurried through the airport and out to the pick up area. She stood on the corner and watched for Bill's car. He pulled up and Blair jumped in.

"I'm so glad to see you," he said. "I can't believe that you were able to make it out there and back so quick."

"I was lucky that the flight schedules worked in my favor. I can't tell you how much I appreciate you doing this for me. I need to get back to Thomas' house as soon as possible."

"I talked to Thomas this morning and he said that the other FBI people were leaving Bridgewater. I hope that is good news."

"I think they have headed to New York because of developments in this case."

"Do you want me to drop you off on Blue Bird or in front of the house?"

"To be safe just drop me off on Blue Bird Street. I can walk through the woods to the back of the house. No sense talking any chances now. Plus I don't want to get you involved."

"I'll do anything for you and Thomas, Blair."

Blair leaned over and gave Bill a hug. They rode along without saying much the rest of the way. Traffic was much heavier than on the ride the night before but they were making good time. Blair never wore a watch and she asked Bill what time it was. He looked down and said it was 1:55 p.m. They were just about 15 minutes from Bridgewater and Blair felt the excitement of her findings tingle through her. Finally she would have some answers to the mystery. Bill slowed down as he drove along Blue Bird behind Thomas' house. Blair leaned over and kissed him on the cheek.

"Thanks so much for your help. We will call you later. You've been such a great help."

Bill didn't ask much about the reason for the trip but he knew that Thomas would fill him in. Blair got out of the car and headed through the woods behind Thomas' house. She came in the back door behind the garage and into the kitchen.

"I'm back!"

Allisa came running into the kitchen and Thomas was not too far behind her. They all hugged. Allisa told Blair that Dino and Steve were probably on their way to New York and that no one was looking for her here. Allisa said that Dino told her the L.A. office had spotted Blair coming out of her apartment the night before.

"I got nervous when he told me that because I was afraid that they would stop you from your plan."

"That was a set up my friend Olly had planned to throw them off. It was my friend Ashley that pretended to be me."

"That was a great idea."

"Olly said that they had been looking for me and that the local FBI had men watching The Pub and my apartment. She figured that if she could throw them off the trail it would be safe for my arrival in Santa Monica."

"I'm so glad that you're back safe," Thomas said.

"We have to sit down and I can go over what I found."

Thomas turned and headed into the living room. Allisa and Blair followed him. Thomas sat in his rocker and Allisa and Blair sat on the couch. Blair opened her bag and brought out the bundles of letters inside. Allisa moved to the edge of the couch. Thomas slid his chair closer as Blair started to open the letters inside. "When I opened the package it was addressed to me from Hunter's unit in Iraq but it was not his handwriting. It was addressed to Mrs. Blair Adams and the return address did not have a name just the unit number on it. The only thing inside was these two bundles of letters. I started to go through them and all of them are letters that I sent to Hunter. He must have kept all of them. I didn't open any of them but when I got to the end of the first bundle and started to look at the second bundle this manila envelope was stuck between the two bundles of letters."

Blair held the manila packet up for both of them to see.

"It doesn't have any writing on it. I opened it and this is what I found."

Both Allisa and Thomas were now standing over Blair as she emptied the contents on the coffee table.

No one was talking as Blair removed some papers and then a map. The writing was all foreign and there was a skeleton key taped to the lower right corner with a map on it. Blair continued to tell them about the contents.

"Olly and I looked at everything inside. It seems that someone had hidden this packet between my letters so that it would not be found. Allisa you said that Hunter was sent on a mission the day after he led a search of one of Saddam's Castles. I think he wanted to make sure this was in a safe place so he stuck it in between my letters until he had time to get it to the proper people."

"That makes sense Blair, because he always followed through himself on every mission. He was suppose to go Riyadh, Saudi Arabia for a debriefing the next day. Instead they asked him to go on another mission because one of the men in his group had been injured in a mine explosion."

Thomas picked up the map and studied it.

"I'm not too familiar with the writing but I can tell you that there are two spots marked on this map that designate something hidden or buried."

Both women looked at Thomas.

"How do you know that?" Allisa asked.

"When we were in the Philippines our command was always doing search and rescue missions. Every once in a while we would find a map with some designation like this. It usually was a symbol for items that either had been buried or hidden during raids on villages. The locals would bury valuables so that invading armies would not steal them."

"Blair, I have a friend that I went to NYU with, his name is Baltazar, and he does a lot of interpreting for the FBI. He is willing to come and look at these for us."

"How do we know that he can be trusted?"

"I know him very well and he will look at everything here and give us the answers to what is inside these documents. We can decide what to do once we know what they say."

"That makes a lot of sense. Give him a call."

While Allisa called Baltazar, Thomas and Blair continued to study the documents.

"He said he will be here in a few hours. He will call when he is on his way so I can give him directions to the house."

All three of them sat around the coffee table looking at documents and thinking about what they held.

"Allisa, I also took this picture in the LAX airport. Do you have any idea who these men are?"

Allisa took the cell phone from Blair and studied the picture.

"The man on the right is Dean Curry, the FBI head in Los Angeles; I'm not sure who the soldier is. Dean is the head of the LA Bureau that they told me to turn over all my information on you to. I told you that they were taking me off the case, and he was going to handle it from where I left off. He isn't a nice guy. I'm not sure why he is meeting the soldier at the airport."

"The soldier is Captain Montgomery. He is the one that was on my plane to LA. He had flown in from Baghdad."

They both wondered why Dean was meeting Captain Montgomery at the airport.

Dino told Steve that when they got to New York that they were suppose to meet Don Goth at the FBI Headquarters in Manhattan. We can coordinate our search with his team and the team from the Bronx. New York had one of the largest groups of FBI personnel in the country. With their heavy population and after 9/11 the office of Homeland Security made sure that the ports of entry on the east coast and the city of New York would be as secure as possible. The possibility of a terror cell operating in New York City had many of the agents mobilized and the city teaming with code red security measures.

The desk Officer in the Columbia University station had the backpack that Pat had turned in taken to the detective's office and put it on the desk of Detective Wahid. He would be in and could look through the documents so that they got to the right person. The shift of detective's arrived a few minutes before 10 am and Wahid was informed that a package was on his desk.

"Why did they bring it to me?"

"They said the material inside was Arabic and you might be able to help them figure out who it might belong too."

He went upstairs and saw the backpack. He went over and got a cup of coffee and a donut and talked to some of the other Detectives that were on his shift.

"What's the backpack on your desk Wahid? Forget your homework!"

They all laughed. He tossed the backpack on the floor.

"Funny guys you should all be on television."

He went through his reports from the break-in that he had been working. Bunch of comedians he thought.

Dino and Steve got to Manhattan and parked in front of the FBI center. Dino put his FBI card on the dash and they locked the doors.

"Just let me do the talking," Dino said.

"Don is a great guy and we can be a big part of this thing."

It was close to noon and Don had just got off the phone with the Director who had informed him that he was sending men from the original investigation site to help with the search for the possible terror cell. Dino had the copy of the documents that Kevin had found at the Crosswicks rest area. He hoped that Don would not be offended that the Director had sent him in to help with the investigation.

Don came out of his office and greeted Dino and Steve.

"Welcome to New York. I just got off the phone with the Director and he said that you would be here to help with the situation. I understand that you have some key information that could help us in the search for a possible terrorist cell operating in our area."

Dino thanked Don and showed him the map that he had.

"You can see the area around Yankee stadium is circled in red and there are arrows leading to the stadium."

"We have added about 30 agents to help with the search area and I have sent an APB to every police station in the five Boroughs to be on the alert for anything suspicious. The Director has also issued a code red for the metro area."

Dino was pleased that Don was extending a welcome and seemed to appreciate their help.

Wahid was sitting at his desk when the Captain of the Columbia University station called all his men in for a briefing.

"We have been put on a code red alert for possible terrorist activity. Anyone that has anything suspicious reports it to me immediately. It appears that a possible terrorist cell may be operating in the area and we need to be on the lookout for anything that may help solve this case."

Wahid went back to his desk and reached for the backpack that was on the floor. He opened it and pulled some of the papers out. He immediately realized that he held critical documents that the Captain had just told everyone to be on the lookout for. There was a map detailing the location of a two story house about three blocks east of Yankee stadium. The writing also detailed a search in Pennsylvania that the owner of the backpack was involved in. The names that were highlighted were that of Blair and Thomas Adams. Wahid took the backpack into the Captain's office.

"Captain, I was delivered this backpack from the desk downstairs and it has some very important documents in it."

He took out the map and translated the material for the Captain. The Captain was excited. This may put us in the middle of this search. He contacted the New York FBI headquarters in Manhattan and faxed them a copy of the map. The Captain also put Wahid on the phone so he could interpret the other material. Although the FBI had added to the number of Agents they had in the field, they did not have many that were fluent in Arabic.

Don called Dino and Steve into his office and told them about the map that was being faxed over from the Columbia Police station. They were excited that some possible leads were already coming forth.

"The information contains maps and details that may be the key to your terror cell." When he said that the detective also found information about Blair and Thomas Adams they knew that this was the real deal. It was all coming together Dino thought. The papers must have belonged to the escaped terrorist from the break in at Thomas Adams' place. This was the only conclusion that they could come up with. The men stood at the fax machine and studied each document that came across. Dino was excited and he and Don would consult the Director before they made their next move.

Yawer walked all through the neighborhood without any luck. He had to finally call El Jaafi to let them know that he was close but had lost the backpack with all the documents inside. El Jaafi said he would inform the men in the safe house but first Yawer should get to the house so they could plan their trip to Los Angeles. Jaafi knew that Yawer was upset and felt that he had failed in his mission. El Jaafi told him that their mission was not complete. They would head to the home of Blair Adams to continue their search. Yawer felt better and looked forward to the trip to Los Angeles.

Allisa's friend Baltazar made it to Bridgewater about 3:30 p.m. He called Allisa when he got off the freeway to get directions to the Adams home. Baltazar was in his mid thirties and had been called by the FBI office in Philadelphia many times for assistance in interpreting documents that they had found. Baltazar was a first generation United States citizen. His parents had traveled to the U.S. from Lebanon during the war with Syria. He studied Middle Eastern history at NYU and he had been asked during his senior year to help the local New York police with a case that required an Arabic interpreter. Baltazar was proud of his involvement and help that he had been to local authorities.

He got to the Adams home and Allisa introduced him to both Thomas and Blair. Allisa explained that she was working on a case, and Blair and Thomas were part of that case. She also told him the importance of the documents and that she was to inform the Director of the FBI herself. The information would be top secret. He was stunned to see the documents that Allisa and Blair had showed him. He took a deep breath and started to explain what they held.

"The map must have been drawn by a close member of the inner circle in Iraq," he said. "It may have been done by Saddam himself. It has two specific areas that seems to show the location of a great wealth, probably gold and the other of massive weapons stored outside of Baghdad."

Blair and Allisa were looking over his right shoulder as he detailed the explanation of the maps details. Thomas sat across from Baltazar with a grim look on his face. The letters that accompanied the map had a detailed legend of the map with locations spelled out.

"This map looks like it had been drawn out about three months before Saddam's fall from power," Baltazar said. "He must have felt that there could be an invasion and he wanted to move stock piles of weapons and gold to a safe hiding spot."

Blair was close to speechless and Allisa was teaming with excitement.

"This is the key to why those men were searching your apartment and Thomas' house. They must have known that Hunter found these documents and thought since nothing had happened for weeks after his death he never turned them in to his commanders. They probably felt he was keeping the treasure for himself."

Both Blair and Thomas knew that could not be true.

"He would never do that," Blair said.

"That's for sure," added Thomas.

"I agree," said Allisa. "If he had planned on sending these items to you he would have attached a note with an explanation. He must have just hid them between your letters Blair for safe keeping."

"What do we do now?"

"Blair we have very important documents that can help the FBI with their mission and obviously help the war effort. I think I should call the Director and give him some idea as to what we have found. We could deliver them to him personally." "Allisa I want to think about this for a little first. It is important that Hunter gets credit for this information, and not thought to be a traitor."

"Blair, I agree with you. With this information and especially the fact that Hunter did not send it to you, but it was in the middle of letters that someone forwarded to you no one could think he was a traitor. Hunter will be a hero and you, and I will be off the hook. We will have solved the mystery."

Blair thought for a few minutes and asked Thomas what he thought.

"I agree with Allisa, you and her need to take these to the number one person in charge. Don't let someone else take credit for it. You will make sure Hunter gets credit for finding them and it would make me feel a lot better."

It was settled. Allisa said she would contact the Director and would just tell him that she had found some very important information to solve the case. He doesn't know that we are together here but the fact that we have critical information will be the key to the meeting.

"We will go to Washington together Blair, you can give him the documents and we will explain everything."

"We're going to have to let him think that we are coming to Washington from California. Everyone still thinks that we are out there."

Dino was very excited as he looked at the faxed information with the location of the possible safe house in the Bronx. Don was putting together his team that would head off to the Bronx and they were getting the military that was stationed in the New York area put on alert to their plan. Don contacted the local N.Y.P.D. headquarters to advise them that the FBI would be carrying out a special high level mission. He asked the police chief for support and that they could set up a perimeter around the suspected safe house. Don also had Dino contact the commander of the National Guard so that they could supply the necessary manpower needed for this mission. The N.Y.P.D. was pleased that the FBI had offered to have them involved. Don told Dino that he and Steve should go with him. They took the map and other documents that were faxed to them. They made copies so that they could be distributed to the other agencies involved. They would take Madison Avenue across to the bridge on 3rd Street in the Bronx. The local police station was on 149th Street and they would set up command there. It was just two blocks from Yankee stadium and gave them easy access to the neighborhood east of the stadium.

Yawer arrived at the safe house and he and El Jaafi were in deep conversation. The leader of the group at the safe house wanted to know what had happened. His men had noticed a heavier concentration of police in the area. At first they associated it with the upcoming night game between the Yankees and Red Sox but it seemed too early for this much police action. Yawer told him that he lost his backpack but they should not worry because the location of the safe house was not in there.

This was the night the group had been planning for. They had all of their operatives in place and would plant the explosives in trash cans around the stadium. The timing of the explosion would be about twenty minutes before the ballgame and many people would be trampled to death. They would create not only a master moment for their cause but this would disrupt most sporting events around the country for a long time. They knew that the American people loved their sports, but the constant fear that a bomb might be planted at any stadium was in the back of most people's minds. Every sporting event had increased security and people were always checked before entering stadiums. The group understood this, and that is why they decided to plant their explosives around the outside of the stadium. If their plans worked out the people inside would hear the explosions and start to rush out and trample those trying to enter. They also had hoped that their next step would be to duplicate the bombing that took place in London at subway stations in the New York area.

El Jaafi told Yawer that they should get Abdulla and leave for California so that the local group would be able to carry out their planned attack. They began to pack their stuff and make reservations for a flight to LAX. El Jaafi was using the new set of identification that they had packed away so as not to cause any attention to them.

It was close to 5:00 p.m. and Dino wanted to check in with the Director.

"Sir, we are closing in on the terrorist group in New York City. It appears that they have a safe house just east of Yankee stadium and Don and I have mobilized both the National Guard and the NYPD. We're going to get them sir."

John Martin was a happy man. He had just gotten a call from Allisa Jones that she was on her way to Washington with information that would solve the mystery of the missing documents. Martin had contacted Dean in Los Angeles to inform him that Allisa was back on the case and it might not be necessary for Dean to get Captain Montgomery involved and blow his cover as an FBI agent. Dean Curry was mad that he was being put on the back burner and that Allisa had found favor with the Director. The Director did not give Dean any information and said that he would send out a memo to all the FBI offices after he had studied the information that had just been made available to him. Dean had to contact Captain Montgomery and inform him to just sit still until there was further direction from Washington. John Martin wanted to let the President know that his team was close to solving the case and that he had further information regarding possible activity in New York. John Martin knew that he also needed to contact the Head of Homeland Security. He had wanted to make sure that it was his team that solved this crisis and that he would get the credit.

TWENTY NINE

El Jaafi had carried his bag out to the car when he noticed a police car at each end of the street. He walked down the street toward the corner to see what other activity was taking place. He saw that there was a military Jeep parked on the next corner and that it appeared that the lights were turned on in Yankee Stadium. It seemed too early for the lights to be on. He walked down Second Street closer to the stadium and could see that vendors had set up carts on the streets that led to the stadium entrance. There were a lot of people on the street around the stadium. It was at least two hours before the big game but he knew that the group at the safe house had said that close to 60,000 people would be at the game. El Jaafi didn't understand Americans. Even when he was in New York before 9/11 he found Americans to be superficial and pre-occupied with sports and sex. He walked back toward the safe house and passed three NYPD officers that were walking toward Yankee stadium. El Jaafi was concerned but again related the activity to the big game. He went into the safe house and told Yawer and Abdulla that they should get going.

The terrorist group led by Fahim Wazir was meeting in the large front room in the lower level making their final plans for that evening. They would set the timers to go off in a sequence so that as people ran away from one explosion another one would go off. They had both nail bombs and plastic dynamite. This was the same type of bombs that they used in the Madrid and London bombings. The plan was to get all the bombs deposited around the stadium about an hour and a half before the game. Fahim told them that they should start leaving in groups of two with their backpacks in ten minutes. He issued both Yankee and Red Sox caps to all of them. The cover had to be convincing. They had to look like fans on the way to the big game. Once they had planted their bombs around the stadium another group would place some bombs at subway stations around the stadium. They were set to go off about an hour after the stadium bombs struck. The goal was to create havoc and disrupt all the future sporting events in America.

El Jaafi wanted to bid them good luck in their attack on the Americans. He was thinking back to the group he participated in before the 9/11 events unfolded. His group had similar goals that were centered around the financial district in New York. Yawer and Abdulla went outside the safe house to wait for El Jaafi. Yawer looked down the street toward the Stadium and could see a large group of men standing on the corner. Abdulla pointed to a high cube dark van on the street a few houses from where they were standing. It had what appeared to be a radar dish on the roof. Yawer moved away from the car parked out in front and toward the men on the street corner. He had a Yankee baseball cap on that he got from the safe house and was following another group of fans that had found parking spots along the street. One of them turned and asked Yawer if he knew if Giambi was back in the line-up. He figured that he could walk with them and look like he was part of their group. "I haven't seen the paper today but I hope he's in the line-up," Yawer answered. He knew they were Yankee fans and thought that was the best answer. They continued their conversation and Yawer walked along side of them listening. He had to get a closer look at the men on the corner. Yawer saw that part of the group of men had weapons as he got closer to them. Yawer told the two men he was walking with that he had to meet a friend. They said, "ok," and waved as they continued toward the Stadium. The men on the corner watched as Yawer moved back down the street about two houses. Yawer then walked up to the porch on a house about four houses from the corner. He sat down on the stoop like he was waiting for someone. He took his cell phone out and started to call back to El Jaafi. When Yawer started toward the corner Abdulla had gone back into the safe house to alert Jaafi that more action was happening at the corner and it seemed unusual to both him and Yawer. He said Yawer was heading down the street to check it out.

Dino and Steve were manning the surveillance truck parked down the street from the safe house. The FBI had been using audio transmission surveillance of the neighborhoods around Yankee Stadium. They had picked up the conversation from the safe house via radar and knew the location and had an idea what their plans were. They had to move in and move in quick before any of the bombs were planted. Orders were given by Don who had been on the corner of the block with the NYPD police chief. They were hoping to stop any of the potential terrorists from leaving the safe house. They mobilized all the men available from both the NYPD and State police unit. They had close to 100 men stationed on the street behind the safe house and now were moving into position to surround it. The goal was to arrest the men that were plotting this ill deed and not have any civilians injured. Orders were given to block the street and detain anyone that was walking down the street. The group of men that were watching fans walk down the street was now getting their orders. They called back that a small group of about three men had just turned the corner and headed toward the Stadium. One of them stopped and appeared to be waiting for someone. They were given orders to detain the man that was still on the street and find the men that had turned the corner. They should all be searched as a precaution. The National Guard had set up a perimeter around Yankee Stadium and was on the look out for anything or anyone suspicious.

Don gave the order to move. Do not let anyone out of the house. They had made sure that all the people on both sides were taken out of their houses and put in a safe area. El Jaafi and Abdulla exited the safe house when a loud speaker announced that they should put their hands up and lay face down on the porch. Abdulla jumped over the small wall on the right side of the porch and ran toward the rear of the house. El Jaafi heard gunfire. It sounded like a machine gun. He knew that the only weapon Abdulla had was a pistol. He ducked back into the safe house as bullets rang out around him. Yawer was still sitting on the porch down the street when two Officers approached him. He was about twenty five houses from the safe house and had heard the shots ring out.

"We need to get you out of this area sir."

Yawer just looked at the officers. They figured that they could both remove this man from the area and check him out.

"We have a police emergency and it is for your own safety that we get you behind the police line on the corner."

Yawer got to his feet and followed the officers. One of the officers told Yawer to hold his arms up and he was searched. They found nothing and figured that he was just a fan headed to the game. Yawer was being protected by New York's finest.

The National Guard along with the NYPD moved in to cover all the escape routes from the house. Fahim Wazir yelled orders to his men. They would fight to the death he told them. El Jaafi had an unfinished mission. Where was Yawer he thought? He had to escape this mess so that he could continue to search for the documents that brought him back to the United States. He figured that Abdullah was lost to the cause. Gunfire was loud and seemed to come from all directions. Fahim ordered his men to toss the nail bombs into the police that had mobilized around the safe house. As his the men moved toward the windows to achieve this order they were chased back by a wall of bullets. It seemed hopeless for the terrorist. All the men that surrounded the house were ordered to keep anyone from escaping. The hope was that they could arrest these men. The reality was that they would stop them at any cost. The military men that joined the FBI and NYPD had brought the most sophisticated weapons available.

News of the raid on the safe house had spread to the news media that had gathered for the ballgame. FOX was covering the game and had their T.V. blimp move into position over the suspected area for film footage. Television stations around the country picked up the feed and now it was being carried live across the country. More people would watch this than those that watched O.J. evade police on the LA freeway. It was close to 6:00 p.m. and the National Guard had covered all the entrances to Yankee Stadium. They requested that the game be called off due to the possible terrorist attack on the stadium. The American League president was being called by George Steinbrenner with the information. George didn't want to cancel the game, but would do whatever he had to protect the players and fans. The fans that were arriving were told that they would not be let into the stadium until it was searched for possible bombs. All those that had entered were being removed and some protested because their tickets had already been torn in half at the gate. Everyone was being told that a bomb threat was called in and safety of the fans was more important than the individual game.

"You will all be allowed back in once we have cleared the area," the officers were telling the fans.

Dino had called the Director from the van he was in and told him that they uncovered the terrorist safe house and were moving in to arrest everyone. John Martin was excited. He would make sure that everyone knew that it was the FBI that uncovered this plot. He told Dino that he had heard from Allisa Jones and she was headed to Washington with news of the missing documents. John Martin was excited. It looked like he would have news of both the secret documents that they were looking for and a key terrorist cell uncovered in New York. Dino was glad that he was off the hook with Allisa and Blair Adams being in Bridgewater. He had his glory moment in New York and the director was happy with him.

The safe house was now ablaze with bullets coming from both inside, and ones being delivered into the house from the National Guard. The Guard had a tank being mobilized and it was headed down the street into position. There were four military vehicles including a rocket launcher now parked behind the safe house in the alley. Don had the NYPD Police Chief and the Commander of the National Guard with him, as Dino and Steve watched from the FBI Swat truck. They were still monitoring the action inside the safe house and although voices could be heard nothing they were saying could be made out. There was a lot of yelling and the conversation was in Arabic. At times there would be a lull in the action and then it would resume with retaliation from inside the house. The Swat truck had been moved further down the street as the action picked up. Dino had a unit just like this one available to him in Philadelphia so he was experienced in its operation. He had told Steve that they should continue to monitor what was happening inside the house so that he could relay that to Don and the units surrounding it. He was hoping to get the men inside to see that there was no hope and to surrender. The trial and glory would last for years he thought.

The Army had brought a tank to the front of the safe house. It had a short cannon type of a gun on the front that was about four feet long and maybe a foot and a half wide. Dino had never seen anything quite like this before. It had to be a new military weapon. The cannon on the front of the tank was raised and pointed at the target. Don had hooked up a loud speaker and called out to the terrorists in the safe house.

"This is the FBI. You are surrounded and must toss your weapons out. We will give you five minutes and if you do not respond we will blast the front of the house and kill everyone inside."

It was very quiet for what seemed like an eternity. Crowds had been pushed back as far as possible but the strain of onlookers pressed their way along the police lines. The NYPD police chief had ordered his men to make sure that no one got closer than two blocks from the action at the house. It was a mess. Over 60,000 baseball fans and media were present for the big game and now they had to keep them away from both the Stadium and the blocks that surrounded the house under siege. Reporters had found their way to the front of the throng of people. They demanded some access or at least a response to their questions. Everyone was now aware that not only was there thought to be a bomb planted at Yankee Stadium, but now there was a group of terrorist located just blocks away.

Don called out again for a response from the terrorist inside.

"This is your last warning, you have two minutes to respond."

Just then a man stepped out onto the porch and held a machine gun in the air. It wasn't clear if he was giving the signal that he was about to surrender or was he going to fire on the police and guard unit outside of the house.

"Death to the infidels," was his cry as he pulled the machine gun into position to shoot. Bullets rang out from the gun, but all of them went straight up in the air as snipers positioned across the street on a roof top shot him through the temple and into the chest. More bullets rang out from the house and a package was tossed out from the porch. The bomb rang out a loud blast that made everyone on the street hit the ground. Steel flew from the bomb and penetrated everything for fifty feet. It was a nail bomb, like the ones used in the subway attacks in London just weeks ago.

The response was fast and loud. The smoke from the gun on the front of the tank left a small cloud that rose over the street. The noise came almost a full minute after the smoke was seen. It sent people running from their position two blocks away. The devastation was unbelievable. The whole front of the house had collapsed. The National Guard that was in positions both in the front and rear of the house fired a hail storm of bullets into the house to insure that anyone that survived was taken out.

Dino and Steve had dropped their listening devises and fell to the floor of the Swat truck. Their ears rang with a terrible buzzing. What had happened? Who gave the order? Dino struggled to his feet and looked at the viewing screen that had the house on closed circuit. It was leveled!

The Guard had moved in and was positioned all around the house with weapons drawn. Nothing was moving from inside. The tank had fired a devastating blast that exploded on contact. That is why no one heard the blast right away. It only happened when it penetrated the interior of the house. The explosion came from inside and caused the house to blow up and out from the interior. This caused total devastation and eliminated everyone inside. The block was covered in ash but none of the homes on either side had any structural damage. There were some broken windows on the block and bricks and wood shattered all over but this type of a devise limited the extensive damage to just the target area.

Dino climbed out of the truck and stood almost stunned as he looked at the blast area. It looked like a picture you would see from a war zone. Nothing remained from the terrorist hide out. Steve followed Dino and both of them held their hands over their ears. The noise was still ringing in their head from the blast.

People had run from the police lines when the first blast took place. The nail bomb had been loud. When the second blast that came from the cannon happened many people just fell into a crouching position. The FOX blimp had been moved out of the area before the first blast to a position further away. It appeared that the guard had informed them that it would be dangerous to stay put. They caught the whole thing on film for the country to watch. Millions of people were glued to their televisions around the world. The incident had been fed via satellite to over 100 world news agencies.

John Martin and the Head of Homeland Security had tuned in along with the President. John Martin was taking credit for the position that his men had taken when the blast had hit the house. The President was startled, "What the hell," he said. It became obvious to the others that he had never seen any real action. John Martin explained the type of blast and how the military had developed this for urban warfare. The President was impressed when he saw how the damage was limited, but had taken the target out. John Martin was telling everyone that he had one more surprise. He was meeting with one of his top Agents that may have discovered critical material that they were searching for.

Allisa was telling Blair how they would precede. She would tell the Director that she and Blair discovered the map and packet of information among a package sent to Blair from someone in Iraq. The package was not sent by Hunter. He must have hidden the documents to protect them when he went on his last mission. His original plans would have let him deliver them to his commander in Riyadh, Saudi Arabia.

"Blair, I will make sure Hunter is known as a hero. He uncovered this critical information and you helped get it to me." Blair was happy that she trusted Allisa. Her trust was right and Allisa would make sure that the information he found was credited to him. Blair was proud. She was proud of her husband and what he had accomplished.

Thomas had told Blair that they could use his car to go to Washington.

"We are planning on telling the Director that we found the packet in Santa Monica and brought it to him first. Allisa doesn't want to get you or her friend Baltazar involved."

"Guess your right," Thomas said. "Sounds like a good plan."

Allisa said that they should rent a car to drive to the Capital.

"I don't want to get anyone into trouble or cause further suspicions."

Thomas agreed and said, he would drive them into Philadelphia to rent a vehicle. Blair said she had to call Olly and her parents to fill them in. Allisa said, "be careful not to tell them too much until we get the documents into the proper hands." Blair understood.

THIRTY

The FBI building in Arlington, Virginia was very impressive. The long corridor leading to the office of the director seemed to go on forever. Blair and Allisa had changed clothes before leaving the Adams home. Allisa suggested that they might meet some high ranking personnel in Washington and they should look as professional as possible. This would be Allisa's moment. She had lost the confidence of the director just a few days ago when he gave her assignment to Dean Curry in Los Angeles. He was so concerned that the information would not be found that he arranged to fly Captain Montgomery from Iraq to Santa Monica so that he might get the information out of Blair Adams. She had not told the Director about bringing Ms. Adams with her. This would be the icing on the cake. Not only did she solve the case and find the documents but she had the confidence and support of the person the FBI thought might be hiding the secret material.

Blair was impressed when they entered the building and Allisa showed her badge and announced that she had a meeting with the Director. The military personnel at the entrance called someone and they were both escorted into the lobby through a large metal detector. Allisa had her FBI badge on and made sure Blair had left hers in Bridgewater. Blair was given a visitors badge that she placed on her jacket. Blair held the package tightly as the military personnel requested to scan it before they proceeded. She looked at Allisa and was told it was ok; they will give it back once they run it through the scanner. The package was handed back to Blair and the military guard escorted them down the long winding hall to the office of John Franklin Martin,

Director of the FBI. This was so unreal to Blair. Here she was in the inner sanctum of the Federal Bureau of Investigation.

Allisa and Blair had discussed their plan on the ride from Bridgewater. They would tell the director how they found the map and key information in the middle of Blair's letters to Hunter. They would also tell him that Blair had some Middle Eastern studies in college and had a little knowledge of what the map entailed. She was not able to interpret the foreign language but did understand a couple of the symbols on the map. They knew the FBI would have experts analyze every piece of the documents and take action according to what it held. Allisa wanted Blair to get credit for part of this. They had become friends. Allisa told Blair on the ride that she should consider a career in the FBI.

"You would be a great agent Blair. You handled so many stressful things. Not everyone in the bureau gets involved in stuff like this. Many Agents live normal lives and never have a case that sees danger."

"I'll admit that as it went along and I watched you work I did get a thrill out of the search. When I remembered about the package that came from Iraq it all came together."

The military guard had been walking about two steps ahead of the two women as they both held hands. Blair was nervous and Allisa wanted her to be as calm as possible.

"We're going to be in a lot of meetings with key people so just remain calm and keep to the facts."

They approached an office that had a large entrance. The mahogany door had to be ten feet tall and four feet wide. The military guard knocked on the door and they heard a click, then it opened. There must have been an automatic release that someone pushed because no one was standing on the inside. The two women walked inside and they were in an outer office area. It had three large leather chairs and two couches with assorted tables and a large conference table with twelve chairs around it. The guard positioned himself at the door as it closed behind them.

Allisa had been in the building many times in her career but never in the office of the director. Not many field agents ever made it this far. It seemed like something out of a movie to Blair. She said that once in a play that she was in they had a set that was very similar to the office they were in.

"What was the play about?"

Before Blair could answer the large inner door opened and John Martin walked into the outer office. He walked over to Allisa and shook her hand as he turned to Blair with a questioned looked.

"Allisa, I'm so glad to see you again."

"Sir I'm glad to be here. I want to introduce you to Mrs. Blair Adams."

The Director stepped back and smiled at Blair.

"Mrs. Adams, I'm so sorry for your loss. We all hope that all of our military men return from their assignments safely but sometimes that doesn't happen."

John Martin did not know how much Blair knew but wanted to remain on the safe side of his conversation when referring to her husband. He did not know who Allisa was bringing with her but when the closed circuit T.V. scanned both guests he knew who Mrs. Adams was from her pictures that he had in the file. He wasn't sure why Allisa had brought her but also saw the package that Blair held under her arm. She was a beautiful woman. He had seen some of her photo's that the bureau had in her file from various plays she had been in. He thought she was even better looking in person.

"I'm glad to meet you, sir. I know that my husband was a good soldier. He never told me about what he did or where he was when he was on any assignment, but now I am able to put it together. He must have been an agent of yours and I'm sure a good one."

Allisa was pleased that Blair had been direct with John Martin and had not said that Allisa told her about Hunter's FBI involvement.

"Yes Mrs. Adams, your husband was an excellent field agent for us. He was very brave and always willing to help his country. I see that you have a package. Is it for me?"

"Yes sir, but we need to discuss the contents with you. Allisa and I found the package after all the strange things started to happen to both Hunter's dad and myself. We have to be sure that your people understand the way the package got to me and that Hunter was a hero not a rogue agent."

John Martin was surprised with the comments but impressed with Ms. Adams straight forward approach. She was no dummy. Not the Hollywood starlet he had pictured when reviewing her file. She had attended the University of Mississippi and was involved in both Journalism as well as the School of Performing Arts. This was a smart cookie he thought.

"Mrs. Adams, your right, your husband was a great agent and had many successful missions for us. We are saddened with his loss as you are and we will remember him as a hero. Can we have a seat and look at the package you brought me?"

Allisa was surprised at how calm Blair was, and that she was handling herself very professionally. She figured that the Director would overwhelm Blair with his presence and the office would be overpowering to her. They moved over to the conference table and John Martin pulled out two chairs for the women. He had positioned himself in the middle seat at the end of the table. Blair sat on his right hand side and Allisa moved to the seat on the left side. Blair put the package on the table and said that she would explain the contents, but Mr. Martin should understand that without the help of Allisa none of this would have come to light.

"Sir, Allisa stayed in contact with me the last few days and suggested that I might have something that was sent to me of critical importance. I had received this package a few days ago from Iraq. I went to the post office to claim it but it was the same day that I found out that there had been a second break in in my apartment and men had been shot and killed. I left the package at my work and forgot all about it."

"I felt that Blair was being very honest with me about not having anything from her husband sir but we knew that the documents had to be somewhere. You said that the people had not found anything in Bridgewater and it made more sense that the package would be sent to Hunter's wife not his father," stated Allisa.

The Director was sitting in the middle of two women who were leading him down the path of their adventure the past few days. He was usually the one in charge but he just sat back listening to the developments as they unraveled the story.

"I remembered about the package yesterday and called Allisa right away. We got it from The Pub where I left it, and found this information inside."

The Director moved to the edge of his seat as Blair started to open the package.

"At first, I could not understand why there was not a name on the return label. Hunter always put his initials on anything he sent to me. The handwriting was also different. It wasn't from him. We opened the package," and Blair continued to take the bundle of letters out of the package, "the only thing we found was two bundles of letters that Hunter had saved. These are all letters that I had sent him while he was away. We looked through the first bunch when an envelope stuck to the bottom of the first bundle fell on the floor. Here it is."

Blair handed John Martin the manila envelope. He held it in his hands as Allisa added.

"Sir you will notice that there is nothing written on the envelope and we were not sure what was in it."

John Martin opened the envelope and his excitement rose as he saw a map on the top of the other notes.

"We are not sure what the map means sir, but Blair said that she had a mid-eastern studies class and the two symbols showed that there was something hidden in these two spots."

"Holy shit this is it."

John Martin could not contain himself. He jumped up from his seat and the two women looked at each other. John Martin grabbed his phone and called to someone to get it his office right away. They were successful in weaving their story without the Director asking questions. They were in the lead and the package would be his focus.

Two men knocked on the door and John Martin reached under the table and the door opened. They came into the office area and John Martin introduced Allisa and Blair to them. He told them to sit at the table and look at the map and other paper inside the package. They moved to the middle of the table and spread the documents out to review them. The map was their main focus. They were talking fast and thenDlooked at the director. "You might want us to study these for a while sir." John Martin knew that they did not want to tell him the contents with the two women in the room. "You both have been through so much. How about if we get you into a hotel and let us go over these documents. I know you have had a long day already with the trip here from California." "That is ok with me sir," Blair answered. "But I must remind you that my husband did not send these to me and he was killed before he could get them to his commander. They came from Iraq but not from him."

"Mrs. Adams, I will assure you that we know that your husband was a hero and will be remembered that way. I will also tell you that you and Allisa have done a great service to your country. Allisa you have my apology for not believing in you. You have done a great job and I will be putting you in for a well deserved promotion. Mrs. Adams I would like you to get some rest. Allisa will go with you and I want to talk to you more about our organization."

Both women walked to the door and John Martin told the guard to please escort the women to the lobby and he would have someone meet them and take them to a hotel. We will take care of everything he told them. Allisa mentioned that they heard about the incident in New York and hoped that it had gone well.

"I'm not sure if you remember Dino Tuchy from the Philadelphia Bureau, but he and his people were instrumental in that effort. We were very successful in removing a large terrorist threat in New York."

They were pleased that they had been successful in protecting Dino from being involved with Allisa in this mystery and that the Director never questioned why Blair had not been seen for the past day and a half. The two women walked back down the hallway holding hands smiling at each other. The guard led them to the lobby area and they were met by a woman who identified herself as Diane Roper, special agent with the FBI. She said that she would escort them to the Marriott in Arlington. Allisa said that they had parked their rental car in the visitor's lot.

"It will be ok. Give me the license number and description and I will make sure they tag it as being ok for the night."

"I think we would like to take the car with us to the hotel," Blair said.

Ms. Roper said that would be ok and she would go with them and have someone follow her to bring her back.

The women walked to the parking lot and Allisa smiled at Blair.

"You did a great job in there. I was very impressed and so was the Director." "Thanks Allisa, but I could not have done it without you."

They got into the rental car and Ms. Roper was giving someone instructions. She got into the back seat and said that she would give Allisa directions to the Marriott. "The Director wanted me to tell you that he has called to reserve rooms for both of you and anything you need please charge it to the room. We are taking care of everything."

Blair and Allisa had packed small bags in case the question came up about their travel from California without any luggage. They also weren't sure how long they would be in the nations Capital.

The ride to the Marriott was short. Ms. Roper asked Blair some questions as they drove to the hotel.

"Is this your first trip to Washington?"

"No my parents had brought me here before and I always enjoyed sight seeing around the area."

"If there is any place in particular that you would like to see please let me know," Ms. Roper added. Blair sat in the passenger seat and was pleased with the results of the meeting with the director. She hoped that she accomplished what she had intended to and that her trust in him would be as fruitful as her trust in Allisa had been.

The view of the Capital's building from the Virginia side of the Potomac was grand. They could see the Washington Monument and the top of the dome of the Lincoln Memorial. Blair listened to Ms. Roper and Allisa talking about their colleagues that they both knew. The Director was right. She was tired. She would call Hunter's dad when they got to the hotel and fill in her parents and Olly in on the meeting with the Director. The package was in the hands of the FBI and her mission was over.

THIRTY ONE

The view from their rooms was of the Potomac River and Blair could see some of the buildings in Washington. She looked out of her window and could see the Arlington Memorial Bridge and the top of the Lincoln Memorial. She knew that they had done the right thing. She had felt a rush of emotion as she looked out over the view. She had told Allisa that she needed some rest but didn't know if she could calm down enough to actually rest. She had called her parents on the way to Washington and told them an abbreviated version of the events that had happened. They wanted to come to meet her but she said she was "ok," and she would call them a little later. She also had called Olly and told her everything that had happened. Olly was pleased that it was over and Blair was safe. Hunter's dad was happy that Blair and Allisa had delivered the package in person and told their story to the Director.

Allisa sat in her room and was very content with the direction the case had taken. She wanted to call Dino but she knew that wasn't the best idea. He was deep into the incident in New York and had been on the news channels constantly with a recap of the terrorist threat to blow up Yankee Stadium. He was a hero and would get the respect of every agent. She was sure that he would be promoted and she would probably never see him again.

Washington was especially beautiful in the spring. The trees were full of cherry blossoms and they had a fragrant smell that filled the air outside. The Marriott was located on George Washington Memorial Parkway and had a great view of the river and downtown Washington. Blair sat on a large leather chair by the window and just looked at the view. She remembered that her parents had brought her to Washington when she was about ten and they went to see all the tourist sites. It was even more beautiful than she remembered.

Her phone rang and she got up to answer it.

"Hello," it was Allisa.

"Blair I'm still so pumped up that I can't rest, how about you?"

"Me too!"

"Come over to my room and we can talk."

Blair walked down the hall to room 2412 and knocked on the door. Allisa opened her door and the women hugged. They had truly become friends and were bonded together by the events of the past few days. They moved over by the window and sat across from each other on the two chairs.

"Allisa, I'm so glad that you talked me into going with you to Bridgewater. You are a good friend."

"Blair, I felt you could handle yourself and what had to be done but you surprised me. You are very strong and have a great sense of what has to be done. You adapted to the situation that came up and took charge when necessary."

They both looked out of the window. The sky was a deep blue and made the Potomac look clear, especially from the 24th floor. The phone rang in the room and both women jumped up. Allisa answered and a wide smile came across her face as she listened to the conversation. She finally said something back to the caller.

"Sir, I'm glad that the information is that important to our effort. Yes we would be glad to meet with you and the President."

Blair sat stunned as she heard Allisa mention the President.

"When do you want to come get us sir?"

Allisa hung up and jumped up and down. Blair just looked at her and seemed in a daze.

"What else did he say?"

"They had experts look at both the map and the other documents and we may have uncovered storage of weapons and a pile of gold that Saddam Hussein had hidden. The information is being fed to our forces as we speak and they are planning raids to check everything out."

"What about the meeting with the President?"

"The director said that they informed the President and he was very excited about the findings and wanted to award Hunter a medal of honor. He will want to present it to you at a special event once they check out the map's details."

Blair sat stunned as Allisa was talking. So much had taken place and now the President wanted to meet them.

"The Director wants us to meet him for dinner about 7 p.m. He said that the head of Homeland Security and a couple of other Washington dignitaries may also be there. Details of the dinner were still being worked out."

"I need something nicer to wear and these shoes will never do."

Allisa started to laugh and Blair laughed with her.

"You and your shoes."

"We can go downstairs, they have a few shops in the lobby area and we can just charge the stuff to the room. Remember they said the FBI is taking care of everything."

Dino and Steve had been on a whirlwind of news media stations covering the mission in New York and the terrorist threat that they uncovered. Don had told Dino that he was just a year from retirement and that Dino should take the lead in the case.

"You will have to follow up with this for the next year because of its implications. This is the first major terrorist cell that has been handled in front of the whole world on our soil."

Dino was happy and always mentioned Don and the NYPD when he was giving details of the events. Steve would be promoted along with Dino and viewed as instrumental in this case.

Back in Bridgewater, the local police had completed the final task of recording all the details of their involvement with the FBI. Captain Douglas had given Kevin Reese from the FBI credit with helping organize a joint effort to solve the investigation in his town. Kevin had stayed back as instructed by Dino and made sure that all the loose ends were taken care of in Bridgewater. He stopped in at Mr. Adams house to thank him for his help. Thomas told him that Allisa and Blair had gone to Washington to meet with the Director. They both sat and watched the news coverage of the events that had unfolded in New York and now more information about a large scaled effort that was taking place in Iraq.

Kevin said, "Everyone was a winner in this." He was glad that this case was over and he would be headed back to his home and his wife and two girls. He was always happy to be going home.

Allisa and Blair had been in the lobby shops in the Marriott and were pleased to find so many places to purchase clothes and accessories. Blair wasn't sure how much would be ok to spend but Allisa said that they needed to be prepared to meet some very high ranking officials. They had been able to rest and Ms. Roper had called to tell them that a driver would pick them up about 6:30 p.m. from the hotel. He would pull up in front and take them to dinner. Allisa and Blair were waiting in the lobby for their driver to pick them up. They weren't sure where they were going to, but they both looked beautiful. People that passed by took a second look. Allisa thanked Blair for helping pick out an outfit for her.

"You have a great sense of style."

"In my business when you get a break you have to look the part."

Blair had only been lucky enough to be in a few plays and one small part in a movie, but she was once asked to be an escort at the Oscar's by the studio and she made sure that she made a splash on the red carpet. The experience was unbelievable. She was to walk along side of one of the presenters for that evening. Until she got there she didn't know who she would be walking with. To her surprise it was Ron Howard and Tom Hanks. They were up for an Oscar and Tom's wife was out of town. The studio just wanted a young actress to be seen with them as they entered the pavilion.

The driver pulled up in front of the Marriott and Blair and Allisa came out of the hotel. He opened the doors for them and the women got in the back of the limo. They crossed the Potomac River and headed down Constitution Avenue to 17th street. They had asked the driver where they were going to but he said he wasn't supposed to tell them. It was suppose to be a surprise. The driver turned right on Pennsylvania Avenue and entered the gate to the White House. Both women turned to look at each other and just stared at the entrance. The driver opened his window and the guard opened the gate. He pulled around to a side entrance and got out and opened the car door for them. Blair and Allisa got out of the car and the Director was there to meet them.

"Why didn't you tell us where we were going to?"

"The President was told about your involvement and that you were both here in Washington and he wanted to meet you and have you here for dinner. It all came up quick."

They entered past a metal detector and into a lobby area. The house was just beautiful and both women were looking around when the President came into the lobby. They were speechless as he shook their hands and extended his thanks for the great service they had performed for their country. His wife came out and was very gracious to them. She shook both of their hands.

"You are both so beautiful. Please come in. Honey you didn't tell me that they were so beautiful."

They walked down a small stairway and the First Lady had one of them on each side of her.

"I hope that you like what the staff made for dinner. I didn't have time to find out what you like to eat so we had to come up with something that I hope is ok?"

"We are so honored to be here," Blair said.

Allisa expressed that the evening was very special and what an honor it was to be invited to the White House.

At dinner the President asked the two women about themselves and he had conveyed to Blair that he and his wife were sorry for her loss. Blair felt a rush of warmth come over her and she didn't know what to say. The President said, "that the Director would give the women more details about tomorrow but he would like to present Blair with a medal of honor for her husbands work in Iraq. The presentation would take place on the lawn of the White House." He told Allisa that she should be there too, because she is the one that made sure the documents got to the right people.

"You both are very brave young women and represent the people of the United States.

The evening was magical. They had a gracious dinner with the President and First Lady and now were being told that they would be honored in a special event on the lawn of the White House tomorrow. The evening was great. After dinner they were escorted to the Lincoln room for coffee and dessert. The First Lady talked to the two women as the President was meeting with John Martin and the Director of Homeland security. They were discussing something very important and had to excuse themselves from the Lincoln room. The First Lady continued to converse with the two women.

John Martin returned to the Lincoln room and said that he would get them back to the Marriott. He had called the driver to come back to the White House and take Allisa and Blair back to the hotel. John Martin walked the women out to the limo that was waiting for them.

"You need to watch TV tonight for developments in Iraq. It is directly related to your information. We will be carrying out missions in Iraq and Pakistan over the next few days."

That news was exciting. Blair was surprised that the government was able to act so quickly on the information.

They asked him what time are they were suppose to be at the White House tomorrow. "We will pick you both up about 10:30 a.m. and the President is calling a press conference for around noon on the White House lawn. Go down to one of the shops in your hotel if you need. "We already purchased some items today, are you sure we should buy something else?" Blair asked. "What you have done is tremendous and I want to make sure you are treated with first class attention. Please get something special for tomorrow's occasion. It will be carried live across the Nation." John Martin put his hand on Blair's right arm. "Blair, I would like to talk to you after all of this about joining our group. You are a bright person and would make a great field agent." "I appreciate your confidence in me, but I love where I live and would not want to move." "We could arrange to keep you right where you are and you would be surprised how many agents we have that are living what appear to be normal lives."

The limo pulled up to the side entrance and the women climbed into the back seat. It would follow the same route that it did when they were on the way to the White House. The driver took them back to the hotel and the women sat in the back talking a mile a minute. They had experienced so much that day and now tomorrow would bring more. Blair had to call her parents and Olly and she wanted to tell Hunter's dad what had happened.

When they got back to the Marriott they went to Blair's room and turned on CNN. Details of events were unfolding about the discovery of weapons of mass destruction being found in Tikrit, Iraq close to Lake Tharthar near one of Saddams Castles. The reports showed the 5th

Army removing boxes of material and putting them in trucks lined up in a convoy to return to their headquarters. There was also information about a missile attack near Islamabad, Pakistan where reported al-Qaida leaders were holding a meeting. The reporter said that key terror group leaders were meeting and that this would be a significant blow to al-Qaida in the region. The evening was full of news reports on every station and both women were pleased with what they had accomplished. Allisa said she was going to her room and Blair said she had some calls to make.

Blair called her parents first and filled them in on the whole story. They were happy that everything turned out ok but wished she had gotten them involved. They knew that their daughter was strong willed and would follow the action that she thought was right. She had been through so much and now some positive news was great to hear. She talked to Hunter's dad and he was pleased that his son was going to be awarded a medal for his work. Her next call was to Olly. With the time difference from the East Coast to LA she knew she would be able to get Olly at home. They discussed the events and Blair said that she wanted to talk to Blake and Ashley before the news came out. She didn't want them to hear about it first from television. They were great friends and had been there for her through it all. Olly agreed that they would like that.

The night had been a whirlwind of excitement. Tomorrow would be the same she thought. After talking to Blake and Ashley she turned on the television. Blair did not have a television in her apartment. It seemed an expense that didn't make any sense to her. She was rarely home and when she was she loved to listen to music. She had a collection of albums that featured jazz and show tunes. Her friend Blake was an avid collector of rare albums and she often would go with him to the flea market and buy some for herself.

It was hard to put the evening into perspective. First hearing news that the President was going to want to meet them and present Hunter with an award, then having dinner at the White House with the President and First Lady. She knew that tomorrow would be a big day but the emotion she was feeling sent adrenaline pumping through her veins. She had to get some rest. She had made plans to call Allisa around 8:00 a.m. They would go down for breakfast and to buy a new suit for the White House event. Blair watched the CNN broadcast that was unfolding a story about events in Iraq and that the President would have a press conference the next day. Blair turned the channel to a local station to see if they had any other news. The local evening news had the story about the press conference that would be held tomorrow on the White House lawn. The reporter said that the President would honor a fallen hero and two women that were instrumental in helping find some important documents. He also said that there would be further details about military action in both Iraq and Pakistan. Sleeping would be difficult but Blair had to get some rest.

She got into bed and listened to a recap of the terrorist situation in New York. She smiled as Dino gave the reporters the timeline of events. He said that his team had been following leads that took the FBI from California to the east coast. He never mentioned her or Allisa, but said that a couple of Agents had been involved and were instrumental in solving the case. She turned off the television and turned over in bed. She wasn't sure what to expect from tomorrow, but how could it top today's dinner with the President and First Lady.

THIRTY TWO

The sun was high as the alarm went off in Blair's room. It was 7:00 a.m. and she had to shower before meeting Allisa. Blair knew that she was too excited to eat but wanted to talk to someone. She dialed Allisa's room. Allisa, like Blair was very exited. She had been awarded special accommodations before but never anything like this. They talked and decided to move their meeting time up. The shower felt great and she put on some clothes and walked down the hall to room 2412. Allisa was waiting and they jumped on the elevator. Allisa had contacted the hotel manager and he arranged to have someone open the boutique in the lobby early for them.

"We need to shop for something for today's ceremony," she told Blair.

Blair said that she felt funny about buying all this stuff.

"With everything you have been through it is the least thing the FBI can do for you Blair."

She said, "ok" and they looked through the shop with the help of a sales lady. They were the only two in the shop and the sales lady knew that they were VIP's of some sort. The shop usually didn't open until noon but the manager said he would have someone help a couple of dignitaries that the FBI had staying at the hotel. It was not unusual for them to get requests like this from a government agencies. Blair found a navy suit with a bright blouse.

"I have shoes that will go with this." Allisa started to laugh. Both women were nervous and the laughter was great medicine to calm their nerves. Allisa settled for a basic black suit.

"This is something that I can use for meetings."

The sales lady rang up their purchases and thanked them for shopping at the boutique.

They had planned on having breakfast but neither of them felt hungry. Blair suggested that they get a carryout from the coffee shop.

"Sounds good to me," Allisa said.

They ordered coffee and Blair got tea plus an egg sandwich. "We have some time before they will pick us up," Allisa said.

"I want to go up to my room and get ready. Do you think that I should have something prepared to say in case I have to?" Blair asked.

"That's a good idea."

"I'm sure once the President finishes he would let you say something."

"I can work on that and want you to read it over before we go."

They had truly become good friends and trusted each others opinions.

They went to their rooms to get ready for the trip back to the White House. Blair called Allisa about 10:00 to see if she was ready.

"I'm pacing around the room, "she told her.

"Ok, let's go down to the lobby and you can look over what I have written."

Allisa and Blair met at the elevator on the 24th floor and headed to the lobby. They sat near the entrance and Allisa looked at the notes that Blair had prepared.

"This looks very good. I think that the President would appreciate what you have written.

The limo pulled up in front of the Marriott about 10:20 a.m. and the driver came inside to find his passengers in the lobby. They got into the back seat and were now feeling like veterans. Blair looked at Allisa and said softly, "to the White House young man." They both laughed as the ride took them on the same route as the night before. The driver didn't hear what Blair had said but smiled when he heard them both laughing.

It was a beautiful day. The sun was high and the entrance to the White House was just ahead. You could see a orange hue around the sun as they passed along the government buildings off of Pennsylvania Avenue. The trees that lined Pennsylvania Avenue were all in bloom. Everything was perfect. They pulled into the gated area as the limo pulled to the side entrance. They noticed that a large crowd had gathered around the front gate of the White House. They asked the driver if that was normal.

He answered, "Anytime there is a press conference on the lawn of the White House we have large crowds gather hours before to get a view of the event. Sometimes we have more protesters than onlookers but today's crowd seemed to be very quiet," he said. They both got out of the limo and John Martin was there to meet them. He introduced them to the Homeland Security Head and the other men that were waiting in the outer lobby of the White House.

"We will want to meet with both of you for a few minutes before the press conference. I want to go over the details of the event with you and if you have any questions please now is the time to ask."

Blair asked who would be present during the press conference.

"The President wants to make sure all the news media is there and he will cover events from last night before he introduces you.

"We saw a large crowd along the gated area. We were wondering why so many people were out in front when we pulled up to the gate."

"After the events last night and the CNN coverage it is not surprising to see this big of a crowd."

Both women knew that the President's approval rating was very low and the war had not helped. He hoped that this would be a turning point in his Presidency and by allowing people to gather at the gated area it would help him seem more of a People's President.

"Will I get a chance to say anything?"

"Yes but I would need to see what you have in mind. Most times people being given an award just thank the President."

Blair gave John Martin the note she had written and he looked it over.

"Blair this looks ok to me but I will have to give it to the Presidents Press Secretary," he said. "If they approve they will give you a cue when you will be able to give your response."

They were escorted to sit in an outer office. It was getting close to the time the press conference was supposed to start. Blair was nervous and asked if she could get some water. They brought her and Allisa bottled water and a young man entered the room. He introduced himself and said, "he had the notes that Blair had written." Blair got up and introduced herself and Allisa. "I have gone over your planned remarks with the Presidents Press Secretary and there is no problem with what you plan to say. Please make sure that you look into the cameras when you are talking," then the President and the First Lady came in. Both women jumped up and exchanged hello's.

"I hope you are not too nervous," the First Lady asked.

"We should be ok," both of them answered.

The President spoke to both of them.

"Ms. Jones, you have been instrumental in this case and I want to recognize you for your efforts. The Director said that he is putting you in a new position that would keep you in Washington. I hope that is ok with you?"

"Yes sir."

Allisa was in awe and found it hard to speak. Blair and Allisa were holding hands as the President was talking to them.

"Mrs. Adams, you are a very brave woman and I cannot tell you how important your efforts and the information your husband found has helped our cause."

"Thank you sir. He was very dedicated to his country and his father will be pleased to know how that he will be honored here today."

"I called his father last night after dinner and invited him to be here today but he said that this should be your moment. We will send him a copy of the medal that I will present to you today. You both should have one."

Blair was speechless and had a tear in her eyes. The First Lady moved closer to the girls and gave them both a hug.

"My Press Secretary will be in here in a few minutes and go over the details of the presentation. I understand that you have a planned speech Mrs. Adams!"

"Yes sir, I gave it to Mr. Martin and your people said it was ok."

"I appreciate your wanting to contribute and think the remarks are very good." "We will be going out to the lawn in about ten minute's, sir," the white house aide said.

They moved toward the West Wing of the White House and were told that the Secret Service would have men in position along the grassy area. The military stationed outside the door of the west wing would open the doors and that they should follow the President and First Lady out to the lawn. There would be a small platform with microphones mounted on it and they should stand to the right of the President. The First Lady would be on his left hand side.

The doors opened and the President stepped out followed by his wife and the two women. Flash bulbs went off as they took their position on the platform. The President addressed the crowd. His speech detailed the events of the past evening and that morning. He talked about the events in New York, Iraq and Pakistan. Reporters clamored for answers to questions but he said that he had a presentation to make first.

"I would be happy to answer your questions after that."

He then turned the conversation to Allisa Jones and congratulated her on being instrumental in finding the critical information to help the war efforts. He handed her a plaque and she posed with the President for pictures. The press was asking for comments but the President waved them off.

"I still have one more special guest to introduce you to."

The President put his hand out to Blair and she stepped forward.

"This is Mrs. Blair Adams. It was through her husband, Hunter Adams efforts in Iraq, that the information we needed was found. She made sure that information got to the proper people and it has been instrumental in our efforts. It is with great pleasure to present Mrs. Adams with the Medal of Honor for her husband Hunter who was killed in the line of duty in Iraq."

The photographers were moving forward and pictures were being snapped of the presentation.

"I also want to present Mrs. Adams with a plaque of appreciation from the people of the United States for her efforts. Mrs. Adams has some remarks she would like to make."

Blair had both the plaque and the Medal of Honor in her hands and the press asked for questions to be answered. She moved toward the microphone.

"I want to thank the President and First Lady for this honor. My husband, Hunter Adams, was a hero and his father and I are glad that he is being recognized for his work. I am just a normal citizen who did the right thing. Regardless of your views we are all American's, and when the opportunity is there we all need to do the right thing for our country. My husband died in the line of duty and he is being honored as a hero. He is not the only hero we have. The brave men and women in our military and the civilian contractors that are helping to rebuild Iraq are also our hero's. I want to share this award with all the family members that have lost someone in the conflict."

The press was in love with her. She stood tall next to the President and the photo op would be good for his approval rating and she would be in the limelight for a long time. As the people along the gated area watched and many of them cheered, one man just seemed to stare at the events that unfolded. He had no expression on his face but seemed to be taking the events in more than anyone around him.

Yawer watched as Blair took the medal and plaque from the President. He knew that she had helped to destroy what his group had built and he would not forget her.

The End

ABOUT THE AUTHOR

Mr. Aued is a new author. He attended college in Michigan, Kentucky and Georgia with degree's in English, History and Secondary Education. He spent most of his professional career working for a major corporation in the Southeastern United States. Mr. Aued has lived in many Southern and Mid-Western States, and that has helped him develop a unique prospective on people across the United States.

The story that unfolds in The Package comes from today's headlines. Over 2,700 men and women have died since our involvement in Iraq. Although a fictional character, there are many Blair Adams among all of us. Young men and women searching for answers as to why their loved ones were killed.

I hope her story gives you good feelings as why our men and women have sacrificed their lives.

LaVergne, TN USA
31 August 2010
195360LV00003B/20/A